STOLEN
HEARTS

Elise Noble

Published by Undercover Publishing Limited

ISBN: 978-1-912888-06-1

Edited by Nikki Mentges, NAM Editorial

Cover design by Abigail Sins

www.undercover-publishing.com

www.elise-noble.com

Some men will unlock your heart,
Others will release the devil inside.
- *Emmy Black*

CHAPTER 1 - EMMY

"DIAMOND? DO YOU want the good news or the bad news?" my husband asked from the cockpit of our jet.

We'd just boarded at Cairo International Airport, ready for a short hop over the Med to Italy to dispose of a particularly pesky oligarch's son who'd developed a penchant for bumping off competitors to his daddy's business. Whether it was to help the old man or simply to protect his inheritance, we weren't sure, but either way it didn't matter. Sonny boy's last murder had been on American soil, and the powers that be had deemed he needed to go.

"Gimme the bad news."

Get it over with.

"We're not getting paid a million and a half bucks to dispose of Anton Ludovich."

"Oh?"

"That's the good news. He died all by himself."

"How?"

"Drove his Ferrari off a bridge. Cocaine was mentioned."

"So where does that leave us? Should I file a new flight plan?"

More bloody paperwork. The bane of my life. What do you think it's like to be a jet-setting assassin? All glamorous parties and car chases and silenced pistols?

I wished. No, mostly it was meetings and planning and occasionally, I got to crawl in mud. Then there was the time I almost died in the desert, but that's a whole other story.

"Yes. We need a new flight plan."

"Virginia?"

Virginia was home. Or at least, it had been for the last seventeen years—more than half of my life. At heart, I was a London girl and always would be, but I'd moved to the US after a job offer I couldn't refuse, and look at me now—I'd clawed my way to the top of the ladder, leaving chaos, destruction, and piles of bodies in my wake. And still inconsiderate assholes dicked with my plans.

"We'll need more fuel," Black said, followed by a tiny hesitation. Most people wouldn't have seen past my husband's poker face. Me? I sensed there was a "but" coming. "But we do have a gap in our schedules now."

See? "And?"

"We could take a...vacation?"

He said the word tentatively, testing it out. Black didn't take time off as a rule. The occasional minibreak, maybe, or undercover work in sunny climates, but not proper holidays. In the fifteen years we'd been married, we'd only been on one bona fide vacation, and that was more of a recuperation period than anything else.

"Are you feeling okay?"

"We've got two weeks before our next job starts." A joint security exercise with the Secret Service. We'd been hired to play the bad guys, hurrah. "We're apart too much, and just for once, I'd like to spend some time doing nothing. See how it feels."

"What do you have in mind?"

"Since we're already in Egypt, why don't we go to Dahab? How long since we visited?"

Two and a half years had passed since I last set foot in the tiny town, but the memories of dragging myself up the beach in my underwear after trying to start World War III on the other side of the Gulf of Aqaba were as vivid as if it had happened yesterday. For Black? It must've been three or four years since he'd been there.

Together, we ran Blackwood Security along with two of Black's old Navy buddies, and over the years, it had grown to be the second-largest security and investigations firm in the world. Thousands of employees and offices on six continents meant vacations were something other people took, although Nate, my husband's best friend and one of our business partners, did threaten to send me to Antarctica on a regular basis.

Sometimes, I felt tempted to take him up on the offer. Business was booming, which meant our schedules barely allowed enough time to shit in the mornings, let alone go sightseeing. Black oversaw the investigations division while I ran Special Projects, which basically meant I got sent all the crap nobody else wanted to touch. Everything from rescue missions to spying to common or garden assassination came across my desk.

And I was tired.

"It's been too long. A vacation? Are you serious?"

Stupid question. He was always serious.

"Change the flight plan. I'll call Bob and let him know we're coming. Actually, speaking of coming..." He eyed up the tiny bedroom at the back of the plane. "The admin can wait for ten minutes."

"Only ten minutes? What happened to your stamina, old man?"

He picked me up and threw me over his shoulder, slapping me on the ass with his free hand. Any other man would have died for that, but with Black, I only giggled. *Giggled*. What was wrong with me? This whole vacation thing was already messing with my mind.

But who cared? A fortnight on the beach doing nothing but my husband sounded like heaven to me. Sun, sea, sand, and sex—the perfect combination as long as we didn't mix the sand with the sex, because that could get painful.

I landed on the bed in a heap, but I was smiling. "Love you, Chuck."

"Love you too, Diamond."

Three hours and as many orgasms later, we sped along the dual carriageway between Sharm el-Sheikh and Dahab. Not so long ago, the town had been nothing more than a Bedouin fishing village clinging to the coast halfway up the South Sinai Peninsula, but over the last few decades, it had morphed into one of the world's premier water sports destinations, although it still managed to retain a lot of its original charm. And its goats. There were goats everywhere.

I glanced in the rear-view mirror, and the driver Captain Bob had sent with the pickup didn't look particularly happy in the back seat. Neither was I. The "too fast" warning chimes had been going for thirty minutes now, and I didn't have any earplugs. But eighty kilometres of smooth tarmac with only half a dozen other vehicles in sight was too good an opportunity to pass up, and if it hadn't been for the tour bus we got stuck behind at the second police checkpoint, I might have beaten my record for driving the route.

Beside me, Black tapped away at his tablet, letting everyone know of our change in plans. There'd be a few raised eyebrows at Blackwood, and probably some cursing too, but it was time to practise what we preached and improve our work/life balance. They'd cope.

At last, the third and final checkpoint came into view, and I smiled as we were waved through.

"Such incompetence," Black muttered.

"Good for us."

Although we'd left most of our hardware on the plane, there were still two guns and a selection of sharp things in the luggage strapped down in the bed of the truck. Be prepared, that was our motto. Or at least, it would have been if the Boy Scouts hadn't trademarked it.

The whole town was just a couple of miles square, and it wasn't long before we drove up to the gates of the Black Diamond Hotel. As you can probably guess by the name, we had an interest in it. A decade ago, we'd provided the bulk of the money to purchase and renovate the sprawling estate on the edge of the laguna, a beautiful blue bay sheltered from the worst of the waves by a spit of sand reaching across its mouth in the distance. The renovation project had been the brainchild of Captain Bob Stewart, a colleague of Black's back in his days as a Navy SEAL, and Bob still ran the place with his wife, Sondra.

When we first laid eyes on the place, it had been derelict, the victim of an investor who'd mortgaged himself up to the hilt then made a series of spectacularly lousy business decisions. Not many owners had wanted to buy chicken-flavoured water for their pets, and his range of fashion burkas flopped too.

We'd picked the land up for a song and rebuilt, and now sixty guest villas nestled amongst tropical gardens, complete with a spa, two restaurants, two bars, a tennis court, and a conference centre. No high-rise buildings for us. We kept it traditional with arched windows, domed roofs, and mosaics made by local craftsmen.

Honestly, I loved the place. It had a feeling of peace about it, and my only regret was that I didn't get to spend more time there.

Of course, we had an emphasis on security too—it was in our blood—and Bob strode towards us as a guard stepped out of the gatehouse with a mirror to examine the underside of the pickup. Blackwood's people were slightly better trained than the police.

"Chief Petty Officer Black."

"Captain Stewart."

Black climbed out of the car, and the two men saluted each other while I turned to check on the dude in the back seat.

"It's okay—you can get out now."

A tiny nod.

"Shall I help you with the door?"

Another nod.

The instant he got free, he scuttled into the main building. Captain Bob stared after him.

"What happened to Ahmed?"

"He's not such a good passenger."

Bob gave a surreptitious sniff, but the smell of burning rubber had all but dispersed by then. I grabbed my suitcase out of the back and headed for the tiled path at the side of the lobby with Black and Bob following behind. Both knew better than to ask if I needed a hand with my luggage.

The smell of the sea air soothed my senses, and that tight knot of tension that lived in my gut—the force that drove me—loosened just a little. Despite being in the desert, the gardens were lush and green thanks to a sprinkler system that came on each day before dawn. Fragrance washed over me as I strode along the path to our seafront villa.

"I haven't touched the place since you were here last," Bob said. "Let me know if you want me to send housekeeping over."

I took a mental inventory of the place. Yes, anything interesting was locked up in the floor safe.

"If someone could give the place a freshen-up while we have dinner, that'd be good. Want to join us?"

"And ruin your romantic getaway?"

I refrained from pointing out that Black had fucked me quite thoroughly before we left Cairo airport. A sideways glance, and his tiny smirk showed he'd had the same thought.

"Always good to catch up with old friends," he said.

"Wish I could, but I can't." Bob overtook me as we walked up the steps to our Egyptian home, the key in his outstretched hand. "Lynn's here, and I promised I'd eat with her tonight. But I could ask the chef to set a couple of extra places…"

Lynn was Bob and Sondra's only daughter. In her

mid-thirties, if I recalled correctly, with a high-pitched voice, a love of crochet that bordered on an obsession, and a tendency to sniffle if things didn't go her way. The last thing I wanted to do was share a table with her.

"No, it's fine. You enjoy your family dinner, and we'll drive into town. We've already planned to go to that Mexican place by the bridge if it's still there?"

"It's still there. The tacos are still every bit as good as they used to be."

"How long is Lynn staying?"

My real question: could we put off a Black-Stewart get-together until after she left?

"A month."

Shit. "That's a long trip."

"She's here to get married. The pair of them figured they could combine the wedding and the honeymoon to save money. They're tying the knot on the beach in two weeks, and you're invited of course."

Black raised an eyebrow. "I thought she was already married?"

"She was. This had better be third time lucky because I was this far..." Bob held his thumb and forefinger a millimetre apart. "From a murder charge with number two."

"You could've made it look like an accident."

"I'll pretend I didn't hear that."

The door to the villa creaked open, heat radiating from the thick wood in the afternoon sun. The inside, with its domed roof and AC unit, would be cooler, but before I could step into the shade, a voice drifted across from the other side of the thick shrubbery that surrounded our private terrace. Dammit, I *really* needed those earplugs.

"I'm not wearing that dress!"

"Zena, you chose the design." No mistaking Lynn's voice, and she sounded exasperated. "Please don't argue with me again."

"No, I said it was the least horrible out of all the ones you showed me, which is totally different. Plus we were in *America*. This is *Egypt*, and it's boiling. I won't be able to breathe."

"Zena?" I mouthed at Bob, and he rolled his eyes.

"My granddaughter. From husband number one."

Ah, yes, the guy who ran off with the babysitter, if memory served me right. Seemed he couldn't stand Lynn's whining either, and if my first impression of Zena was any indication, the attitude was genetic. A funny thing, genetics. Bob was a legend, Sondra was sweet as cotton candy, and somehow, they'd ended up with Lynn. If it weren't for the fact that Lynn had Bob's pale blue eyes and Sondra's delicate chin, I'd suspect a mix-up at birth.

"You only need to wear it for a couple hours," Lynn told her daughter. "And it's real pretty."

"If I have to truss myself up in that thing, I'm not going to the wedding at all."

"But where are we gonna get a different dress? There aren't any bridal shops in Dahab, and that one took me weeks to make."

"Can't I just wear shorts?"

"No, you can't."

"Why not?"

"Because it's a wedding."

"So? That's not a proper reason."

"Okay, so how about because you're sixteen years

old, and I'm your mother. In two weeks, I'm going to become Mrs. Christopher Holt, and I want you there to celebrate with me."

"I hate you. You're determined to ruin my life!"

Running footsteps signalled Zena's departure, and I began to wish we'd gone to Italy after all. Planning a risky, high-profile assassination was infinitely more fun than dealing with a stroppy teenager.

Captain Bob let out a long sigh. "I'd better go and mediate."

Black edged towards the threshold. "Rather you than me. See you tomorrow."

The door clicked shut, and I flopped back on the sofa. A cloud of dust puffed up as I landed, and if I wasn't mistaken, that was a pile of dead ants in the corner under the TV. Yup, the place definitely needed a clean.

"Should've gone to Milan," Black muttered.

"Don't worry; if we're out on the water, they can't get us. I guess we should probably pick up a wedding present, though. I'll email Bradley."

Bradley was our personal assistant, a self-confessed shopaholic who wouldn't bat an eyelid at the request. The small matter of an ocean and a language barrier wouldn't stop him from finding the perfect gift.

"Good plan."

"Is the door locked?" I asked.

"Of course."

"In that case, you're wearing too many clothes. Get 'em off, Mr. Black."

He peeled his T-shirt over his head, and I'd never get sick of the sight of that chest. And the abs... *Don't drool, bitch.* We'd had our ups and downs over the years as a marriage of convenience turned into something altogether more sweaty, but now that we were together, properly together, nothing could prise us apart. Occasionally when I drank too much, I was liable to ramble on about two souls joining and becoming one, at least until Black told me to shut up and carried me to bed, but it was true.

Black had stolen my heart.

CHAPTER 2 - BLACK

CHARLES BLACK LASTED thirty minutes on a sunlounger. Sitting still for any longer than that left him bored. Irritated. On surveillance duty in the field, he could control the twitchiness, tamp it down, but it was always lurking in the background, niggling at him. With Emmy reading peacefully beside him, he tried checking his emails to distract himself, but when the damn phone threatened to overheat in the morning sun, he shoved it under his towel and stood up.

"I'm going for a swim. Join me?"

The sea was right there, calling to him. His time in the Navy SEALs had turned him amphibious. Two or three miles in the open water and he'd be calm again, ready to do whatever else a man was supposed to do on a vacation.

But Emmy didn't look too enthusiastic.

"We're supposed to be on vacation. You literally used that word yesterday."

"And?"

"If I wanted to die of exhaustion, I could've done that in Virginia. And I'm already shattered from last night."

No, they hadn't made it out for dinner, but he had eaten well.

"Swimming isn't exhausting."

"It is when I'm trying to keep up with you."

"We both need to stay in shape."

"I'll give you a blow job if you don't make me swim."

Black hesitated. Emmy sucked like an inverted hurricane and took pleasure in a job well done. Which was why he called her bluff.

"You'll give me a blow job anyway."

"Dammit, you know me so well. Okay, I'll go if you agree to let me do nothing all afternoon."

"Deal."

"And bring me drinks."

He wasn't a fucking waiter. "There are staff here to bring you drinks."

"That's not the point."

Of course it wasn't. Black liked to be in control. Emmy knew that, and so she pushed the boundaries at every available opportunity. He pretended to be annoyed, but secretly, he enjoyed the challenge. He'd concede on this point, but he wanted something in return.

"Fine. I'll bring you drinks if you wear a bikini."

"Sure. I'll wear a bikini."

Hmm. That was easy. Almost too easy...

Black's phone buzzed, and he moved to the shade of a carob tree to check who'd messaged. Nate, his former Navy SEAL swim buddy, checking whether Black would be available for a videoconference with a client the day after tomorrow. He almost answered in the affirmative, but then he thought of Emmy. The whole reason he'd suggested this trip was because the last three times he'd tried to take her out to dinner, work had got in the way. And he'd noticed the tiredness in her eyes this last month. She'd never have said anything, but perhaps Anton Ludovich's untimely death had been fate's way of telling them to take a break.

He tapped out a reply to Nate.

Black: Unless it's an emergency, neither of us is available for anything for the next two weeks.

But Black still needed to swim.

"Ready?" he asked Emmy, sticking his head around the villa's front door.

"Almost. Where are we swimming?"

"In the laguna?"

"Can't. The banana boat's bombing around, and I like my head where it is, thanks. We'll have to walk over to Baby Bay."

She stepped out of the bedroom, and Black let out a groan. He hadn't thought this through, had he? Emmy had gone with a violet two-piece to match her eyes, and that wasn't the only thing it enhanced. If she ventured out in public dressed that way, he might be forced to murder someone.

He went inside and rummaged through the closet.

"Here. Wear this."

"A kaftan? Are you fucking kidding me?"

"In case you get sunburned."

"Bullshit. You wanted me in the bikini—now own it."

Black made a grab for her because at that moment, he had absolutely no desire to swim but a hell of a lot of desire to fuck his wife. But Emmy sidestepped and darted out the door, leaving him to lock it behind them.

Logically, Black knew Emmy was his. They'd renewed their wedding vows not so long ago, and she'd never cheat. But every time a man's gaze lingered on her body, he still wanted to dig the asshole's eyes out with a spoon then lock her in their bedroom so nobody else could look at her.

Did that stop her from flirting? No. Sometimes, he thought she did it deliberately to wind him up. Like now, for example. She grinned as she strode along the beach, and Black stalked behind her like a shadow, glaring at anyone who so much as looked in her direction as they headed for the spit of land on the far side of the laguna.

Think of the water, he told himself, *not Emmy's ass*.

They'd first come to Dahab in her early twenties—his early thirties—before they'd invested in the hotel. Black had wanted to dive at the Blue Hole, a sinkhole just a few yards offshore that plunged almost 370 feet into the depths. It had a reputation for being one of the most dangerous dive sites in the world, and it was true that a number of people had lost their lives there—the wall of memorial plaques right before the entrance was a testament to that—but much of the risk could be mitigated with proper equipment and training.

Almost halfway down the Blue Hole, a long arch led out to the open sea. At that depth, with air much denser and the effects of narcosis hovering around the edges of your consciousness, it was all too easy to burn through the contents of your tank and do something stupid. Beyond forty metres—a hundred and thirty feet—was technical diving territory, not recreational, but too many people still attempted the arch on a single tank and without proper backup. Those were the people who died most often.

Black preferred to think of the process as natural

selection.

Back then, he and Emmy had dived the arch and spent the next few days exploring the town. Emmy told him she loved the place, and that was why he'd handed over a million and a half bucks when Bob Stewart came up with a crazy plan to renovate a wreck of a hotel. For Emmy. Because until Black met her, love had just been a word in the dictionary. A mythical mix of chemicals that messed with a man's mind and destroyed his ability to think rationally. Then he'd stumbled into his future wife on the streets of London one rainy evening —or rather, she'd stumbled into him—and she'd stolen his heart as well as his sanity, the mental bitch.

On the other side of the bay, Emmy cannonballed into the sea, then trod water as Black dove in beside her. Perhaps they'd only do one mile today. Half an hour, and he'd have her back in the bedroom where he wanted her.

In the meantime, Black made an effort to enjoy the swim. Stroking lazily through the water with his wife beside him was better than stalking a junior oligarch, and the Red Sea sure was warmer than the places he'd trained in his SEAL days. But that ass...

A quarter mile along the coast, he grabbed Emmy's hand.

"Let's go back."

"You're quitting already? Are you kidding? I need to do at least another mile."

"Why?"

"Because of the amount of dinner I want to eat tonight."

"I can think of another way to burn calories."

Emmy wrapped her legs around his waist, and his

cock hardened instantly.

"And what might that be?"

She released her grip and sank beneath the waves. Black braced for the feel of her lips, maybe the scrape of her teeth, because it wouldn't be the first time she'd pulled that trick and he knew how long she could hold her breath, but she popped up again almost instantly.

"Shit."

"What?"

"There's a group of scuba divers down there."

Fuck. And now he had a damned daggerboard in his shorts. Emmy was laughing as they took off for the laguna, and he let her set the pace at first, but the sight of her smooth legs didn't help a certain part of his anatomy, so he soon scooted in front.

How long would it take to get back to the villa? They could jog, but then Emmy's tits would bounce, and— Wait. Why was Bob waving at them from the beach?

Black didn't know, and he wasn't sure he *wanted* to know either.

But since Emmy was already heading for the shore, Black followed, mentally rehearsing excuses not to go for dinner with three generations of the Stewart family. Bob was a good friend, Sondra was tolerable, but Black would rather be waterboarded than spend an evening making small talk with Lynn, fiancé number three, and a teenage brat.

"Is there a problem?" he asked his old boss.

"Always so negative."

"What can I say? People come to me when shit goes wrong, and you've got the look of a man who wants something."

"This isn't a problem, more of an opportunity. The small boat's free, so how would you two like to go diving this afternoon?"

Black glanced in Emmy's direction, and she flicked her gaze towards the villa. Message understood.

"Emmy wants to take the afternoon off. We can dive tomorrow."

"Both boats are booked by tour groups all day."

"Then we'll dive from the shore."

For a rare moment, Bob hesitated. This was the man who'd led special forces into battle and received the Medal of fucking Honor for bravery, so why did he seem so nervous?

"Uh…"

"So there *is* a problem?"

"A small issue."

"Which is?"

"Lynn wants me to drive her and Zena to Sharm el-Sheikh to go dress shopping. I don't mind paying for the damned outfit, but I'd rather get shot in the gut than go on that trip."

"And you told them you were taking us diving instead?"

"I might have said that."

On a regular day, diving came second only to swimming on Black's list of favourite things to do, but with his schedule otherwise clear and his wife gagging for it, he struggled to muster up the enthusiasm. Emmy managed a smile.

"I hate shopping for clothes too."

"You'll go?" Bob asked.

"You owe me the mother of all desserts for this."

"Ice cream, waffles, chocolate brownies… Just

name it."

"Yeah, that lot'll do for starters."

CHAPTER 3 - EMMY

IT TURNED OUT Captain Bob hadn't been entirely forthcoming about the extent of his deception. When Lynn had questioned him over why, exactly, he couldn't just send the regular boat captain on our trip, he'd trotted out some bullshit about needing to escort us personally because we wanted to dive deep and the added danger was something only he was qualified to handle. And since Lynn was watching us from the beach bar as we prepped our equipment, we had to go with the whole shebang. Extra tanks, extra-thick wetsuits, and extra backache.

Out of the three of us, only Bob was smiling as he dragged a super-sized picnic cooler on board the *Blue Tang*. I'd named the boat after a particularly vivid variety of surgeonfish I once saw on a dive, then Disney Pixar released *Finding Dory* starring, you've guessed it, a blue tang, and now everyone thought I watched too many cartoons.

When Bob described the *Blue Tang* as small, he was talking relatively. She was nowhere near the size of the *Stingray*, the live-aboard boat that took guests on overnight trips to dive the wreck of the *Thistlegorm* and explore the waters of Ras Mohammad National Park, but she still catered comfortably to groups of ten divers. The wet area took up the back two-thirds of the main deck with a salon at the front, and the upper deck held sunbeds and a shaded seating area. The galley and engine room were on the lower deck, as well as a sleeping area for emergencies.

"How long are you planning to stay out on the water?" I asked, eyeing up the giant cooler.

"It's important not to get dehydrated, and I haven't eaten lunch yet."

Neither had I, and I was starving, but I also hated eating right before a big dive. Once again, I cursed weddings in general and Lynn in particular.

Black dodged past me carrying yet more air cylinders. With technical diving, redundancy was key. If a recreational scuba diver suffered an equipment failure, they just needed to swim to the surface in a controlled manner, remembering to breathe out slowly as they went so their lungs didn't rupture as the air in them expanded.

For a technical diver, life wasn't so simple. Because of the depths involved, decompression stops were needed on the ascent. If your equipment failed without proper backup in place, you had the choice between drowning or surfacing too fast and getting decompression sickness. To avoid that unpleasant decision, we carried two of everything. Two cylinders connected by a manifold, two regulators to breathe through, two air bladders in our inflatable wing, two masks, two computers, two torches, two slates, two knives... Think of a cross between a pack pony and a Christmas tree, and you'll get the picture.

Now do you see why I wanted to sit on the beach instead?

"So, where are we diving?" I asked. "Ras Abu

Gallum? Gabr el Bint?"

Gabr el Bint in the south—its name translated as "Grave of the Girl"—ranked as one of my favourite places in Dahab, but the highlight was the shallow lagoon filled with table coral and pufferfish. Diving there with technical equipment would be the very definition of overkill. Ras Abu Gallum in the north was pretty but twice as far, and I really, really wanted lunch.

"Gabr el Bint's busy today. Six boats have gone down there already. We could go to Abu Gallum, or..."

"Or?"

"The dive team and I have been working our way along the coast hunting for new dive sites. The old ones are so crowded nowadays, and damage from all the visitors is starting to show. A safari boat from Hurghada pulled over the big coral pinnacle at the Canyon three weeks ago." He shook his head, frowning. "If they try anchoring there again, I'll be the one to cut their damn line."

"Assholes."

"The tour operators just see the dollar signs. Anyhow, the last time anyone did a full-scale mapping exercise was two decades ago, and that focused on the shallow areas. I want to know what else is down there."

New reef growth, earthquakes, overfishing—they all changed the underwater landscape. If the Black Diamond dive centre could offer its clients something different, that would give us an edge over the competition, plus it would take some of the pressure off the busier areas.

"Where have you got up to?"

"Next on the list is a spot between the Caves and Shahira."

Closer even than Gabr el Bint. Perfect. "Great. Let's go."

Black rolled his eyes behind Bob's head because he knew exactly what I was thinking. So what? V-a-c-a-t-i-o-n. Ice cream took priority.

Sweat was rolling off me by the time I got into my wetsuit, and I tore a fingernail trying to work the sleeves up my arms. As you can imagine, when I eventually staggered off the edge of the swim platform, I wasn't in the best of moods. Black didn't feel the cold as badly as I did—probably because he had Superman genes—so he'd opted for a thinner wetsuit, and since he stood at almost six feet seven, the equipment didn't dwarf him as it did me. He stepped into the water smiling.

"Don't forget the camera," Bob said, bending on one knee to hand Black his GoPro.

On any other day, we'd have preferred memories to pictures, but since Bob wanted everything recorded for posterity, we'd agreed to film. Cold water seeped into my suit as I descended under the shallow waves.

The reef wall dropped straight into the depths. This site was no good for shore diving because although jumping in from land was a piece of cake, there was no easy exit. Without a boat, the only way out was to scramble up vertical rocks—difficult at the best of times, but almost impossible for a diver weighed down by twenty kilos of equipment.

But with a boat... Yeah, it had potential. The reef wall teemed with life, from anemones to shoals of orange anthias fish, sea stars, moray eels, cleaner wrasse. A turtle shot out in front of me and made me jump. I glanced behind, and of course Black had got that on film—the git was grinning as wide as his regulator would allow. He was happy here in his undersea world, and I suppose that made all the effort worth it.

Ten metres... Twenty... We went through a thermocline, a line in the water where the temperature dropped markedly, and the colours dulled. The brightest fish and corals lived near the surface, where the sunlight was strongest.

A huge grouper swam past in the blue, and Black reached out to squeeze my gloved hand. We'd agreed to go straight down to sixty metres to see what was there, then shallow up slowly, swimming south with the current as we went. Once we surfaced, we'd inflate a bright orange signal tube, and Bob would come to pick us up.

Thirty metres. Forty. The water got darker, and holy fuck, that was the biggest school of barracudas I'd ever seen. The predators of the ocean, although they rarely attacked humans. Why were they there? What were they hunting?

Black, of course, couldn't resist getting in closer with the camera. The shoal parted, and... Oh, shitting hell. Just one time—*one time*—couldn't I have a freaking day off?

Sightless eyes stared back at me, the sockets swarming with tiny shrimp-like creatures. Under a torn T-shirt, tattered flesh hung in ribbons—the remains of the barracudas' chosen meal—and white glimmers of rib shone in the light from Black's torch.

I checked one of the computers strapped to my wrist. Forty-five metres down. If the backpack the corpse wore hadn't snagged on a piece of coral, it would have sunk farther into the depths, another twenty or thirty metres at a guess. Even now, another attack by overly enthusiastic fish could easily dislodge the body. How long had it been there? No more than a week, surely, or there'd be nothing but a pile of bones.

Black shooed barracudas out of the way as I pulled out my dive slate and printed a single word.

FUCK.

Black pointed his thumb upwards: ascend.

Since we'd only been underwater for a few minutes, our decompression stop was short. To avoid damage to the reef, the *Blue Tang* used a ropeless anchor system that kept the boat in place using GPS rather than a physical anchor, but Bob had hung an actual rope over the stern with depths marked and a pair of oxygen bottles at five metres. Breathing pure oxygen in the shallows reduced decompression time, but deep down, too much $O2$ caused oxygen toxicity that could kill you. At depth, we used a combination of oxygen, nitrogen, and helium, known as trimix.

Black switched his regulator over, then wrote me a message.

Sorry about the vacation.

I hooked an elbow around the rope as I scribbled out my reply.

You take me to all the best places.

He smiled with his eyes. *Should've gone to Abu Gallum.*

Right. Instead of Gabr el Bint II?

Bob was relaxing in a fucking deckchair when we surfaced, reading a novel with his feet up on the deck rail. Next time, he could dive and I'd do the supervising.

"That was fast. Nothing down there?"

I left it to Black to explain this one.

"There's a good variety of coral, a reasonably large sea turtle, an army of barracudas, and a corpse."

"A corpse? What do you mean, a corpse?"

"Do you want the dictionary definition or the photos?"

I sat on a bench to release my tanks. Boy, that felt good. "Look on the bright side—at least we weren't a group of tourists because that would've been awkward."

"A fucking corpse?"

"Dude, you can keep asking the question, but the answer won't be any different. Yes. It's a half-eaten, spectacularly ugly corpse."

"I'm retired. I don't do corpses anymore."

"So who do we call around here?" Black asked. "Do you have a contact in the police?"

"I do, but they don't know a whole hell of a lot about dead bodies either. The last time there was a murder around here... That was the debacle in Fidda Hilal two years ago." Fidda Hilal was a similar-sized town a half hour north, and although Blackwood hadn't been involved, one of our clients had got tangled up in the mess, so I was familiar with it. "They got rid of the bad apples, I gather, but they still lack any kind of investigational expertise."

"How about diving expertise? Somebody needs to bring the body up."

"By the time they get around to organising that, there'll be nothing left but bones."

Bob looked at Black, Black looked at me, and I looked at Bob.

"We're on vacation," Black said. "I thought you

wanted to get ice cream?"

"I've lost my bloody appetite now. And whoever's down there, they've got family."

"We don't have jurisdiction."

"When has that ever stopped you before?"

"We can't do everybody's jobs for them. We had precisely this discussion yesterday with Lieutenant General Fakhry."

Ah, yes, our meeting in Cairo. With all the rumblings going on in the Middle East and North Africa, the Egyptian government wanted to hire a contingent of Blackwood's former special forces operatives to run an advanced training program for some of their troops. The problem was, their basic training wasn't good enough, and you couldn't teach soldiers to sprint, climb, and jump before they mastered walking or they'd fall flat on their fucking faces.

Last month, we'd run a trial, and it had been a disaster. We weren't about to risk our reputation or the morale of our people until the Egyptian army put some effort in, and we'd told them that in no uncertain terms. So I kind of understood where Black was coming from, but he had a tendency to think in cold, hard facts when sometimes a little empathy was needed.

Bob was on the same wavelength, it seemed.

"Remember the day after Eid al Adha in Northern Iraq?" he asked. "When Briggs got shot by a sniper and you insisted on going back for the body?"

"I was young and stupid then."

"Young, yes, but never stupid. You said you wanted him to have a proper burial."

Black didn't much like to talk about his time as a

Navy SEAL, but I knew he'd been nineteen when that incident happened. He still had the faintest scar on his thigh from the bullet wound he'd received that day, plus a Silver Star tucked at the back of our bedroom safe back in Richmond.

"I can't argue with both of you." A pause. Black liked space to think, to mull things over. "Fine. We'll bring the body up." He glanced around the boat, and I could see the cogs turning. "Diamond, you'd better empty that fucking ice chest."

CHAPTER 4 - EMMY

FOR THE SECOND time that sunny Wednesday, a chill ran through me, partly due to the water seeping into my wetsuit but mostly because this time, I knew what awaited us at forty-five metres.

We'd spent the last hour and a half talking over our plan to recover the body, watching the footage Black had filmed on our first dive and discussing the logistics, the potential problems, and how to mitigate those problems before they happened.

One thing we all agreed on was that Captain Bob wouldn't notify the authorities until Black and I were back underwater. The only thing worse than manhandling half a corpse while on vacation was attempting to do that with a dozen men who didn't know what they were doing barking opposing instructions on the matter.

Black carried Bob's camera this time, a professional setup with lights that cost more than a small family hatchback and weighed about as much as one too. I guided the picnic cooler into the water, now modified with drainage holes in the bottom and a sturdy rope cradle we'd use to haul it back to the surface again. The cradle hooked to a winch on the back of the *Blue Tang*, and when we set off the submersible flare Black carried in his pocket, Bob would slowly, slowly start reeling our haul in.

We descended quickly—going down was never the issue, rather it was coming back up that slowed things with pesky decompression stops. Take Ahmed Gabr's world-record dive if you want an extreme example. Three hundred and thirty-two metres deep, fifteen minutes to get there, and thirteen and a half hours to safely ascend again.

At forty-five metres, the body was right where we left it, but minus another pound or two of flesh. Since I hadn't eaten lunch yet, I figured it was safe to take a closer look. Was it a man or a woman? Difficult to tell, but from the size, I guessed at a female, or perhaps a teenage boy. Light brown hair curled around the edges of the skull, wafting in the current. The clothes didn't give much away. Blue jeans and a red T-shirt hung in tatters, floating eerily in the blue, and the feet were bare. One scrap of the T-shirt had a logo—two fish fashioned into a heart shape.

It was Bob who'd asked the inevitable question: accident or murder? I didn't know the answer to that yet either. Could the body have drifted with the current? Had a tourist slipped on the rocks above and drowned before they managed to escape? If they'd hit their head...curtains. Or had some sick freak tossed our victim into the sea, assuming their remains would sink straight to the bottom of the abyss?

Our plan called for me to act as barracuda-blocker while Black documented the scene. I got all the good jobs. Even though I wore gloves, their teeth could still do plenty of damage, so I carried a knife just in case. A five-inch clip-point with a matt-black blade. Barracudas were like magpies—attracted to shiny things—and I didn't want to encourage them over.

With better lighting, I saw details I'd missed on the first trip down. The silver ring on a bony finger. The pair of flowers embroidered below the left-hand jeans pocket and pink nail polish on what was left of the toes that suggested our victim was female. The words printed on the purple backpack: *Love Life, Love Dahab*.

That philosophy hadn't worked out so well for her, had it?

The tiny shrimps crawled over her exposed flesh, hundreds of them, thousands even, and Black used his spare hand to sweep a bunch of them away before he resumed filming. Odd. The straps of the backpack were tied together with a piece of yellow cord, making it harder for her arms to slip out. Had she done that? Or had somebody else done it for her?

Something silver flashed in my peripheral vision, and the mother of all barracudas swam at me. I turned in what felt like slow motion and punched the bloody thing as it shot past an inch from my face. One chance. I'd give it one chance.

In front of me, Black focused on the task at hand, panning slowly from left to right, recording every detail of the scene for posterity. Another barracuda—or maybe the same one—glided past me towards the reef wall, and I spotted something twinkling, half-buried in the sand on a ledge just below the girl's feet. A hair clip. Hers? And where were her shoes? I looked above and beneath us, but I couldn't see them, so either they'd tumbled to the bottom or she'd gone in barefoot.

Black beckoned me forward, and I let a little air out of my wing to make myself heavier, then hooked myself to the reef wall. He did the same—we needed stability for the next part—and also clipped the camera onto the rope to free up his hands. Now came the tricky part. First, we manoeuvred the cooler into position underneath the girl's legs, and I held it steady while Black worked out how best to free her. He tried lifting her backpack, and I caught the surprise in his eyes as he shook his head. Whatever she had in there was heavier than he'd expected.

How was our air? A third gone. At these depths, every lungful was denser than at the surface, so we went through it much faster. Black's gauge would say about the same as mine, I knew from experience. He may have been bigger, but practice meant he was also better at conserving air.

Now, he studied the scene, head slightly tilted and a knife in his hand. He needed to cut something, but what?

A barracuda got curious, swimming up to take a bite of its favourite meal as though it realised the table would soon be cleared. I batted it away, and it glared at me through beady little eyes. Good thing we weren't dealing with piranhas. Finally, Black sawed through the cord, and I grabbed it off him and stuffed it into a pocket as the girl slid free from her bounds and concertinaed into the makeshift casket. Not exactly the ideal procedure, but with time and location against us, it was the best we could do.

I made sure to pick up the hair clip too, then went for the backpack. What the bloody hell was she carrying? Rocks? Black held out a hand, ready to secure the bag to the winch cable, when my hook came loose and I plummeted towards the depths. Ah, fuck. *Think,*

Emmy. I blasted more air into my wing, which slowed me down, but it wasn't enough. Whatever was in the bag had to weigh at least fifteen kilos. Fifty metres, fifty-five... My ears began aching, and my dive computer beeped helpfully to let me know I was too deep. No way was I letting go of the evidence, though, so with little other choice, I sacrificed my weight belt to the sea. Nine kilos gone, and with a bit of kicking, I began to ascend. At a maximum safe rate of nine metres per minute, it took me two minutes to get back to Black, and when I drew level, the asshole fucking laughed. I gave him the finger as he set off the flare and sent the school of barracudas bolting into the blue.

Since I'd lost my weight belt, I had to hold on to the backpack as we made our way to the surface, and my impromptu adventure meant I had a longer decompression time to look forward to. At ten metres, Bob had hung two small bottles of oxygen to help us out. The winch cable had depths marked at intervals, and he paused the ascent of our grisly cargo too, three bodies hanging in the water while we counted down the minutes.

Black rolled onto his back and studied the ripples on the surface. When I followed his gaze, I saw a shadow off the *Blue Tang*'s stern, what looked like a small dinghy tethered to the bigger boat.

Black wrote on the slate strapped to his arm.

Police?

I nodded. That seemed the most likely scenario. Suddenly, a longer decompression stop didn't seem so bad. The prospect of answering questions for hours when I *still* hadn't eaten lunch didn't spark joy, as that TV cleaning lady Bradley loved so much kept saying, and it was tempting to leave the cops with the body and swim a little way up the coast. We could hide the gear, walk into town, and come back for it later. Probably no one would steal it. Crime rates were low in Dahab, apart from a possible murder, obviously.

Black scrawled on his slate again. *Don't even think about it.*

This was the problem when you met your soulmate. They knew you as well as you knew yourself— sometimes better—and maintaining an element of surprise was almost impossible. But the good times far outweighed the bad. If I hadn't met Black, I could've become an accounts assistant or a marketing executive or an HR administrator, another faceless desk jockey working forty hours a week to afford the rent on a one-bedroom flat in a shitty part of London, a Netflix subscription, and the occasional package holiday to the Costa del Sol. That was a best-case scenario. More likely, I'd be dead on the streets I'd tried so hard to escape.

With little else to do underwater, I got to wondering what was in the victim's bag. I really wanted to open it, but I held back in case some vital piece of evidence got loose and floated away. The last thing I fancied was another swim to retrieve it.

No, I had to wait, and patience wasn't my strong suit. For long stops, I usually liked to read. Nonfiction, mostly—science, politics, history, stuff that made me sound intelligent at parties. I pushed the boundaries with my waterproof e-reader case as well as with everything else in my life. But today, there were only fish to look at.

After a minute or two, Black pulled out a torch and

signalled to Bob in Morse code. I didn't follow everything, but my fuck-up was mentioned, as was the resulting delay. After what seemed like forever, we were on our way upwards again, water pouring off us as we emerged in front of Bob and our two new guests, neither of whom appeared too thrilled by today's developments. While the younger private chewed his bottom lip in apprehension as he glanced at the cooler, his boss, who wore the three-star epaulettes of a captain, looked plain ol' pissed off. Both stepped back as puddles spread across the deck.

"The body is in there?" the captain asked.

Where else would it be? "Yup."

"You shouldn't have moved it."

"Captain al-Busari's going to be running the investigation," Bob told us. "He trained at the Police Academy in Cairo, and apparently, we shouldn't have moved the body until the police documented the scene."

"Were you planning to go down and document it yourself?" Black asked.

"We have a specialist team."

"Really? Then where are they?"

"Alexandria."

For fuck's sake. The man was a grade A idiot.

"By the time they got here from Alexandria, there wouldn't have been anything left of the woman," I pointed out.

"It's a woman?"

"Yes. Want to take a look?"

I didn't bother to wait for an answer, just opened the cooler lid then stifled a laugh when the younger cop tripped over his feet running to the side of the boat to puke. The horror on the captain's face didn't escape me either. Had he even seen a dead body before?

"There you go. Guess you can start documenting everything now."

A shout came from the shore, around thirty metres away, and another cop waved something black and plasticky in our direction.

"I have it! I brought the body bag."

Good grief.

"That area's also part of your crime scene," Black pointed out. "Since it's where the woman went into the water. You need to secure it and search it, not trample all over it."

The captain swallowed hard, then yelled at the newcomer in Arabic. "Get back, you fool. Stop anybody from coming near." Then to sidekick number one, who was wiping his mouth with his sleeve: "And Khaled, start documenting. Write everything down."

What a charmer. Did he realise we foreigners spoke Arabic? Probably not. I usually preferred not to let on— that way, I could listen in on all sorts of conversations I wasn't supposed to hear.

Khaled pulled out a notepad and stared around, pen paused over the page. I took pity on him.

"It's easiest to start with photos," I said. "We've filmed the scene underwater, but you'll need to have a record of what we've brought up. Chain of custody. The body can stay in the cooler until it goes to the morgue, but you'll need evidence bags for her backpack and a couple of other bits. Do you have any of those?"

A quick shake of the head. Of course he didn't.

"Bob, do you have any plastic bags? We'll need a big rubbish sack plus two smaller ones. The kind you put sandwiches in."

"Around here, we use Tupperware for sandwiches. It's better for the environment."

"Okay, two boxes."

"What are you doing?" the captain asked. "This is my investigation."

"We appreciate that," Black told him. Until that point, he'd managed to stay diplomatic, but the little tic in his jaw said he'd had enough of the good chief. "But since you've come woefully underprepared, we thought we'd help."

"Thank you," Khaled whispered, but the captain didn't seem to share his sentiment.

"I will handle it," al-Busari snapped. "You're civilians. Foreigners. This is not your business."

"Then get the body off our boat, and we'll carry on with our vacation."

Black turned his back on the man. Dismissed.

I took a small measure of joy at the shock on the captain's face. Evidently, the big cheese wasn't accustomed to being spoken to like that, but my husband didn't suffer fools gladly. Me? I was conflicted. On the one hand, instinct told me the girl had been murdered, and I wanted to see her killer brought to justice. But on the other hand, this *was* our vacation. Perhaps that sounds selfish, but we couldn't solve every crime in the world, and the thought of spending the next two weeks butting heads with the Egyptian police didn't exactly fill me with glee. We'd offered to assist, and they'd turned us down.

"Here—you'll want these." I fished the piece of knotted cord and the hair clip out of my pocket and placed them on the cooler. "And this."

I picked up the backpack, but without the water to support it, the flimsy fabric tore under the weight of its contents. Rocks tumbled out. One landed on my foot, and the rest scattered across the deck. Rocks? *Actual rocks?* I'd been kidding when I suggested that earlier. Who the hell went hiking with a bag of bloody rocks?

Black paused halfway up the ladder to the upper deck, and our eyes met. Well, we were both certain of one thing now—the girl's death was murder.

Chapter 5 - Emmy

"WHAT DO YOU want for breakfast?" Black asked. "Fruit? Cereal? Toast?"

"Waffles." I hesitated, rubbing feeling back into one wrist where he'd just removed the handcuffs, which sounds a lot kinkier than it was. "And I'm sorry."

"Waffles," he repeated, tugging on a T-shirt to cover the bruises on his chest. "And there's nothing to be sorry for. It's not your fault."

But it was. I never meant to hit him, but my nightmares were so real, so vivid, that I lashed out without being aware of what I was doing. Last night, I'd watched a girl's murder, a brunette about my height fighting for her life against a monster in the sea. Then I became the girl, and when the shadowy form wrapped its tentacles around me, I'd fought back, clawing and punching until Black slapped me hard across the face and I woke up.

I always used to sleep alone, but now that we were together, Black refused to let me. Whenever I suggested it, he said he'd rather deal with the consequences than have us spend a night apart.

Which left me to deal with the guilt. At three a.m., I'd dabbed antiseptic cream onto the gouges in Black's back and handcuffed myself to the headboard, then spent the rest of the night wide awake while Black tried to find a comfortable position beside me.

The front door clicked behind him, and I paced the room. Should I try sleeping pills again? I hated them because they messed with my mind, not to mention put me in danger by slowing down my reactions, but I also hated hurting the person I loved most. It was days like this that I wished I'd never accepted the job with Blackwood. Wished I'd taken my chances in London. Wished I hadn't seen so much death.

Black was right. We really did need this vacation.

"How about we go kitesurfing?" he suggested when he came back with breakfast. After scuba diving and swimming, kitesurfing was Black's favourite water sport, and with the latter, we had a much lower chance of coming across a body. "It's good and windy today."

"Maybe."

"You're still fretting about the girl we found yesterday?"

"How can I not?"

No matter how many corpses I saw, they still affected me. Think that's hypocritical considering I was in the business of death? Perhaps. But every contract I took, I accepted because I believed it was for the greater good, like cutting a cancer out of the world. Anton Ludovich, the speed-loving oligarch-in-training? The American he'd had killed was a journalist writing an exposé on the Ludovich family's business empire, which happened to include the illegal dumping of toxic waste that had seeped into rivers and poisoned thousands.

A small group of people like Black and me fought in the shadows to maintain the balance between right and wrong, although we sometimes had to ignore a few laws to do so. And if you reckon governments didn't condone our activities, then you'd be wrong. They were our biggest customers.

But my job took its toll on my psyche. In the daytime, I could force the dark thoughts away, squash them to the back of my mind and get on with the task at hand, but after sundown, all bets were off. This morning, I'd woken with a mixture of guilt and foreboding gnawing at my mind. Maybe it was the unexplained nature of the girl's death, or perhaps it was the police captain's attitude, but I had a horrible feeling the worst was yet to come.

"We don't have any kind of authority here," Black reminded me. "We can't right every wrong we come across. This case is somebody else's job." Sometimes, I envied his ability to compartmentalise so effectively. The worst of his world got sucked into a black hole, never to be seen again. "So, kitesurfing?"

"Aren't you tired?"

"I'm fine." He crouched beside me. "But you're tired, aren't you?"

Yes, which was my own fault. And dammit, why did he have to be so sweet about stuff like that? I didn't deserve him.

"A little tired," I admitted.

Plus my waffles had cream *and* chocolate sauce, which meant a double helping of guilt niggled at me. A triple helping when Black leaned over to kiss me on the forehead.

"We can kitesurf tomorrow," he said. "Let's lie in the sun this morning."

"You hate lying in the sun."

"I can pretend to like it for a day."

"No, we're going kitesurfing." Whether I enjoyed it or not. Decision made. "I'll be fine."

And that was how I found myself standing in the spare bedroom, yawning as I stared at the mountain of water sports equipment stacked beside the French windows. Scuba tanks, a wakeboard, fins, boots, a windsurf sail…

Black sucked in a breath as he tugged on the arm of a stray wetsuit. "I think we need to tidy up."

"Or get an Egyptian version of Bradley."

This was the first break I'd had in ages. The last thing I felt like doing was wasting any of that precious time rearranging all the shit I'd avoided rearranging on past visits. Come to think of it, the main reason the pile was so high was because I hadn't been able to find anything on my previous trip, so I'd bought more stuff instead of digging through the mess.

"Diamond, if we had an Egyptian version of Bradley, we wouldn't be able to move from incense burners and shisha pipes, and I fucking hate wind chimes. Let's just buy another closet instead."

"Fine. A closet. A really big closet." Great. I hated shopping almost as much as I hated pineapple on pizza. "Have you seen a furniture store in Dahab?"

"No, but logically there must be one. We'll ask around." He passed me a rolled-up kite. "Here, you'll need this."

When I wasn't so tired, I really did love kitesurfing. A cross between parasailing and wakeboarding, it was tricky enough to keep me sharp. In Dahab, the semi-enclosed laguna attracted enthusiasts from the world over with its glorious wind conditions, and when we finished breakfast and went outside, we were two of a dozen people arranging our gear on the beach.

First, we had to blow up our kites using a foot pump. The kites attached to waist harnesses via long lines, ready to propel us over the waves. Speed and direction were controlled using a bar in front of our chests. One small move of the wrist could mean the difference between resting while the kite hovered in place above you or shooting forward at fifty knots.

Black launched his kite first and accelerated away from me as I positioned myself in the water, feet strapped to my kiteboard. A moment later, I followed, and the wind whipped through my hair as I sped after him.

Sometimes, I wondered what life would be like if I retired. Just quit the security business and spent my days having fun. Fuck knows, I'd earned enough money over the last decade to never have to work again. Maybe my nightmares would even go away?

But every time that thought crept up on me, I dismissed it almost instantly. The truth was, I was a junkie. An addict. I needed my drugs of choice—oxytocin from the friendships I'd made at work, endorphins from keeping fit, and dopamine from the occasional sneaky donut. But my real vice was adrenaline. Sure, kitesurfing was a rush, but it didn't come close to walking that fine line between living and dying while keeping my balance all the way to the end. No, I'd stick with the odd vacation. The sun stimulated serotonin production, after all.

My kite caught the wind, and I left the water, knees bent as I somersaulted. This was what it felt like to be free, not a care in the world, at least until I realised I'd gone too far out to sea and was fast heading for Saudi

Arabia. The Hijaz Mountains were just visible through the mist that hung over the Gulf of Aqaba, hulking brown lumps seemingly devoid of character from twenty-seven kilometres away, although at night, the twinkling lights at the foothills signalled the existence of towns and villages.

Er, best to turn around.

Chapter 6 - Emmy

MY ARMS AND legs ached when we hauled our gear up the beach at the end of the day, but Black was, well, not smiling exactly because he rarely did that in public, but content. The effort had been worth it, even if I could hardly keep my eyes open, and a little of my guilt trickled away.

"Dinner?" he asked as we walked up the path to the villa.

"Yes."

"Where? Do you want to stay in or go into town?"

We'd stayed in last night. By the time we'd cleared the diving gear away, downloaded the video footage onto a memory stick for the police to pick up, and tried to scrub away the feel of rotting flesh in the shower, neither of us could be bothered to leave the hotel complex, so we'd gotten room service to deliver sustenance.

Truth be told, I was still shattered, and all I wanted to do was crawl into bed alone and avoid another night like the last one. But that wasn't fair on Black.

"Let's go out. Pick a restaurant."

"Italian."

"We had pizza last night."

"So? We're..."

"On vacation," I finished with him. And of course

my husband picked Italian. He *always* picked Italian. It was his favourite kind of food. Secretly, I suspected he'd been looking forward to our now-cancelled assassination job in Milan because it meant he could've spent two weeks living on ravioli and osso buco. "Okay, we'll have Italian."

Italian meant a walk up the coastal path to Maurizio's, a restaurant on the beach near the local sheikh's house. At that time of year, the evenings were cooler, and with enough wind to blow any bugs away, the walk was a pleasant one, albeit dark. Years ago, the town council had tried installing solar lights, but despite the amount of sun, they'd never worked properly. Nobody worried; Dahab was safe. But as we strolled along, hand in hand, I couldn't help wondering whether the recent murder would change things.

Not much had altered since I last visited. The vegan restaurant was still there, the Lebanese restaurant, the weird bar that always played loud music but which never seemed to have any customers. The place by the Sweet Dreams Hotel was new. Or at least, the beachside seating area had had a makeover. Gone was the tired blue-and-white decor, replaced by gaudy red and green glass-topped tables and low benches with enough cushions to give Bradley a wet dream. But the bright furniture wasn't what caught my eye. No, that was the new logo. Two fish in a heart shape, the name *Happy Fish* written underneath.

I ground to a halt.

"Do you recognise that?"

Black didn't need to ask what I was talking about because of course he'd seen it too. His charcoal eyes missed nothing. "We're not having Italian tonight, are we?"

"I'm curious. Aren't you curious?"

For a moment, he didn't answer, because he was trying to decide whether to lie. See, I knew him well too. He didn't want to get involved with any official inquiry, but the innate sense of nosiness that had led him away from the Navy SEALs, first to the CIA and then to a career in investigations, meant he wanted answers.

Finally, "Okay, I'm curious."

A waiter sidled up to us. "Would you like to eat here tonight? We have daily specials—fresh fish, steak, Black Forest cake."

I offered him a smile. "Table for two?"

"This way, please."

The logo on his shirt matched our victim's, but the colour didn't; his was navy blue. He showed us to a table in a prime spot by the water and held my chair out while I sat down. The actual cooking was done in a building on the other side of the promenade, and the staff dodged pedestrians as they hurried across to their customers, carrying trays of drinks and dishes aloft.

There appeared to be three waiters, all male, plus a cheerful German owner—a middle-aged man with thinning hair and a Star of David on a chain around his neck—who came out to check our food was okay.

"Delicious, thank you."

"And the service is also good?"

"Yeah, great."

Black conjured up a charming smile. "A lady we met on the beach suggested we try this place. She said she was a waitress here, but I don't see her?"

"Carmela?"

"We didn't get her name. About my wife's height, short brown hair, wearing one of your T-shirts in red."

"Sounds like Carmela. She quit last week."

"Really? She was singing the place's praises not so long ago, and we're keen to thank her for the recommendation."

When in doubt, flatter the target.

"*Ja*, but she didn't turn up for work, and when I called her, she didn't answer."

"So she didn't actually hand in her notice?"

"No, but the population is so transient here. It's not the first time a person has left without saying a word."

A waiter wandered over. Omar, according to his name badge. Egyptian, kind of nervous-looking.

"Is everything good with the meal?"

Did he know anything? "Wonderful, thank you. We were just discussing one of your colleagues. Carmela? She quit suddenly last week."

"Oh? I thought maybe she had some days off. She quit? That is surprising. She didn't tell me."

The German shrugged. "Probably because she hates difficult conversations. The number of times she made excuses for that boyfriend of hers rather than sticking up for herself..."

"They had problems?" Black asked. "She seemed happy when we spoke to her."

"That's Carmela—always putting on a smile. The customers loved her."

"But the boyfriend?"

"He didn't like her working here. Said she was too good for waitressing and she could get a better job in Italy, but she always told me her heart is by the sea."

And in a horrible twist of irony, that was where it

had ended up for eternity, stolen by a barracuda.

"So that was it? They disagreed over her career ambitions?"

Our German friend glanced around, but the only other occupied table was right across the restaurant. A party, it looked like, with a dozen or so people all talking too loud. Still, he leaned in closer.

"Worse than that. I think he gets violent on occasion. A while ago, she came to work with a big bruise on her face. She said she walked into a door, and we all know what that means."

"Did you ask her about it?"

"*Ja*. I drove her to the hospital for X-rays, and the whole time, she swore it was the truth. But I also overheard her on the phone to her friend later, and she said it was Youssef's fault."

"Youssef was her boyfriend?"

Omar nodded. "Yes, Youssef. He works in his father's chicken shop on the far side of Assalah Square."

"What about the friend? Will she take care of Carmela?" Black glanced at me. "We just hate hearing tales of violence against women. Back home in Virginia, Emmy volunteers at a women's shelter."

That part was sort of true. Our charitable foundation funded the place, and my good friend Dan, who'd many years ago been a victim of domestic violence herself, spent hours there listening to the women pouring their hearts out. Sometimes, for the worst cases, I tagged along when she visited the offenders with a reminder that women weren't always the meek little creatures they thought we were.

Now the German's cheeks reddened. "I think so. I

should've checked before that she was okay, but...but..."

I went for sympathy. "But you were annoyed because she left you in the lurch? That's understandable."

"*Ja*. Now I feel as if I should have done more."

Omar fished around in his trouser pocket. "I will call Aurelie. That's Carmela's friend," he explained to us. "She's a nice lady."

A group of tourists walked in, three couples, the women cooing over the view of the sea and the shells glued to the wall in the shape of the restaurant's logo. The German backed away apologetically.

"I need to seat these people. Please, enjoy the rest of your meal."

The waiter scuttled off too, but he already had his phone to his ear. Black took a sip of water.

"That should set the ball rolling. Once they realise Carmela's disappeared, either Omar or the friend will report her missing. Assuming the dead girl *is* Carmela, only a fool wouldn't manage to connect the dots between her death and her hospital visit, which means they'll hand the police a viable suspect too."

I held up my glass and clinked it against Black's. "To sticking our noses in where they're not wanted."

"To fighting for justice."

"Awesome. Now that's done, what are we having for dessert? I was gonna go for ice cream, but the Black Forest cake sounds good too."

"Have both. We're on vacation."

"Did you really just encourage me to eat two desserts? Are you feeling okay?"

"Don't expect me to do it again."

"This must be my lucky day. Love you, Chuck."

"I'll love you more if you stop calling me Chuck," he said, but he was smiling.

"Charles?" That was his real name, but he didn't like that much either.

"Sure, if I can call you Amanda."

Amanda. My given name, and a reminder of the mother who'd done such a bad job of raising me that I'd run away aged twelve. I hadn't used it since I was fifteen.

"Fine. You win. How about I use my mouth for something else instead?"

"Let's get dessert to go."

"And give a whole new meaning to *Black* Forest cake?"

"I'm good with you eating cake off me, but forget the ice cream."

"Fair enough. I wouldn't want anything to shrivel up."

Black waved a different waiter over since Omar had vanished. "Can you put a whole Black Forest cake in a box?"

Oh, this was definitely my lucky day.

CHAPTER 7 - BLACK

BLACK GROANED AS he stretched his arms to the sides. Half a Black Forest cake sat heavy in his gut, and he'd overslept by two hours. Was this what regular people did on vacation? Let their discipline slip, then regretted it afterwards? If the answer was yes, he wanted to go home already.

But Emmy was smiling in her sleep, her blonde hair spread over his chest, so he'd stick out the two weeks if it made her happy.

Where was his phone? He could catch up on emails, check the daily logs, help with any questions his team might have... Maybe review the crime scene footage from yesterday...

And it *was* a crime scene. No woman went hiking with a backpack full of fucking rocks. Well, Emmy did when she was working out with Alex, the ex-Spetsnaz personal trainer who kept her in shape. Rephrase: no *sane* woman. Coupled with the odd way the bag's straps had been tied and the lack of footwear... Yes, she could have been wearing a pair of flip-flops that had drifted away, but she'd have shredded her feet climbing over the sharp rocks on the shore before she got near the water.

Black knew he should leave the case alone, but it'd piqued his curiosity. Was the boyfriend guilty? What kind of man killed a woman rather than showing her the door?

"Chuck? What are you doing?" Emmy mumbled.

"Nothing."

"You're incapable of doing nothing. Are you working?"

"Not exactly."

She lifted her chin to take a better look. "You're going through murder photos? It's not even seven a.m. No death before coffee."

"Thanks for offering. Make mine a double espresso."

Curses were muttered, but Emmy still got up and stumbled through to the kitchen. She'd never been a morning person, and the vacation had left her drowsy. Or perhaps that was the cake. Or the sex. Never mind— she was easier to deal with that way, so Black wasn't about to complain.

He took one last look at his phone and shut it off. How was the police investigation going? Next time he saw Bob, he'd get an update. Bob was well-connected, and he'd know somebody involved.

"What are we doing today?" Emmy asked.

"Whatever you want."

"Wakeboarding, then. All I need to do is find my wakeboard."

"Where did you leave it?"

She jerked a thumb towards the mountain of shit in the third bedroom. "Uh, I think it's in there."

Which was why at eleven o'clock, they found themselves driving into town in Bob's pickup to buy a fucking closet.

"Where to?" Black asked Emmy.

"How the hell should I know? Dahab doesn't exactly have a department store. Just drive around, and we're bound to come across somewhere sooner or later."

Later, it turned out. After an hour, they'd gotten stuck behind a herd of goats and helped a lost group of German tourists to locate their hotel, but the only furniture store they'd found was filled entirely with wicker.

"This is hopeless," Emmy said. "It's easier to buy a new villa than a new bloody wardrobe. I'm calling Bradley."

"No, you're not." Black plucked her phone out of her hand before she could dial. "We can do this ourselves."

"I need a donut."

"You don't need a donut."

"Fine, a pastry. A croissant. Some sort of carbs."

Black had slowed to steer around a stray dog, and Emmy leapt from the car before he could negotiate a healthier lunch, landed like a cat, and jogged straight into the nearest bakery. That crazy bitch. He had little choice but to wait for her, and she strolled back a minute later, clutching a family-sized paper carrier bag.

"I bought you a cookie."

"I don't like cookies."

"No, you don't like the *idea* of cookies. One won't kill you. And take the road on the left up there—I got directions to IKEA."

"IKEA? Here?"

"Apparently so." Even Emmy didn't sound convinced. "The dude at the bakery swore they sold wardrobes."

In the embodiment of Dahabian enterprise, IKEA

turned out to be a small room containing one man and a laptop. You picked whatever you wanted from the IKEA website, and he dispatched his brother to Cairo to pick it up. Their Platsa modular storage system would arrive the day after tomorrow, together with a chair shaped like a giant egg, a set of kitchen storage canisters, and a cactus.

Black edged towards the door as Emmy handed over a sheaf of hundred-pound notes. Was it over? Could they go back to the hotel now? Even festering on a sunlounger was more tolerable than this.

"Done?" he asked Emmy.

"I think so. Perhaps we should've ordered that hammock too…"

"Out." Black half carried his wife to the door. "We're leaving."

"But—"

"Hey, wait!" The shout came from their left. "Please?"

Was the woman yelling at Emmy and Black? He turned to see a twenty-something brunette dressed in yoga pants running towards them in that funny gait that only came with flip-flops. Knees high, heels dragging along the ground. He glanced sideways at Emmy. No, she didn't know the girl either.

"Hi, sorry, excuse me…" American, but with the apologies, she sounded almost British. "But were you…?" She paused to suck in a breath. "Were you in Happy Fish last night?"

"Why do you ask?"

"Omar said it was a big guy, like a giant, and his wife was really pretty with blonde hair. And when I saw you, I just thought…"

"Perhaps you could start at the beginning?" Emmy suggested.

"My friend Omar called to say Carmela was missing, then he and Gunther told me you saw her, and now the police are saying she's dead, that she killed herself, but she'd never have done that, and I need to know when she died because her boyfriend went to Cairo, and so they said he couldn't have been involved, but if it happened *before* he left—"

"Ease up." Emmy's demeanour softened. "Slow down a bit. Who's Gunther?"

The cops thought Carmela killed herself? Had they lost their fucking minds?

"Gunther Krause. He owns the Happy Fish restaurant."

"And you were friends with Carmela? Are you Aurelie?"

"Yes, I'm Aurelie. How did you know?"

"Omar mentioned your name. I'm so sorry about Carmela."

"It's *insane*. She'd never have killed herself."

"What makes them think she did?"

"They said the doctor did an autopsy yesterday, and she drowned because she deliberately wore a backpack filled with stones to make herself sink."

How did the *doctor* come to the conclusion that she'd drowned? The rocks were merely circumstantial evidence. And more to the point, how did a medical professional come to that conclusion so quickly?

When a person drowned, there were several signs, the most obvious being water in the lungs, stomach, and frontal and ethmoidal sinuses, followed by haemorrhaging in the mastoid air sinuses. But

Carmela's stomach and lungs had been devoured by a school of hungry barracudas, and there wasn't a whole lot left of her face either. Her head had been teeming with small shrimp-like creatures, lysianassid amphipods if Black wasn't mistaken, and they'd been snacking on her flesh.

Which meant the only sure way to determine if she'd drowned was through analysis of her bone marrow. The sea contained diatoms, tiny unicellular organisms, and during the late stages of drowning, those got circulated to all the organs. Diatoms weren't normally found in bone marrow, so if they showed up, that was an indicator of how she'd died.

But they'd only had the body for a day. Checking for diatoms meant digesting the bone marrow with strong acids first, and the process took time. Black wasn't totally ruling out drowning, but rather questioning the authorities' handling of the case. If he had to guess, he'd say it was more than likely that the police captain had pushed for a quick resolution in order to avoid any bad publicity, both for himself and for the town. The death of a foreigner in Dahab wouldn't exactly boost tourism revenues.

"Interesting," he said, more to himself than anybody else.

"Interesting? You think this is interesting? This... this is *devastating*."

A tear rolled down Aurelie's cheek, and Black gritted his teeth. "Interesting" had perhaps been the wrong word to use. Maybe he *should* go on the sensitivity training course that Logan, Blackwood's development coordinator, was always emailing him about.

"Tell us more about Carmela," Emmy said. "Why do you think the police are wrong?"

"Because she was happy. The week before last, we were planning a trip to Jordan to visit the ruins at Petra, and she was looking forward to it."

"Sometimes, even those who seem the happiest can be depressed inside."

"Not Carmela."

"How long had you known her?"

"Eight months. We arrived in Dahab on the same day and ended up sharing an apartment until she moved in with her boyfriend. She was my best friend."

Best friends, yet nobody had been aware of her disappearance before the body was found.

"Did you report her missing?" Black asked. "Before yesterday, I mean."

"No, because I thought she'd gone to Cairo with Youssef."

The boyfriend. And Aurelie's curl of the lip when she mentioned his name betrayed her opinion of the man, which appeared to be in line with Gunther's.

"You didn't get on with him?" Black asked.

"I always thought she could've done better. And now... Now..."

"You think he might have killed her?"

A nervous shrug. "Well, somebody sure did. Can you tell me when you saw her on the beach?"

That was the problem with lies. Occasionally, they came back to bite you in the ass. Now, should he tell a bigger lie or revert to the truth? Say they saw her last week, and Aurelie would go chasing after Youssef, which could be dangerous if he was the culprit. Say they saw her this week, and they risked ruling out a suspect.

"We didn't," Emmy said.

"Huh?"

"We didn't see her on the beach. It's a long story. Basically, we were the people who found Carmela's body, and we told Gunther a small fib because it seemed like the fastest way to join the dots and steer the police towards her identity."

"Why didn't you just call them yourselves?"

"Honestly? Because we didn't want to get wrapped up in a murder investigation on our vacation."

"If you're only here on vacation, how do you know Carmela? How did you work out it was her?"

"She was wearing her work shirt. We recognised the restaurant's logo and figured she might be an employee."

Another tear, this time accompanied by a trembling lip. "You shouldn't lie. It wastes people's time, and it's... it's *rude*."

Aurelie turned away, mousy brown hair flying in the wind. She didn't look like much—five feet nothing with delicate features and big hazel eyes—but her attitude, fiery with an undercurrent of fear, would get her into trouble if she wasn't careful.

"We're sorry, okay?" Emmy said. "Where are you going?"

"To talk to Youssef."

"That's probably not a good idea."

"What else am I supposed to do? And don't tell me to speak to the police again, because they won't do anything. They never do. Gunther's bicycle got stolen, and he knew who took it because the asshole was riding it around town, but the cops wouldn't even file a report."

Ah, fuck. Black glanced at Emmy at the same time as she cut her eyes sideways towards him. He knew that look. His beloved wife couldn't stand by and watch while a woman walked into jeopardy alone. And how did he feel? Although two weeks of vacation had sounded like a nice idea, three days in, and he was bored already.

"We'll come with you," he said.

Aurelie paused mid-stride. "You will?"

"Yes."

"Why? Because you feel guilty?"

Guilt wasn't an emotion that had ever bothered Black. "Because neither of us wants to fish another corpse out of the sea."

Aurelie wiped her eyes on the bottom of her T-shirt while Emmy pursed her lips. What was the problem now? The woman had just told him not to lie, no? So he hadn't, for once.

"What he meant is that we'll help because Carmela deserves justice," Emmy said. "And we don't want to see you get hurt either."

"What if *you* get hurt?"

"Don't worry about us. Back home, we do this for a living."

"You're cops?"

"No, we run a security and investigations company."

"But w-w-what about your vacation?"

"Some things are more important than getting a suntan. Come on, let's find a quiet spot and talk over what we know."

CHAPTER 8 - BLACK

PREDICTABLY, AURELIE WANTED to go steaming over to Assalah Square and question Youssef *right now*, but Black quickly vetoed that idea.

"You only get one shot at questioning a person for the first time, and you want to do that armed with as much knowledge as possible."

"But—"

"How can you catch him in a lie if you don't know the truth yourself?"

"And nobody can work on an empty stomach," Emmy put in. "Have you eaten lunch yet?"

Aurelie backed down easily. Too easily for this job. "I haven't even eaten breakfast."

They ended up back at Happy Fish. In mid-afternoon, the place was as popular as 1987 Chernobyl, and they settled at a table near the water's edge. There was no sign of Gunther, but Omar materialised with an order pad.

Scrawny, nineteen or twenty years old, cheap clothes, but the shirt was spotless and ironed. Yesterday, Omar's eyes had been worried but hopeful. Today, they'd dulled. He reminded Black of another kid, the son of a café owner in Fallujah he'd met in another lifetime. Syed. Twenty years on, Black still remembered his name. On the first visit, Syed had smiled as he served coffee that was too sweet in a cup that was too small, full of optimism that Good Samaritans like the businessman Black was pretending to be would rebuild his country. The second visit, after Syed's parents had been killed by a suicide bomber and his sister had disappeared, he looked a decade older than his nineteen years. On Black's third visit, he'd sipped weak tea as Syed ran across the street to the grocery store to get more sugar, only for the teenager to get picked off by a sniper hell-bent on eliminating infidels. Black had taken a certain satisfaction in dispatching the terrorist to meet his god in person.

"I almost can't believe the news," Omar said. "Are the police certain it's Carmela?"

"That's what they told me, but they said..."—a sniffle from Aurelie—"they said there wasn't much left of her to identify. I don't know what to do. I mean, I guess someone should organise a funeral, but how? Nobody close to me ever died before."

Black didn't see how they could've confirmed Carmela's identity for sure. Not yet, when they hadn't had time to run a DNA test. And had they even obtained a sample for comparison?

"What about her family?" he asked.

"They live in Salerno. What am I supposed to tell them? I've only spoken to her mom a handful of times."

"Salerno? You should contact the Italian Embassy. They'll be able to assist with the arrangements and advise on repatriating the body if that's the route the family decides to go down. The Italian police should go and break the news."

"What else did the police here say?" Omar asked. Was that a tremble in his voice? Sadness over Carmela, or a hint of nerves? "Do they have any suspects?"

"Suspects?" Aurelie shook her head, frustrated. "They're not even looking. They think she drowned herself. Captain al-Busari told me I was misguided when I said Carmela wouldn't have taken her own life. Mis-freaking-guided!"

"She did seem down lately. Sort of quiet."

"She wasn't *suicidal*."

"Last night, Gunther mentioned problems with her boyfriend," Black said, digging gently.

"What problems?"

"An incident with a door? Apparently, she said she walked into it, but also that it was Youssef's fault."

"That happened months ago! Youssef decided to take the door off its hinges to repaint it, and he left it propped against the wall in the dark. Carmela came home late after work and walked straight into it. Sometimes, Youssef just doesn't *think*."

"So he wasn't violent towards her?"

"No, more...more...pushy."

"Pushy?"

"Carmela just wanted to make everyone happy, and sometimes that meant she didn't stick up for herself enough. But she was getting better. Last month, Youssef..."

Ah, shit. Aurelie looked as though she was about to cry again. Black grabbed a handful of napkins from the dispenser and shoved them in her direction. She dabbed at her eyes a bit, and Emmy reached across to squeeze her free hand. Thank fuck his wife was here. Over the years, he'd learned how to do a passable imitation of sympathy, but it always felt awkward on him, as if he'd bought the emotion in a half-price sale but it didn't quite fit.

"Youssef asked Carmela to marry him," Aurelie finally said.

"They were engaged?"

Aurelie's hair stuck to her damp cheeks as she shook her head. "She told him she wasn't ready. I mean, she was only nineteen, and she wanted to see the world before she settled down and got a job."

"And Youssef wanted her to stay in Dahab?"

"No, he wanted to move to Italy. Her parents wanted her back home too. Her father always said she was dumb for living out here on a shoestring when she had a good job waiting for her in Salerno."

"What kind of job?"

"Her parents own an accountancy firm."

Yeah, Black saw how life by the water beat being shackled to a calculator. "How did Youssef take the rejection?"

"Like I said, he was pushy."

"Pushy enough to get nasty when things didn't go his way?"

"I don't think so. And she never gave him an outright 'no,' more said that she wanted to wait."

"Youssef drinks," Omar said softly. "Sometimes too much."

"Isn't that against his religion?"

"Yes, but...it happens."

"And how does he act when he's been drinking?"

"I saw him shove a man once."

"Any idea why?"

Omar shook his head, taking a pace back as though he regretted opening his mouth in the first place. Black understood why—locals stuck up for locals. There was an informal code, something he'd seen the world over. Omar had just broken it.

"Can I take your order?" he asked. Buyer's remorse.

Black decided to let it go—for now. Years of work with covert informants had taught him when to probe and when to back off. Omar might be useful in the future, but not if they scared him away now.

"What fruit juices do you have?"

"Mango, strawberry, guava, orange, or lemon with mint."

"Mango mixed with strawberry, plus the chicken salad. Emmy? Aurelie?"

Predictably, Emmy did *not* go for the salad.

"Orange juice, no straw, a chicken-and-cheese pizza, and fries."

Aurelie ordered lemon juice with a vegetable kebab, and Omar hurried off, leaving Black time to send a message to Bob before he contemplated their next move.

Black: Can you find a friendly cop who'll give us an update on that body? $$ on the table if needed.

If there was one good thing about operating in this part of the world, it was that people were easier to bribe. A hundred bucks could buy you a cop, and once he'd sold out, the leverage was there forever. Back in the US, a much more cautious approach was needed. Getting a politician on side—the president, for example —took years of careful planning, not to mention deep pockets.

"Tell us more about Youssef and Carmela," Emmy said, taking a sip of her orange juice, which had arrived remarkably quickly. Seemed the kitchen staff didn't have much else to do that afternoon. "How did they meet?"

"Cleaning the beach. There's an environmental group that organises teams of people to pick up litter every so often, and we both went."

"They began dating straight away?"

"A few weeks later. He started bringing us free chicken, except Carmela was a vegetarian, and when I saw the tiny cages the birds are kept in, I stopped eating it."

"Was he offended?"

"No, not really. He brought us mangoes instead. And dates. So many dates. That was when Carmela agreed to go out with him—she said she'd go for dinner if he'd quit with the fruit."

"Did she feel pressured?"

"No, she treated it as more of a joke."

"So when did he get pushy?"

"Later, when they got serious. He kept telling her that she could do better for herself, that she was too smart to wait tables and she could have a good career if they moved to Italy. More money, a big house, a car. One time, she told me he sounded like her father."

So far, Aurelie hadn't painted Youssef out to be a murderer, more a man with ambitions he couldn't fulfil alone. A man who wanted to live vicariously through his girlfriend.

As Aurelie walked them through what she knew of Carmela's life over lunch, a picture of a girl who was happy with the little things emerged. No known enemies, didn't owe anybody money, no issues with her family other than a desire to fulfil her own dreams rather than theirs. Outside of work, she liked to go to yoga classes and read books on the beach. A simple life.

The only noteworthy point concerned her backpack, the one she'd been wearing when she died. Aurelie recognised it as Carmela's, so either she'd been carrying it when she vanished, or the killer had somehow obtained a duplicate, or worse, whoever took her life had access to her apartment. Which put the spotlight back on Youssef again.

Tomorrow, Black would speak to the man and form his own opinion.

CHAPTER 9 - BLACK

BY MORNING, INFORMATION had begun trickling in, the results of an overnight search performed by Mack, Blackwood's head of all things computer-related, who was based in Richmond, Virginia. Carmela Conti, one month shy of her twentieth birthday and the middle child of three, had grown up in Salerno and showed little inclination towards adventure until she'd decided to explore the world. Local news articles detailed her winning a local talent contest aged five, baking cookies for the homeless aged nine, and celebrating an excellent set of exam results aged eighteen. Her sole indiscretion had come soon afterwards when she got arrested for handcuffing herself to a fashion designer's gate to protest his use of fur. No charges were brought, and within a month, she'd left the country, travelling first to Greece and then to Egypt.

Her parents were two of six partners in a well-established accountancy practice, and both of her brothers worked there too. The firm's website showed four corporate clones, a world away from the relaxed photos of Carmela that Aurelie had scrolled through on her phone after lunch yesterday.

Youssef al-Masri didn't appear to have an official record of any sort, hardly surprising in this town. What did you have to do to get arrested? Either insult the government or play your music too loudly outside the chief's house, if recent rumours were any indication. He posted on social media most days, usually arty pictures of the town, and his composition wasn't bad. Carmela popped up a few times, the latest three weeks ago, and in that photo, they'd both been smiling, arms around each other.

"Ready to go?" Emmy asked.

They'd woken early and gone running before the sun came up. Ten miles, and when they finished, Emmy had taken a shower, settled on a sunlounger with a book, and begun counting the minutes until the bakery opened. Black felt she was taking this whole vacation thing a little too seriously.

"I've been ready for an hour."

The chicken shop gave its address as Assalah Square, although in reality, it was on one of the dusty side streets nearby. Stacks of wire cages outside held the live birds, and as they parked in front, a woman left carrying a rooster by its feet, wings flapping. Eating chicken in Dahab was more of a DIY affair—no ready-plucked, plastic-packaged carcasses there.

Emmy paused to examine the bedraggled creatures in their tiny prisons, timid and picking at their feathers. No food, no water. The top cage held a single white rabbit, cowering in the inch of shade provided by the sign above its head. *Best Chicken in Sinai.*

Inside, Youssef sat behind a dusty counter, smoking as he studied his phone.

"You want chicken?" he asked, head still down.

"Actually, we'd like to talk."

Now he looked up. And up. And up. Black stood six

feet six and three quarters, and he'd had to duck to walk through the door. Youssef's eyes widened, then dropped to Emmy's chest. Asshole.

"Talk? What about?"

"Carmela Conti."

Youssef flipped the phone in his hands. A nervous gesture, or habit? When he saw Black looking, he shoved it into a pocket.

"What about her?"

"We're friends of Aurelie's and also private investigators. She's asked us to look into Carmela's—"

"I didn't kill her! I loved her!"

Interesting. Youssef's first reaction was to deny the crime, not be thankful for an additional investigation into the death of the woman he claimed to love.

"That's not what we're saying. Not at all. But we'd like to find out a little more about what happened."

"The police asked these questions."

"When did they visit?"

"Yesterday. I already tell them I wasn't here. I was in Cairo, and I didn't come back until Thursday evening. You can ask the bus driver. He's my cousin's friend."

"We'll ask him. Can you give us his details?"

Youssef read out a name and phone number, and Emmy jotted them down, which was all for show since they were both recording the conversation anyway.

"And how long were you in Cairo?"

"A week. Two weeks."

"Which one?"

"Why does it matter? The police said Carmela—" Youssef's breath hitched. "They said she died six or seven days ago."

That at least fit with Black's guess. He'd studied death extensively, both the best ways to effect it and the processes surrounding it, and when they found the body, he'd estimated she'd been in the water for three or four days. The temperature of the water, the activity of the marine life, the amount of flesh left—they'd all pointed to that time frame.

"It matters because we're trying to establish a timeline. Humour me."

"Humour? There is nothing funny about this situation."

Uh-oh, lost in translation. Black switched to Arabic, pleased by the look of surprise on the kid's face. "The more time you waste, the further we are from finding Carmela's killer."

Youssef hurriedly counted on his fingers. "Eight days. I was in Cairo for eight days. Plus two days on the bus."

"And why did you go there?"

"To visit friends."

"For eight days?"

"I have a lot of friends."

"Hmm." Black nodded noncommittally. As far as he'd been able to ascertain, Youssef had lived in Dahab his whole life, and although people moved around, it seemed unlikely he'd built up a vast network in Cairo. "Can you give us their contact details too?"

"What right have you got to ask that? You're foreigners."

"None whatsoever, but innocent people generally cooperate. Don't you want to see Carmela's murderer found?"

"The police will do that."

"The police have stopped looking. They think she killed herself."

No, Youssef hadn't been aware of that little snippet of information. He opened his mouth, closed it again, then stared at the far wall as he tried to digest the new development. Black gave him space. There was something pleasing about watching a man squirm. Not happiness, exactly, more self-satisfaction. For a contract killing, an execution, the feeling was intense but oh-so-fleeting, but in a carefully planned investigation, the high could be achieved over and over. Perhaps that was why Black preferred to focus on detective work nowadays, although if anyone asked, he had a pre-prepared spiel extolling his desire for justice.

A woman came into the shop, dressed head to toe in a burka, and there was an awkward silence while she counted out a handful of grubby notes to pay for that day's dinner. Finally, she ambled off with a trio of squawking chickens. Must've been a special occasion.

"So, where were we?" Black asked. "Your friends?"

"I can't give you their details. GDPR forbids it."

For fuck's sake. "That law doesn't even apply in your country."

"But the sentiment is there. I do not feel they would be happy with me sharing their personal information."

"Perhaps you could ask them? Since it would help to clear your name."

"I already told you—"

"Eight days? You could've gone to Cairo and back twice in eight days. Think about it."

Youssef gave that some consideration. "Okay, I will think about it. I will call them."

So they could all get their story straight?

"You say you went to Cairo and you returned on Thursday. Did you speak to Carmela while you were away?"

"I called her every day."

"Every day? Presumably she stopped answering at some point?"

"Yes, on...on..." He dug around in his pocket for the old-model iPhone, the screen cracked in a starburst. "Last Saturday I speak to her. See?"

Sure enough, there was a call to Carmela's phone that lasted twenty-three minutes just after four o'clock in the afternoon. Black held out a hand.

"May I?"

He wanted to check the number behind the name. More than once, he'd seen suspects change the names of their contacts to disguise the true nature of their communications. But the number matched the details they'd gotten from Aurelie, and while Black was at it, he checked the call log. Youssef's next attempt to speak to Carmela had been at eleven the following morning, and that call had gone unanswered.

Although there was a possibility Carmela had been alive on Sunday but decided not to answer her phone for whatever reason, it seemed more likely, considering the state of her body, that she'd died sometime between last Saturday afternoon and Sunday morning. If Black was forced to guess, he'd say Saturday evening because then her killer could have loaded her body into a vehicle and driven it to its watery grave under cover of darkness. Nobody wanted to keep a corpse around all day, especially in the Egyptian heat.

"Why didn't you report Carmela missing when you came back?" Black asked. "Weren't you worried?"

"Some, but Carmela was a free spirit. She say she was going to Italy to visit her family, so I thought that was where she'd gone."

"What about her luggage? Is that missing from your apartment?"

"I checked. One of her bags was missing, and she never carried much stuff."

"Which bag? What did it look like?"

"A backpack she buy here. Purple coloured, and it say 'Love Life, Love Dahab' on the back. Carmela always say she loved Dahab." For the first time since they got there, Black detected a hint of wetness in the man's eyes, and he wiped them with one grubby sleeve. "I already tell the police she took the bag. What can you foreigners do that they can't? You should leave me and my friends alone."

Black sensed they weren't going to get much more out of the man today. Better to leave him to marinate in discomfort while they did some digging, then come back for another shot if necessary.

"How long have you worked here?"

"Since I was eight. My father owns the shop."

"Family business? You have siblings?"

"A sister, but she's too young to work with the chickens."

"Must be a tie, having to look after the animals every day. Did Carmela help you out?"

An emphatic shake of the head. "She didn't come here."

Another premature denial?

"What, never?" Emmy asked. "Why not?"

"She hated seeing the chickens in cages."

"Can't say I blame her. Why haven't they got any

food and water?"

"My father only allows it once per day, otherwise they make too much mess."

"That's cruel."

A shrug.

"How would you like it if you were locked in a cage and fed once a day? Get them some damn water."

"I can't. It is not—"

But Emmy was already on her way through the door at the rear of the shop. Nice power play, plus they could get a look at what was back there. Youssef skirted the counter and hurried after her, but not fast enough. Black heard a faucet running.

"This is private," Youssef snapped. "You must leave."

"Hey, I gave you a chance, and now I'm giving you a hand," Emmy told him. "Where's the birdseed?"

"My father will not be happy."

"I don't give a shit. If he gets pissy, send him round to talk to me. I'm staying at the Black Diamond Hotel. Bowls? Where are they?"

"Under the sink." Youssef turned sulky.

"Good. I'll fill them, and you can put them into the cages."

Dirt streaked the walls of the back room, together with some reddish-brown stains that looked like blood. Feathers drifted across the floor in the breeze from the open door. How long since anyone had cleaned the place? Black could practically taste the E. coli, although the room smelled like death. Could somebody have killed a woman in there? It bothered Black that they hadn't yet ascertained a cause of death. He wanted to see a copy of the autopsy report, but since the police thought she'd drowned, he wasn't sure it warranted the effort. Would it be worth the paper it was written on?

What were the other options? Engage a new medical examiner? Tricky without stepping all over the police chief's toes. Black could possibly engineer it through his contacts, but the power struggle would undoubtedly impede the rest of the investigation. How feasible was it to steal a body? They'd need a refrigerated truck, and—

"What's with the rabbit?" Emmy asked from the front of the store.

"My father thought people might like to try an alternative to chicken, but it wasn't popular. Nobody wants to buy the last one."

Hardly surprising. When Black strolled outside and squinted into the grimy cage again, he realised how scrawny the creature was. Somebody ought to put it out of its misery. He had a knife with him. Should he offer?

Hmm, possibly not. Emmy had her sad face on, and with a sinking stomach, Black realised what she was thinking.

"Diamond, no."

"How much?"

Oh, hell. In past years, his darling wife had come home with a horse possessed by the devil, a Doberman puppy, and a damn jaguar. They already had enough animals, and as she kept saying, they were on vacation.

"Emmy, no way. You're not buying a fucking rabbit."

CHAPTER 10 - EMMY

ZENA OPENED THE gate to our terrace at the hotel, speaking before she got fully inside. We really ought to put a lock on that thing. What if we'd been indulging in a few extracurricular activities? She'd have been scarred for life.

"Grandpa said to tell you that the chef's doing a barbecue tonight. Hey, is that a bunny?"

I glanced up from my spot on the tiny lawn. "Yup."

In the space of a little over a minute, I'd managed to acquire both a rabbit and a pissed-off husband. When I'd bundled the trembling bag of bones up in a spare sweater from the car, Black had given me that thin-lipped look he normally reserved for politicians he didn't like very much and muttered something about stew. Still, he'd stopped at the veterinarian's on the way home and waited while my accidental acquisition had a check-up and fluids, so I'd make it up to him later.

Nowhere in Dahab sold hutches since rabbits tended to be dinner rather than pets, so I'd cobbled together some shade with an old wooden fruit box, bought a bale of hay, and raided the hotel kitchen for fresh veggies. Now the rabbit was staring at me, eyes wide as she contemplated her new-found freedom.

"I used to have a rabbit," Zena told me. "Back when we lived in Portland. He was called Eddie. I still miss him."

"How long do rabbits live?"

"Seven to ten years, usually."

"Ah, shit."

"Why? What's wrong with that?"

"I'm meant to be on holiday, and now I need to investigate a crime and also work out how to export a rabbit to Virginia. Any ideas?"

"Nuh-uh. Can I pick it up? Is it a boy or a girl?"

"A girl. Be my guest, but don't blame me if you get bitten."

Zena dropped to her hands and knees, strawberry-blonde hair dragging in the dust as she crawled towards the rabbit. Every time I'd tried to get near, it'd hopped off, but Zena managed to get close enough to stroke its head before it wriggled backwards.

"Does she have a name?" Zena asked. "Aw, she's so sweet."

This was a different Zena to the one I'd first seen. Gone was the stroppy teenager, replaced by a carefree girl with a broad smile on her face. She liked animals? Okay, I could work with that.

"Nope. Want to pick one?"

"Really?"

Black wandered out of the villa, phone in his hand as usual. "What about calling it Stifado?"

No, he still wasn't happy with me, and I couldn't do anything to fix the problem with a teenager three feet away.

Zena's mouth twitched. "Stifado? That sounds more like a boy's name."

Oh, such innocence. "It's a kind of Greek stew."

Now she gasped. "How could you?"

Still no smile from my husband. "Would you like a practical demonstration?"

Zena somehow scooped the rabbit into her arms and backed away. "Leave her alone!"

"It's okay, he's joking." At least, I thought he was joking. "How about Thumper?"

"That's so lame."

"Fine, then you think of something. This barbecue you mentioned—are we supposed to be going?"

"Grandpa said he wanted to talk to you. Is it about the dead girl?"

"He told you about that?"

She took another pace back. "Not exactly."

"Then how did you find out?"

"He was talking on the phone, okay? Nobody ever tells me anything."

Mental note: Zena had sensitive ears. "We won't know what it's about until we speak to him. What time is the barbecue?"

"It starts at six. Where's the rabbit hutch?"

"There isn't one. I figured she could run around in the garden."

"You know rabbits dig, right?"

Logically, I suppose I did. I'd almost broken my ankle in one of their fucking holes last year while I was out running. But somehow, I hadn't thought of that little issue when I was handing fifty Egyptian pounds over to Youssef. In fact, I hadn't thought at all. And Black would be just thrilled if craters started appearing in the lawn. Thumper would find herself on the barbecue.

"How would you like to earn some money? I'll pay you to rabbit-sit."

"Rabbits are nocturnal. Well, actually they're crepuscular, but—"

Bloody hell. I'd ended up in a discussion with the love child of David Attenborough and that woman who presented *Countryfile* on the BBC.

"Crepuscular? What's that?"

"They're most active at dusk and dawn. Mom wouldn't be too happy if I stayed up at weird times."

Fuck. Then we'd have to put the rabbit in my old bedroom. The floor in there was tiled, so at least the bloody thing couldn't tunnel out.

"Okay, okay... Plan B. Is it possible to litter train a rabbit?"

"Yes, but I've never done it. And Chris won't let me have any pets."

"Chris? As in Christopher, your mom's fiancé?"

"Yeah." Zena screwed up her face, leaving me in no doubt about her feelings on her new stepfather. "He made me rehome my snake before we moved to Seattle."

"Why?"

"He said Basil creeped him out, but he lived in a vivarium in my bedroom. Chris didn't even have to *look* at him."

"Basil?"

"Short for Basilisk."

While I didn't love snakes—nearly getting bitten by a viper would do that to a girl—I found myself growing less fond of Chris as well. I'd only met him briefly, a quick introduction when we'd detoured to the main building to pick up breakfast after our morning run, and he'd struck me as a bit of a snake himself. Not the good kind. No, the type of man who slithered into your life and said all the right words, only to bite you on the ass when things didn't go his way.

And while I was busy evaluating people, perhaps I'd been slightly hasty in my judgement of Zena's character. I began to wonder whether the whining over the dress was less because she cared what she looked like and more because she didn't want to go to the wedding at all.

"Did you talk to your mom about it?"

"I tried."

"And? What did she say?"

"That I was ungrateful, that Chris had given us a beautiful home, and that I couldn't bear to see her happy. Which isn't *true*. It's not my fault she keeps dating assholes. Just because he's got money doesn't mean he's a nice guy."

Lovely. Kinda reminded me of my own mother. When I'd complained about one of her many, many boyfriends molesting me, she'd warned me who filled our fridge. When I said I'd rather go hungry, she'd locked me in my bedroom for three days without food to teach me a lesson. He'd made my life hell for another two months before I realised he'd skipped bail and reported him to Crimestoppers. While Zena and I chatted, I emailed Mack at our head office and asked her to take a look at Christopher Holt. His details would be in the hotel database.

"You're sixteen, right?"

"Almost seventeen."

"So you've got a little over a year before you can leave home. Are you going to college?"

Because if Zena went to college, she wouldn't have to put up with Chris anymore.

"If my grades are good enough."

"Why wouldn't they be?"

"Every time we move, I have to go to a new school, and I just get further and further behind."

"How many times have you moved?"

"Three times in the last four years. Mom gets bored. I want to go and live with my dad—that's all—but she won't let me."

Could that be an option, even temporarily? Lynn didn't seem particularly enamoured with her daughter, and they spent most of their time fighting. A break might do both of them good. But focusing on the negative wouldn't help Zena, so I tried another tack.

"What subject do you want to study?"

"Zoology. Which, to quote Chris, is a waste of time with no career prospects."

"If you can get the grades, I'll help you to find an internship." There, that gave her an incentive. "How about that?"

"Really?"

Black and I had donated money to various projects, including a breeding program for endangered species at the Richmond zoo and conservation efforts in Zimbabwe. It shouldn't be too difficult to find someone who'd do me a favour.

"Sure. But in the meantime, you need to think of a name for this rabbit."

CHAPTER 11 - EMMY

AT A QUARTER past seven, Captain Bob beckoned us into his office, and I struggled to suppress a smile when I saw who was sitting in the chair opposite his desk. Were we going to get some information?

"Khaled, isn't it?" Black said, holding out a hand.

Captain al-Busari's sidekick. The guy from the boat.

Bob nodded. "Khaled's cousin is one of our gardeners. I told Khaled about your background, and he's agreed to answer a few questions."

Khaled looked spectacularly uncomfortable, and it wasn't only because Bob's visitor chair had the lumpiest cushion I'd ever seen. But he still shook Black's hand, although he didn't make eye contact.

"Yes, Khaled Sabry."

"Black. And this is Emmy. Can you give us an update on the investigation?"

"It is closed."

"Closed? That's it?"

"Captain al-Busari says she killed herself."

That much we knew. Khaled didn't seem particularly convinced by the assumption either.

"How did he come to that conclusion?"

"The doctor who examined the body said there was no evidence she was murdered, but I saw his report on the captain's desk. There was no evidence she wasn't murdered either."

"And what do you think?"

The young man looked down at his feet. How old was he? Twenty? Twenty-one? "It is not my place to say."

"We just want your ideas."

Khaled shifted in his chair and glanced at Captain Bob, who nodded.

"It's okay. Nothing'll get back to al-Busari."

"I have watched *CSI*—every episode—and never before have I seen a lady sink herself with rocks on purpose. Plus I checked on the internet, and the statistics say women are more likely to take a drug overdose or cut their wrists if they want to commit suicide."

Well, at least there was one vaguely conscientious cop in the Dahab Police Department, even if *CSI* wasn't the best place to get bona fide information.

Somebody had brought in a tray of drinks, and I poured little glasses of hot karkade for myself and Black. Khaled hadn't touched his water, but Bob's beer was half-finished. In the absence of gin, I was tempted to steal the rest.

"Any guesses why the captain ended the investigation?" Black asked.

Another glance at Bob, another hesitation before Khaled spoke. "He doesn't want to lose his job. The last time a foreign lady got murdered in Sinai, the chief of police in Fidda Hilal got fired for arresting the wrong person. Captain al-Busari doesn't want to make the same mistake."

From what I'd heard, there was a bit more to it than merely arresting the wrong person, but that was a whole other story. Clearly al-Busari would rather sit around drinking coffee than put the slightest effort into hunting down a killer.

"So his approach is to not arrest anyone at all?" Black asked.

"Yes, exactly."

Good grief.

"And how do you feel about that?"

"I do not want to walk along the street knowing that one of the people I pass could be a murderer."

"Good answer. The question is, what do you propose to do about it?"

"What *can* I do? I am just a private."

"You could help us."

Something flashed in Khaled's eyes. Fear? Excitement?

"Bob says you are a private investigator?"

"That's right."

"And you are going to find the lady's killer?"

"We plan to have a poke around. Call it professional curiosity. But we're only here for another week and a half, and we've got a tough job since your captain doesn't want us involved."

"I could share information."

"And what would you want in return?" I asked.

In our world, nothing came for free. Favours, influence, or cold, hard cash—everything had its price. What was Khaled's?

"I want you to teach me what you know."

A mouthful of karkade went down the wrong way, and Black thumped me on the back as I coughed. Khaled wanted to play sidekick? Well, that was... unexpected.

"How about we pay dollars instead?" Black suggested.

"Education is more important to me than money."

So the boy had scruples. That was a good sign.

I watched Black as silence filled the room. Although he was excellent at training people—not wanting to toot my own horn, but I was an example of that—he was also notoriously fussy about who he worked with. Last year, he'd interviewed seventeen people for a vacancy in our Richmond office and rejected them all. The HR lady was on the verge of a nervous breakdown when Black finally poached somebody from the NSA, and that had only been for a junior position.

But what were the alternatives? Sure, we could find out what the local police knew through a combination of hacking, bugging, and good old breaking and entering, but when it came to asking more questions, locals would respond better to one of their own than an American or a Brit, especially a Brit with boobs. If we could get Khaled to do some of our dirty work...

"What could you share?" Black asked.

"Everything I can find, but I can't risk losing my job. My father is sick, and I need to look after my mother and sisters."

"We need a copy of the autopsy report. Did a detective attend? An evidence tech?"

"No, neither. Just the doctor."

Sloppy.

"What about toxicology? Tell me they're running tests."

"I think so. I overheard the captain on the phone, asking somebody to process the samples quickly so he could finish the paperwork and close the case."

"Has Carmela been positively identified yet? Dental records? DNA?"

A quick shake of the head. "I heard the captain say we were waiting for the dental records to come from Italy. You will help?"

More silence. Black didn't move a muscle, but Khaled squirmed in his seat. Like me, Bob had seen the effect Black had on people plenty of times before, and the corner of his lip twitched as though he was trying not to laugh.

Two whole minutes passed like that, but eventually, Black nodded.

"As long as you remember it's a two-way deal. Let's start with what you know about Youssef al-Masri."

"He runs the chicken shop near Assalah Square."

"That's common knowledge. What sort of person is he?"

A glimmer of excitement flickered in Khaled's eyes. "You think he did it?"

"I think he's slippery."

"He's never been in trouble."

"In this town, that doesn't mean a lot. Find me some useful information."

"Like what?"

Black ticked off the points on his fingers. "His phone number. Whether he has a vehicle. The names of his friends. Details of his family. Previous girlfriends. Financial situation. Has he ever got in a fight with anyone? Talked about Carmela? Mentioned plans for the future?"

Khaled scribbled frantically in his notepad, nodding to himself. "I can do that."

"Then we'll speak further tomorrow. Don't forget

the autopsy report."

Nice. Minimal effort on our part to begin with, but we'd get to see if Khaled could deliver the simple things. And if he managed to find the autopsy report Black wanted, I might be able to spend an hour lying in the sun instead of breaking into the morgue.

Khaled finished his water and slipped out the door. I was ready to follow him when Black put a hand on my arm. Now what? I'd skipped dessert for this meeting, and if I got a shift on, there might be cake left.

But Black didn't move, and it wasn't out of concern over my diet. He and Bob seemed to be having a silent conversation with their eyes, presumably in some sort of Navy SEAL language I wasn't privy to, and Black sat down again.

Fan-fucking-tastic.

"Would somebody care to enlighten me?"

Bob waited until Khaled's footsteps had faded into the distance before he opened his desk drawer and pulled out two plastic boxes. Oh, hello. The contents of the one on the left looked familiar. Last time I'd seen that piece of string, it had been tied to a dead girl's backpack.

"Where did you get that?" Black asked, pointing.

"Found it under one of the benches on the *Blue Tang* this morning. The police were meant to clean up after they left, but they didn't do a very good job of it."

Really? The cops had left valuable evidence behind? After meeting Captain al-Busari, I wasn't exactly shocked. They probably just shoved the obvious bits into a bag, then tossed a bucket of seawater over the worst of the bloodstains and called it a day.

"What's in the other box?"

"Some sort of trinket. Looks like one of those scarab beetles they sell in the tourist shops. I don't know if it came up with the girl or not, but I'm fairly certain it wasn't there when I checked the boat over last weekend."

"Who else has been on board since?"

"Couple of diving groups, and a Spanish party hired her for a cruise on Monday evening."

Black took the lids off the boxes, and I leaned forward to take a closer look at the beetle, elbows on my knees. Boy, that was one ugly little pebble. It was black in colour, about an inch long, and when Black flipped it over with the end of a pen, I saw hieroglyphics on the underside and a hole drilled through the middle to take a cord.

"Seems it might have fallen off a necklace," Bob suggested.

Black nodded. "Indeed. But our girl wasn't wearing a necklace when we found her."

"Could have had it in a pocket. Or that bag of hers."

"Yes, she could. I'll ask Aurelie if she remembers Carmela owning a piece like this. We also need to check with Khaled in case the police somehow brought it on board. If we eliminate both of those possibilities, then that leaves two options—either one of your guests dropped it, or the killer did. Mind if we take it with us?"

"That was my intention. You're the detective, not me." Bob's phone vibrated, and he cursed under his breath. "Ah, fuck. Lynn wants to talk about table settings."

"Good luck," Black said. "Give me the dead body any day."

"So, what kind of knot is it?" I asked Black when we got back to the villa. With dessert. I might have made a small detour to the restaurant on the way, and hallelujah, they still had two slices of chocolate fudge cake left. Black umm-ed and aah-ed and said he didn't want one, but when I offered to eat it for him, he changed his mind.

"I don't know."

"But I thought you learned about knots in the SEALs. Didn't you have to tie them underwater?"

"We learned five knots, and none of them were this one." With his fork, he gestured at the piece of cord sitting on the coffee table in its plastic box. "I've sent a picture to the rest of the team. Five bucks says we'll have an answer by the time we finish eating."

Of course we would. No way I was taking that bet, and the buzz of Black's phone proved the decision right.

"It's a surgeon's knot," he read. "Similar to a square knot except you pass the end through the first loop twice instead of once. Most commonly used in surgery, fishing, and jewellery making."

"So we could be looking for a doctor?"

That would be some violation of the Hippocratic oath.

"Don't forget we're in a fishing town. And it's not exactly a difficult knot to tie. But it's a starting point. Tomorrow, let's ask Aurelie whether Carmela hung out with any doctors or fishermen."

"Or jewellery designers," I reminded him. "There's

a lot of handicrafts for sale along the high street, and that would fit with the beetle."

"When you look at it that way, half the people in town should be on the suspect list."

"Sorry."

"I'm not sure what's worse—having no suspects or a surplus of them. We'd better do some research on this scarab too. Miles should be able to help us out there."

Miles was Bradley's boyfriend, an archaeologist who just so happened to be digging things up in Egypt at that very moment. He was farther south, near Luxor, but he had a satellite phone and once he started talking about old dead things, it was difficult to get him to stop.

"You're gonna call him?" I asked.

"That was the idea." Black forked another piece of cake into his mouth and pondered for a moment. "On second thought, it's late, and neither of us needs a three-hour lecture on the Ptolemaic dynasty or ancient burial rites. I'll take some pictures and send him an email."

Thank goodness. "Great plan."

CHAPTER 12 - EMMY

DUST MOTES DRIFTED in the early-morning sunbeam shining through a gap in the curtains. Five thirty a.m. and I was already awake thanks to my husband. With his head between my thighs, I should've been halfway to heaven, but in the stillness, in that quiet time before the world fully came to life, all I could hear was the *shuffle-click-bump* of the bloody rabbit in the next room. Last night, we'd made it a pen by nailing together some old sunloungers, the slats forming a makeshift prison topped by a gauzy curtain we'd borrowed from one of the cabanas on the beach. But it seemed determined to escape.

Usually, Black put his all into making me come, driven to be the best as he was in every other aspect of his life, but this morning, he seemed distracted too. A hesitation here, a sideways glance there. When he went for my clit with his thumb and missed, I levered my head off the pillow.

"What's up?"

"That fucking rabbit. It walks into everything."

"I know—it kept me awake the whole damn night." Weirdly, I could sleep soundly in a war zone, but over the years, I'd conditioned myself to wake at the soft sounds that could indicate unexpected danger. A quiet footstep. A rustle. The squeak of a door. "I'm sorry she's annoying, but I wouldn't have slept if I'd had to think about her stuck in that cage either."

"An assassin with a heart. I love every facet of you, Mrs. Black, even if it ends in coitus interruptus."

"Perhaps I could put some music on?"

"I'll do it."

He rolled out of bed, and the sunbeam sliced across his bare ass as he headed for the lounge. The man had the sculpted muscles of Michelangelo's *David* but with better equipment, and even after fifteen years, I still pinched myself whenever the glint of my wedding rings caught my eye. One plain silver from the original drunk-in-Vegas debacle, the second its fuck-I'm-not-that-cheap platinum companion complete with a hidden handcuff key, and the third a flawless diamond from our recent slightly-tipsy-in-Vegas attempt. Yeah, Black loved me enough to marry me twice, even if I struggled to love myself sometimes.

Perhaps we could put some sort of carpet in the rabbit's run? That would muffle the *click-click-click* of nails on tile. But what about her terrible spatial awareness? Padding? A tiny crash helmet?

I was expecting classical music, maybe R 'n' B. Black preferred piano, Beethoven or Chopin. Rachmaninov when he was annoyed. Bach when he was sad. At home, the music room was his sanctuary like the stables were mine. But instead of the delicate notes I'd been waiting for, I heard the rap of knuckles on wood.

What the hell?

"Who is it?" Black called.

"It's me." The voice was young. Female. A touch nervous. "I brought breakfast for the rabbit."

No doubt because Zena was a teenager, and also because she was a friend's granddaughter, Black tried to temper the edge of annoyance in his voice, but he didn't quite manage it.

"It's five thirty in the morning."

"Grandpa said you always get up early." *Not voluntarily.* "And the rabbit'll be awake now."

How to deal with this one... In all honesty, inviting Zena in was probably easier than explaining the reason why we couldn't. Black's dick had rapidly deflated, and was it my imagination or was the rabbit scratching louder?

Black flipped on the light switch, blew out his cheeks, and exhaled a sigh.

"Perhaps we could get her to take the rabbit outside?" I suggested as he pulled on a pair of shorts and a well-worn T-shirt, a sky-blue one advertising a beachside restaurant in California we'd visited about a decade ago. Sized extra large, but it still stretched tight across his chest. Bradley had regular culls of our clothing, but our Egyptian wardrobe had escaped his attention, thank goodness. Sometimes, the old stuff was the most comfortable and the most comforting, like putting on a hug from a long-lost friend.

"Take it outside—good idea." Black tossed me a shirt of my own and a pair of baggy harem pants I'd bought in the high street on my last visit. Pants I wouldn't be caught dead in stateside, but which somehow seemed to work in Dahab. "Why don't you talk to her? I might get tempted to introduce her to Carmela."

What made him think I wouldn't?

Still, the rabbit had been my fault, and I took

responsibility for my mistakes, even if it meant negotiating with a teenager at daybreak instead of screwing my husband.

"Don't you know about the birds and the fucking bees?" I muttered quietly as I opened the door, but not quietly enough.

"Of course I do. I scored straight A's in biology. And Mom says it's rude to swear."

"It's also rude to get people out of bed when they're on vacation."

"And speaking of bees, did you know that the number of colonies in the US has dropped by sixty percent since 1962? And pollen's full of pesticides now."

"It's too early for this."

"It's never too early to save the planet."

That wasn't a discussion I wanted to get into before breakfast, and certainly not with a kid who knew more about wildlife than I did. If I had to spout statistics like that, say if I was attending a fundraising dinner or a corporate event where I needed to sound smart, I generally wore an earpiece with a research team on hand to assist. And since it was approaching midnight back at headquarters in Virginia, I didn't feel our merry band of IT geeks would be too chuffed if I kept them awake so I could win an argument with a sixteen-year-old. Instead, I nodded at the tray Zena was carrying. It held two plates, one full of fruit and one full of vegetables.

"That's a lot of food for a rabbit."

"It's my breakfast too. Want a grape?"

"No, I want coffee. And if you give me a lecture on caffeine, I'll be forced to shoot you."

"Right. Like you even have a gun." Oh, how little did she know. "Can I come in?"

"How about I bring the rabbit out?"

"I was going to clean her run."

Well, when she put it like that... I didn't want to pick up rabbit poop before I'd had my coffee either. Black would understand.

"Fine. Just promise you won't turn up at this time tomorrow."

"But the rabbit—"

"Will be fine until nine o'clock."

All thoughts of resuming our earlier activities came to an abrupt halt when Black's phone rang while Zena was still down on her hands and knees in my old bedroom, talking to the rabbit in some weird cross between snuffles and baby-speak.

I paused, a perfectly buttery pain au chocolat halfway to my mouth, when I heard him say, "Are you sure they're human?"

Two guesses... Either our friend Jed had held one of his legendary parties at our house again and Bradley was trying to deal with the aftermath—which usually involved people stumbling around the place with varying degrees of hangover—or some kind of body parts had turned up. The pastry turned to cardboard in my mouth as I sidled closer and glanced at the screen. *Khaled calling.*

Black switched to speaker and turned the volume down enough that Miss Satellite Ears in the next room couldn't hear. Neither of us needed her questions when we had so many to answer as it was.

"I haven't seen the bones," Khaled said. "The captain made me follow the tourists back down the mountain. But the woman who found them swears they came from a person."

"Emmy's here now," Black said for Khaled's benefit. "A tourist on a quad-bike safari stopped to answer the call of nature and found the remains of what could be a skeleton lying behind a boulder, and Khaled wants to pick our brains about the investigative process. Khaled, was anything else found nearby? Clothing? Shoes? A bag?"

"Nobody mentioned any of those."

"Can you ask?"

"Captain al-Busari does not like questions."

"Then ask your colleagues. Surely the captain wasn't the only person there?"

"I will try."

"Good. We'll need photos and an exact location too. Is the scene secure?"

"No, it is on a mountain. The captain says nobody will be bothered to climb there."

Apart from the person who found the bones in the first place and, presumably, their friends since I couldn't imagine a tourist taking an early-morning quad-bike trip alone. Black's roll of the eyes echoed my thoughts. In private, he was a lot more expressive than in public. In public, he left people guessing most of the time.

"Fine. Be ready to take us up there when your shift finishes."

"My mother wants me to fix the kitchen tap this afternoon."

"How many detectives on *CSI* do you see fixing kitchen taps?"

Silence.

"Meet us outside the hotel at two, and don't forget those photos."

Another body? Although the circumstances were different, something uncomfortable stirred in my gut. This was Dahab. Crime was normally restricted to problems with unruly dogs and the occasional burglary, which was probably why al-Busari had grown so complacent. Now? I had the horrible feeling our discovery of Carmela's body had been the start of something bigger and a whole lot darker.

CHAPTER 13 - EMMY

TWO O'CLOCK IN the afternoon, and the sun beat down with the intensity of a blowtorch. By rights, I should've been either incinerating myself on the terrace or floating around on the water, but instead, I was rooting around in the room of doom in search of my hiking boots as we waited for Khaled to arrive. Black, of course, had put his away properly last time and found them in the appropriate place.

"How difficult can it be to get hold of some fucking photos?" he grumbled as I pulled out a pair of sunglasses I thought I'd lost roughly a decade ago.

"Khaled didn't have any luck?"

"The captain has them on his camera, and he might download them tomorrow or the day after."

"Sounds about right."

"Khaled offered to help, but the captain declined. Apparently, the camera's expensive and he doesn't trust a mere private to work it properly. Are you up for a little breaking and entering?"

"Do Russians drink vodka?"

"Good." He glanced at his watch. Black changed his timepieces as often as he changed his guns, and this month's was an oversized green thing gifted to him by a sheikh whose kidnapped daughter he'd rescued. According to the leather-bound instruction manual it came with, it had been modelled on a car engine, and if you wanted to reset the time, you had to use a miniature power drill. I hadn't yet worked out how to actually tell the time on it. "Hurry up with those boots. I'm going to find some bottles of water."

"At this rate, I'll be climbing the mountain in flip-flops."

Where the hell had I put them? I'd trekked up Mount Sinai on the trip before last, so there was a good chance I'd had the boots then, but they'd vanished into the Egyptian equivalent of a black hole. In desperation, I rang Bradley.

"It's me. If I was going to lose a pair of hiking boots, where would they end up? And stop rolling your eyes."

"I'm guessing this isn't a hypothetical question. If you had a system…"

"Please, spare me the lecture. I'm about to climb a mountain in baking heat and I'd rather not end up with blisters."

"Climb a mountain? But I thought you were supposed to be on vacation? Let me guess—this was Black's idea."

"Yes and no." I'd jokingly suggested taking quad bikes like normal people, but unsurprisingly, he didn't want to mess up the crime scene any more than the police already had. Hence, we'd be walking, looking for anything out of the ordinary as we went. "That was where the body was found."

"The what? The *body*?"

"Well, possibly. Someone found a pile of bones, and they might be human. We're going to check out the scene."

A small, know-it-all voice came from behind me.

"Oh, they're definitely human."

Zena.

"Don't you ever knock? And how do you know the bones are human?"

"Who's that?" Bradley asked.

"Captain Bob's granddaughter. Can you have a think about the boots and text me?"

"Okay, okay, but only if you dish the dirt on the body. Is it a murder? Are you investigating?"

"Later, Bradley. Just text me."

Zena stood in the doorway, cradling the rabbit in her arms. "She's not so scared now. See? But I'm not sure her eyesight's that good. She keeps bumping into stuff. I'm gonna call her Crash."

Crash the rabbit. Good grief.

"Brilliant. Crash. Now, what were you saying about the bones?"

"That they're human?"

"Yes. How do you know that?"

"Because I spent, like, four years studying human anatomy."

"Can we back up a bit here? When did you see them?"

"This morning. The lady who found them's staying in one of the villas by the pool. She took about three hundred photos, and she showed everyone."

My initial flicker of excitement at an actual clue soon gave way to a sinking dread. Having pictures of body parts in the public domain, out of our control, could cause more problems than it solved. And if the news that today's find was the second body to turn up within a week got out, the reputation of the town would suffer, which was bad for business. Would that spur al-

Busari into action or lead him to put an even tighter lid on the problem?

"Do you know the lady?"

"Not really. But I think her roommate's called Allie. Why? Do you want to see the pictures? Because they're on Twitter."

Oh, this just got better and better. Twitter? Really? For fuck's sake. But yes, I wanted to see those pictures.

"Can you find them on my laptop?"

Boots momentarily forgotten, I dragged an extra chair over to the desk in the lounge, and Zena scooched closer to me with the rabbit on her lap. How did she get the thing to sit still like that? I'd managed to keep hold of Crash in the car when she was terrified, but last night when I tried to pick her up, she bit me.

"Here they are," Zena said. Yup, posted by NorthernGrrrl. She had little hearts on each side of her username. "Look—hashtag Dahab, hashtag corpse, hashtag deadbody, hashtag OMG."

Twelve pictures, and I saved them all to my hard drive before I zoomed in. Yup, that was definitely a femur. And a lower jaw, part of a pelvis, and a fucking skull.

Black was better educated in the ins and outs of forensic taphonomy—the history of a body after death —than me, but I knew that even under normal circumstances, it was hard to determine the time of death once a body was reduced to bones. And by normal, I meant having a fully equipped lab and a police force that actually showed an inclination to investigate the case.

Who did the bones belong to? And were they male or female? How had they gotten into the mountains?

And most importantly from our point of view, had the person fallen victim to foul play or an unfortunate accident? A scrap of faded royal-blue cloth was visible in the corner of one of the shots—was that part of their clothing? If not, where was it? Because naturism wasn't big in Egypt. Nudists would probably be arrested by Captain al-Busari going for the easy wins.

"Where are the rest of the photos? You said she took more."

"I guess she didn't post them all."

"Then we need to look for her."

With the roommate's first name and a rough location for their villa, I could get Captain Bob to go through the guest registrations, then...

"Be right back."

"Where are you going?"

Zena was already halfway out the door with the rabbit, which seemed to have accepted its new role as a teenager's companion with remarkably good grace. A sigh escaped my lips like air from a shanked tyre. The last thing I wanted was for Zena to get involved in the investigation, but what was I supposed to do? Drag her away? When I was her age, I'd already gotten a job, moved to a different continent, and executed my first target. On a scale of one to assassination, tracking down a few crime scene photos hardly tipped the scale. Besides, Zena seemed happier today. Whether it was the distraction of Crash or having to spend less time with her mother, I wasn't sure, but she'd even smiled a couple of times. And heaven help me, I was actually starting to like the girl.

With no sign of Black, I put on a pair of flip-flops and hurried after Zena. Following wasn't tricky—up ahead, I could hear the exclamations of "Hey, was that a rabbit?" and "Do they allow pets here?" and by the time I got to the pool, Crash was eating leftover lettuce off someone's plate while Zena peered at a bikini-clad blonde's camera.

"Over here." Zena grinned and waved. See? She was happy. "This is Danielle, and I underestimated. She actually took four hundred photos."

Now I was smiling too.

"I got a new camera," Danielle explained when I pulled up a spare seat. Ah, a fellow Brit, complete with a Geordie accent and a terrible case of sunburn. "And I've been trying out all the settings. Although I didn't think for a second that I'd find anything interesting on that bloody quad-bike trip. I didn't even want to go, but my boyfriend insisted. If I hadn't tied a scarf over my face, I'd have choked to death on dust, and in a year, it'd be my skeleton people were finding up there."

"I hear those excursions can be kinda rough."

"I should've stayed at the beach bar. They serve the most amazing cocktails. You should try the Devil's Sunset."

Try it? After drinking six of the damn things in a row the night before the hotel's opening party, I'd been the one to name it. Satan gave one hell of a hangover.

"Thanks for the tip—I'll be sure to do that. I hear a rumour you might have more pictures of the bones?"

"Sure do. Your sister here says you're a massive true-crime fan?"

Sister? My self-appointed accomplice gave me a not-so-subtle wink and pointed at the camera. Why me? I already had one genuine sister plus another pseudo-sister who actually belonged to an ex-boyfriend but had stuck around to drive me crazy ever since. I didn't need another. But with little other choice, I had to go along with the story.

"Oh, a massive fan. I listen to every podcast going, even that one where the host has a really droney voice." I managed a giggle. "I can't believe there might have been a real-life crime just down the road from here. Kinda creepy, right? I hear the bones were a little way from the path? Behind a rock?"

"Sort of a big boulder. Oh my gosh, I nearly peed on the skull. My boyfriend said I should hold it until I got back, but honestly, I'd drunk four cups of coffee because we left at an insane time in the morning, and I just couldn't."

"Been in that situation plenty of times myself. Any chance we could download the pictures onto my laptop? It's got a bigger screen."

"Oh, sure, sure. Where is it?"

"In my room. Want me to bring it over?"

"Nah, I could do with getting out of the sun for a bit. I'm turning into a lobster."

CHAPTER 14 - BLACK

IN THE TIME it took Black to find a case of water, Emmy had managed to round up another woman with no concept of privacy and get ahold of the photos Khaled had been busy failing to obtain all morning.

Now there were two females plus the rabbit formerly known as dinner intruding in Emmy and Black's villa, and he forced a neutral expression to override his annoyance before he crossed the threshold. He didn't mind his friends back home hanging out in his house, but virtual strangers invading his personal space tried his patience, even if they did come bearing gifts. So much for spending time alone with his wife.

"That's a scapula," Zena announced.

Since when did Bob's granddaughter know about anatomy? From what Bob had said over a late beer last night, she was a problem child who'd been expelled from two schools so far, had wasted a significant amount of police time when she tried running away from home last year, and who drove Lynn around the bend.

But when Black peered at the picture in question, he had to concede Zena was right. It was a nearside scapula. What else did they have? The skull, mandible, both femurs, part of the pelvis, the sacrum, several ribs... Not so many of the smaller bones, but that wasn't surprising. Animals would have carried those off.

"How big an area were the bones scattered over?" he asked the blonde, who was lounging on the sofa flicking through a dog-eared copy of Homer's *Iliad*. Her glance at his ring finger didn't go unnoticed.

"Uh, fifty metres? A hundred? Something like that. Do you really read this stuff? It's so boring."

"No, I just leave it out on the coffee table to make myself look smarter."

The sarcasm was wasted on her. "Really? That's a great idea. I'm gonna do that when I get home."

"Somewhere between fifty and a hundred metres..." Fifty-five to a hundred and ten yards, if they were talking American. "That's a pretty big margin of error."

"I'm not so good at measuring, and I didn't find all the bones myself. Once I saw the first one, the other quad bikers helped to search. Except for Wayne. He's a lazy arse, so he just sat in the shade and smoked."

"How many people in your party?"

"Uh, eight? No, seven, because Tracey didn't come on account of her hangover. Plus the guide, and there was another Egyptian bloke at the back to make sure no one fell off."

So the crime scene, if indeed it was a crime, had been contaminated by at least nine people before the police even arrived. Fantastic.

Emmy had already uploaded the photos to Blackwood's network, so Black retired to the dining table to review the whole set in peace before Khaled arrived. What did they have? Bones picked clean with little evidence of weathering, a dusty blue T-shirt with dark reddish-brown stains and tears that looked too sharp to be due to simple wear. Were they from a knife? And were the stains blood? The shirt was undoubtedly with the police now, so that would be another question for Khaled.

How long had the body been there? Even for an experienced anthropologist, it was difficult to tell. Factors such as temperature, moisture content, and pH of the soil all came into play, and then there were the individual elements. The weight of the victim, their age, their state of dress, whether they were buried or simply dumped—all were variables that impacted on decomposition time. And all were unknown. In the Florida heat, Black had seen a body skeletonise in as little as two weeks. In cooler climates, protected from wild animals, the process could take years. The only certainty so far was that this person had died before Carmela.

Black's biggest question: was there a connection between the two deaths? He didn't believe in coincidences, and two bodies turning up in one small town in such a short space of time rang alarm bells. Of course, they'd need to identify the victim before they could ascertain whether there was a link, which was easier said than done.

Hmm.

Or perhaps not...

Black zoomed in on another of the pictures, this time showing the humerus, or upper arm bone. Nothing funny about it if you broke that bone, which Black had done as a child when he fell off the roof of the old stables at Riverley Hall, the estate in Virginia where he'd grown up. He'd inherited the place after his parents died, and the stables were Emmy's domain rather than his now. But the broken arm was something Black had in common with victim number two. A metal plate was screwed down one side of the bone, and Black zoomed in close.

Not a recent injury—the bone had grown around the screws—but the plate looked complex enough to be custom. Black searched back and forth for different angles and finally hit pay dirt with the fourth shot. The vacuous blonde went up a notch in his estimation. She may have had no appreciation of literature, but at least she'd bought a decent camera.

He quickly attached the picture with the manufacturer's logo and serial number in an email to Daniela di Grassi, his number two in Blackwood's investigations division.

Dan,
I need to know where this was implanted, and who it was implanted into.
Black

Her reply came almost instantly.

Aren't you supposed to be on vacation?

Yes, he was. Thanks for the reminder.

The dead have no respect for my schedule.

Black held off on updating Emmy while they had company. The less information flying around, the better. The rumour mill would undoubtedly start turning soon, and if the killer of either victim was still in town—assuming for now that some poor asshole hadn't wandered into the mountains and died alone by accident—then Black didn't want to tip his hand too early.

Instead, he closed his laptop, then stuffed half a dozen bottles of water into his backpack and the same into Emmy's.

"Ready to go? Our friend'll be waiting outside by now."

"Going somewhere good?" the blonde asked.

"Just into town. One of the bars is showing a billiard match on TV this afternoon."

"Oh." Unsaid: *boring*. "Tell me if you hear any more about the skeleton, won't you? I love a good gossip."

Mental note: don't tell her anything at all.

"What about me?" Zena asked. "I *love* billiards."

"This is adults-only billiards."

"Really? Too bad. I'll have nothing better to do than stay here and join in with the gossiping."

Black recognised that smile. It was one he'd seen on his own wife when she was Zena's age. Overly sweet. Worryingly confident. A hint of happiness because she knew she had his balls in a vice. And cunning. Call Black a glutton for punishment, but he admired that trait in a woman.

Plus he really didn't want Zena talking. One word to the blonde, and everyone in the hotel would know everything by breakfast the next morning.

"In that case, I'm sure we can find a way for you to join us." Black looked pointedly at her flip-flops. "You might want to change into suitable billiard-watching attire."

"What about the rabbit?" Emmy tried. Oh, that glare shouldn't have turned him on, but it did. "Who'll take care of her?"

"She's tired," Zena said. "She's just gonna sleep this afternoon."

"You need to check with your mother that it's okay to come."

"She won't care. Besides, she went sightseeing in Nuweiba with Chris and left me behind."

"I'll call Bob," Black said. "Explain the situation."

Bob would agree to anything if it meant he avoided getting saddled with a teenager for the rest of the day. And having Zena with them wouldn't be a bad cover story. Their snooping would be less obvious if they claimed they were on a family hike in the mountains with their Egyptian guide. Khaled would just have to keep his mouth shut.

Emmy's phone buzzed, and as Black showed the blonde to the door, his wife crawled halfway under the sofa with a flashlight in her hand. What the hell was she doing?

"Got them!" She held up a pair of hiking boots. "Bradley guessed where they were. The man's a genius."

A genius with a decorating problem. If they got back to the US and found another pink bathroom...

"Well, hurry up and put them on. The daylight won't last forever." He pointed at Zena and then at the door. "You too. Five minutes, and we're leaving. Don't forget your sunblock."

Fuck. Now Black sounded like his mother.

Chapter 15 - Black

KHALED LED THE way as the group of four trudged up the dusty path into the mountains. If one needed a visual of the landscape, Planet Tattooine from Star Wars bore a remarkable resemblance. Pitted and rocky, the route barely seemed wide enough for the quad bikes that had roared along it not so long ago, yet somehow, the police had driven a truck that way to collect the bones according to Khaled. Judging by the smooth rocks on either side, the track had once been an old water channel, not large enough to be a river, but perhaps a stream.

On past visits, Black had hiked in these hills with Emmy, and today's pace was unbearably slow.

"Did you find Carmela's autopsy report?" Emmy asked Khaled. "The toxicology results?"

"The folder is in the captain's desk drawer. I saw him put it there."

"Great. Did you take a copy?"

"The drawer is locked."

"So?"

"I don't have a key."

"So?'

Khaled turned to look at her, panting slightly in the heat. Seemed going to the gym wasn't part of his daily routine.

"Then how am I supposed to get it open?"

"Uh, pick the lock?" Emmy said.

"I don't know how to do that."

"Really?"

Sometimes, Emmy forgot that picking locks wasn't a rite of passage for all teenagers. She'd learned out of necessity to survive on the streets of East London, while Black had taught himself from a book he found in his father's study. The skill came in useful when playing pranks and carrying out other little tasks at the elite prep school he'd attended as a teenager. To this day, the principal didn't know who'd sat at his computer and forwarded half a dozen emails from his mistress to his wife. Black had been of the opinion that the woman deserved to know, and so had James, his best friend at the time, who'd acted as lookout. Of course, there'd been questions, but even back then, Black had been an excellent liar. James too. It was no surprise when he went into politics.

Behind them, Zena snorted, then tried to cover it up with a terrible fake sneeze. Black turned to her. "Do you know how to pick locks?"

"They didn't teach us that in high school. But I wish they had. It'd be a lot more useful than art and trigonometry. I mean, who needs to know about tangents and cosines?"

Snipers, that was who. Calculating range, compensation for bullet drop, wind, and angles when shooting on a slope. And art was pleasing to look at.

"Right, tonight when we get back to the hotel, I'll teach you both how to pick a lock," Emmy said. "A desk drawer won't have anything heavy duty. All you need is a couple of paper clips and practice."

"But the captain—" Khaled started.

"Think of this as part of the investigation, yeah? Bypassing the occasional lock is a useful skill for any detective, and if you do it carefully, the captain'll never know."

Khaled didn't look totally convinced by her argument, but Emmy wouldn't back down. They needed those reports, and Khaled said he wanted training, didn't he? Every good PI cut a few corners now and then.

"How about the rest of the information?" Black asked. "Did you get anything?"

The notepad came out again. "Yes. I got the phone number and the registration details of Youssef's pickup."

So he had a vehicle. "What about his friends and family?"

"He has one younger sister and his parents at home. No brothers. After he met Carmela, he stopped going out so much, but he's friends with Ashraf from the Seahorse Dive Centre."

Hmm. A diver may have known the profile of the sea wall at the first dump site. Only luck had snagged Carmela's bag on an outcrop of coral, and if her body had sunk to the bottom, Black would be fucking his wife in an air-conditioned bedroom rather than climbing this godforsaken hill. Sweat dripped down his back as Khaled bent over, hands on his knees while he caught his breath.

"Any previous girlfriends?" Black asked.

"Nobody serious. He always chased after foreign girls, but none of them lasted long except for Carmela. Probably dreaming of a European visa like so many other Egyptian men our age."

"Are you one of them?"

Khaled shook his head and started walking again. "Dahab is my home. I want to keep the town as a paradise, not run away. How is it you say? The grass is always greener?"

Black understood Khaled's attitude, and not only that, he shared it. That was why he'd spent the past twenty-seven years serving his country rather than taking his billions and buying a really big yacht.

"Yes, the grass is always greener. Except it isn't. Your world is what you make of it. The question is, what did Youssef make of his?"

"I will find out more," Khaled promised. "But so far, there is nothing bad. The chicken shop is a successful business. I also spoke to the bus driver who brought him back from Cairo, and Youssef told the truth about his journey."

"Can anyone confirm he was in Cairo for the whole time he says?"

"Nobody I've found. Not yet."

On paper, Youssef made a great suspect. Dating the victim, fond of getting his own way according to Aurelie, adept at chopping up dead meat, and his alibi was shaky. Black had found him evasive, forceful with declarations of love that had no emotion behind them. But that could fit in with Khaled's theory that Youssef had been using Carmela to get a European visa. In which case, why would he kill the goose that could deliver the golden egg? That was the problem with Youssef as a suspect—no clear motive.

"Are we nearly there yet?" Zena asked.

She hadn't complained much so far, just the

occasional grumble about her boots rubbing and her shirt getting sweaty. When Black spoke to Bob, he'd been only too happy for his granddaughter to go hiking with them. Okay, so Black may have left out the part about visiting a crime scene, but having that discussion would've wasted time, and they didn't have much of that left as it was. Nobody wanted to get stuck on a mountain after dark. Well, Dahab's version of a mountain. In any other country, it would be called a large hill.

"Another ten minutes, *inshallah*," Khaled said. "Maybe fifteen."

Make that twenty. Black recognised an outcrop from Danielle's photos, signposting the spot where the skull had been found on her impromptu bathroom break. She sure had walked a long way off the beaten path. Khaled saw the outcrop too and began to scramble over the crumbling red granite that was the basis of most of the rock formations in the region.

"Stop," Black ordered. "Think."

Khaled halted mid-stride. "This is part of the crime scene?"

"We haven't yet ascertained whether foul play was involved. But if it was, then yes, this is part of the crime scene."

Where it wasn't solid rock, the sandy ground was covered with so many footprints they became meaningless—everything from smooth-soled flip-flops that probably belonged to the tourists to the chunky soles of police boots that matched Khaled's.

"What are we looking for?"

"Anything that doesn't belong." That Khaled's colleagues might have missed. "We'll split the site into zones. Call me if you see anything, and we'll take photos before we move it. And don't touch."

When he went to find the water earlier, Black had raided the hotel kitchen for paper bags and tongs to use as a makeshift evidence-collection kit. Would he hand anything they found over to the police? No. The captain had shown no inclination to work this case properly. If further analysis was needed, Black would send the evidence to either the Blackwood branch office in Cairo or straight to their fully equipped forensics lab in Virginia. He hated to admit it, but this mystery had gotten under his skin.

Black split the site up based on geographical features and assigned sections to each team member. By the time the sun began to drop towards the horizon, they'd bagged up eight more bones, although Black suspected half might be of animal origin, plus a collection of detritus—cigarette butts, candy wrappers, a button, a small piece of metal that looked as if it might have come off something mechanical, and a stray tennis shoe. He'd also spotted a scrape of white paint on a rock along the path, plus a few flakes on the ground below, which most likely came from a vehicle trying to squeeze through. Not the police's truck—that had been dark blue. He'd get the paint analysed, but as most other pickups, taxis, and cars in the region seemed to be white, it wouldn't help to narrow things down much.

"Hey, over here," Emmy called.

Black's ears pricked up, not because of her words, but due to the urgent tone underlying them. What had his wife spotted?

When he reached her side, she was shining a

flashlight into a crack between two rocks. Just visible was the end of a piece of pale blue cord. A clue? He snapped some pictures. Blue cord hadn't appeared anywhere in the case before, so what had got Emmy so excited?

He found out when she snatched the tongs off him to grab one frayed end.

Fuck.

"Recognise this?" she asked.

Yes, he did. Not the cord itself, but the scarab beetle attached to the end of it. This one looked finer than the one Bob had found on the *Blue Tang*, the craftsmanship more delicate, and rather than having a hole through the middle, it was held in a thin metal frame. Not gold, it was too dark for that. Copper, maybe?

And the cord had stains on it, dark brown splodges that might have been dirt or blood. The victim's blood?

While it was hardly conclusive evidence, it did reinforce the possibility the two cases were linked. What were the chances of finding two dead bodies with scarab beetle charms nearby in a small town like Dahab? Could this be the killer's signature?

"What's that?" Zena asked, standing on a rock so she could peer over Black's shoulder. "A clue?"

"Possibly."

"Possibly? That's all you're gonna give me? I'm a part of this team, aren't I? Who identified that last bone as a calcaneus?"

"I did."

"Yes, but I confirmed it."

"We found a similar beetle to this one on the boat after we brought up the last girl from underwater,"

Emmy told her. "Which may or may not be a coincidence."

"A coincidence? Oh, please," Zena scoffed. "In a town this size? You don't really believe that, do you?"

No, Black really didn't.

Chapter 16 - Emmy

"ANYTHING FROM MILES?" I asked Black when we finally got back home. Alone. After I'd taught lock-picking 101 in Captain Bob's office, showing Khaled and Zena how to make a rake and a tension wrench out of paper clips, then use them to unlock Bob's desk drawer, we'd made our escape. Zena had tried to wriggle out of a family dinner and join us, but Lynn had insisted she go and Captain Bob backed his daughter up, thank goodness. I was getting weirdly used to Zena being around, but having a few hours to ourselves was a relief, even if we had to spend the evening poring over clues in what was possibly a double homicide.

Black checked his phone. "He's sent an email. Unsurprisingly, it's long. With multiple attachments."

"I'd better get a bottle of wine."

While I hunted for a corkscrew, Black took pictures of today's find and sent them off to Miles, then opened up the essay he'd penned and began to read.

"It's called a heart scarab, apparently. A symbol of rebirth. The ancient Egyptians believed the sun died each night and was reborn each morning as a scarab beetle."

"A beetle? Why didn't they pick something cool like an eagle? Or a lion? Or a horse?"

"Who the fuck knows? Anyhow, the scarab became

associated with regeneration, and they thought the dead could harness its powers and be reborn into the afterlife."

"With our careers, maybe we should invest in a dozen of these things." I slid a pen through the cord loop and held the necklace up, studying it.

"The heart was thought to be the seat of the mind, of intelligence and emotion, and after death, its owner would be called up before a panel of deities headed by Osiris in a ceremony called the Weighing of the Heart. Anubis, the jackal god, would weigh the heart against the feather of Ma'at, and if the heart was found to be lighter, its owner would proceed to the afterlife."

"And if it was heavier?"

Black took a swig of wine and studied the screen again. "The person would be deemed unworthy, and their soul would be devoured by the goddess Ammit. Nice."

"So how does the scarab fit in?"

"During the funeral preparations, it would be placed over the heart, usually under a mummy's bindings. The scarab prevented the heart from giving evidence against the deceased at the Divine Tribunal. They're usually inscribed with a spell from the Book of the Dead."

"Is that what all those hieroglyphs on the back are?"

Black cracked a rare smile. "Not in this case. Miles says it's mostly gibberish, and the last line roughly translates as 'Made in Egypt.'"

Another email flashed up on the screen. Miles again. Guess there wasn't much to do in his mud hut or wherever it was he slept while he was digging things up. Bradley tried to help out and make things more comfortable for Miles and his team, bless him, but it didn't always go to plan. Last month, I'd spent an hour on the phone to the Egyptian authorities, negotiating for the release of ten kilos of jelly beans and a set of patio furniture from customs. A few well-placed bribes worked, but by the time the jelly beans reached their destination, they'd melted into one giant lump of rainbow-coloured goo, and the archaeologists had been reduced to chiselling bits off with whatever tools they had to hand.

"This is interesting," Black said.

"Really?"

I squashed in closer to read, and yeah, it actually was interesting. Miles reckoned today's heart scarab was the real deal, and he wanted to know where we'd got it from. Apparently, there was currently a thriving black market in stolen artefacts. He'd have to examine it in person to confirm, yada yada yada, but it had all the hallmarks of a three-thousand-year-old artifact, although the copper setting appeared to be modern. The Ancient Egyptians would have used gold.

Miles had even translated the spell on the back.

O my heart of my mother!

O my heart of my mother!

O my heart of my different forms!

Do not stand up as a witness against me, do not be opposed to me in the tribunal, do not be hostile to me in the presence of the Keeper of the Balance, for you are my ka *which was in my body, the protector who caused my limbs to be healthy.*

Go forth to the happy place whereto we hasten, do not make my name stink to the entourage who make men.

What is good for us is good for the judge.
May the heart be happy at the verdict.
Do not tell lies about me in the presence of the god.
It is indeed well that you should hear!

"*Ka* is life force," Black said, reading on. "I guess it's like the Chinese *qi*."

"Shame both of our victims are missing theirs. What are we dealing with here? Some sort of ritualistic killing? A murderer who sees himself as judge and fucking jury?"

"Honestly? I don't know. Nothing about this case makes sense at the moment. Usually, I've got an idea as to motive, but here…"

"Don't feel bad. Hey, why don't we offer to fix Khaled's kitchen tap and let him do the investigating?"

At least that got a smile out of Black, but only a fleeting one because his phone vibrated again, and his forehead creased into a frown.

"What is it?"

"A possible lead on the identity of the victim."

"Oh?"

"The skeleton had a surgical repair to the left humerus. I took the serial number from the metal plate in the pictures and asked Dan to find out more about it. According to the manufacturer, the plate was sent to the Dahab International Medical Center three years ago, but they don't have a record of who it was implanted into."

"So our victim was a local. Can Mack get into the hospital's database?"

"She's trying, but she's starting from scratch so it

could take time."

As a matter of course, our tech department maintained backdoors into a whole variety of computer networks and databases, partly through the high-level security clearances we'd accumulated over the years and partly because certain members of the team enjoyed the challenge of being where they shouldn't. But a hospital in an out-of-the-way town in Egypt? There'd been no reason for them to try cracking that system until now. They'd most likely start with phishing emails, and depending on how security-conscious the staff were, gaining access could take anywhere from a few hours to a few weeks.

"How about Khaled? Could he help?"

"He still hasn't managed to get Carmela's autopsy report. How long do you think it'd take him to get the hospital records? We're only here for another week."

I had to concur, which left one option. Visiting the hospital to try and get the information ourselves.

"Hmm, you know what? I'm feeling a little sick."

"Your daughter needs stitches, but she'll be fine," a nurse told me. Not an Egyptian but a Filipino, judging by her accent, and she leaned in close to peer at Zena's forehead. "The doctor will be here soon."

So much for preparation. I'd gone for an eight-mile run on Sunday morning to bring my temperature up, then eaten half a dozen chillis to keep it high, and I was sweating nicely by the time we left the villa. The plan was that I'd distract the staff with an imaginary fever while Black snuck into the hospital offices to see what he could find in the way of records.

But as we headed for the car, Zena had come running over to see where we were going, tripped down some steps, and landed head first on a fancy metal plant pot. Now she had a cut on her forehead and, I suspected, a slight concussion. When Black and I offered to drive her to the hospital, Lynn had been happy to shirk her parental responsibilities, and in the car just before we ventured into the hospital, I'd said two words to Zena: Drama. Queen. Hence the reason she was now doing her very best to create a scene worthy of an Oscar.

"But it hurts so bad! And my head won't stop bleeding! What if I die of blood loss?"

"Is that possible?" I asked.

"It really isn't bleeding that much," the nurse said, and I pitied her for having to deal with us. Yeah, it wasn't fun being bitchy to the medical staff, but sometimes, doing horrible things was necessary for the greater good. And while we kicked up merry hell in the waiting area, Black had snuck off to get an idea of the layout of the hospital. We needed to know where the records were kept.

"How can you say that?" Zena shrieked. "I'm *crimson*. Look at me!"

"Is it possible to get a second opinion?" I asked.

"The doctor's just finishing up with a patient."

"You only have one doctor here?"

"No, but—"

"Then perhaps you could ask one of the others to help?"

"We have another nurse who can do the stitches."

"Great. Can you find her? Or him?"

"Magdalena. I will ask her to come."

"Thank you," I said, although I hoped Magdalena didn't hurry because there was still no sign of Black. He'd disappeared through a door marked *Staff Only* fifteen minutes ago, and since he hadn't been escorted out by security, I had to assume he was still snooping.

Would he find anything? He'd borrowed one of Bradley's manbags to stash any goodies he came across, and he'd also promised to push my Dodge Viper off a cliff if I ever told anyone he'd gone out in public carrying a genuine ostrich satchel made by Ishmael.

"Am I doing okay?" Zena whispered.

"Perfect. How's the headache?"

"I thought Mom was gonna kill me when she saw the gash."

After a few initial tears, Lynn's biggest concern had been whether her hairstylist friend could hide Zena's injury in the wedding photos. Apparently, the stitches wouldn't match the new outfit they'd bought in Sharm el-Sheikh, which, according to Zena, was as hideous as the old dress but slightly looser.

The Filipino nurse came back, stopping two feet away from us. Opting for a safe distance, from her nervous expression.

"Zena? I can take you to get your stitches now. Do you want your mom to come with you?"

"What, do I look ten? I *can* do things by myself."

Thanks, kid. That gave me a chance to do a bit of snooping myself. Where was Black? I checked the locator app on my phone and saw he was on the other side of the building, by the operating theatres according to the signs. I headed in the opposite direction. The more we learned about the layout of the hospital, the better. I headed past the wards, walking with a purpose because if you looked as though you knew where you were going, nobody would stop you. An X-ray suite, consulting rooms, a staff lounge... When I heard a gaggle of people walking towards me, I ducked into the storeroom just in case. No sign of any filing cabinets, but I did stuff a set of scrubs into my oversized handbag. They might come in handy later.

My phone buzzed.

Black: Found records office but too busy RN.

Not to worry, we'd come back later when the admin team had gone home. Patience was a virtue, and while sin was my speciality, I'd learned to take a step back and wait when I needed to.

At ten p.m., I strolled into the hospital dressed in a pair of scrubs, taking advantage of the chaos only the aftermath of a multi-vehicle pileup could bring. Why me? Simple. Because Black's size made him stick out too much. Zena had offered to help as well, saying that since she'd been poked with a bunch of needles then turned into a human tapestry, she'd earned the right, but I didn't need a sidekick, not tonight. She hadn't been amused when we left her behind, but somebody had to look after the damn rabbit and it sure as hell wasn't going to be me.

Black lurked outside, taking advantage of the shadows left by the sliver of crescent moon that hung low over Saudi Arabia. The records office was on the third floor, or the fourth floor if I were in America, which I wasn't—the soft sitar music drifting out of the room to my left was a testament to that, as was the bill for Zena's treatment that we'd paid earlier. We hadn't been charged sixteen bucks for an aspirin.

We'd only spotted two cameras on our previous visit, and I pulled a surgeon's mask over my face as I strode past them, pausing to wave to the doctor hurrying in the opposite direction. He just waved back.

"So far, so good," I muttered for the benefit of Black and Mack, who were listening via the microphone built into my earring. I could hear everything they said too via a hidden earpiece.

"The admin office should be coming up on your left," Black told me.

Sure enough, there it was. The door was locked, but I carried a set of lock picks like most people carried a credit card—that is to say, I kept it in my wallet and tended to overuse it.

Inside, the narrow room contained six utilitarian desks, lined up in pairs with hard plastic seats behind them. Neat. Impersonal. It reminded me of a classroom except instead of colourful pictures, the walls were decorated with health and safety posters and a reminder that staff fraternisation was *haram*. Forbidden. Under each desk was an old-style tower computer, humming softly, the occasional green light flashing on the front.

Which desk should I pick? Eeny, meeny, miny, moe... I closed the door behind me with a quiet *click* and slid into the seat behind the furthest desk. A nudge of the mouse, and the screen came to life, asking for a password. Of course, I didn't have that, but I did have Mack sitting in Virginia with Wilhelmina, as she'd named her latest computer.

All I had to do was stuff the USB stick containing Mack's proprietary software into the port and wait.

And wait.

And wait.

Funny how two minutes seemed like ten when you were sitting on the floor listening to footsteps in the corridor outside and praying they didn't come in your direction.

"How much longer is this going to take?" I whispered.

"I'm in the system," Mack said. "But it's as if their entire admin team has dyslexia. Nothing's in date order, or alphabetical order—either English or Arabic—so I'm having to run a search on likely keywords."

I should've brought a fucking cushion.

Finally, the tower beside me stopped whirring, and Mack sucked in a breath. What did that mean? It sounded suspiciously like bad news.

"What's happening?"

"I've narrowed it down to six possibles who had their humerus repaired with metal plates."

"Six?"

"They don't keep details of the implant serial numbers on the system. There's a notation in the field that says to see the patient's file for further information. I'm assuming that means a paper file because I can't find anything more on the server."

I glanced around the room, but there were no filing cabinets, only a metal cupboard opposite the door that didn't look big enough to hold a hospital's worth of patient information.

"There's a door at the far end of the hallway that might lead to some sort of filing room," Black told me.

"Try there."

Next time, I'd sit outside and sweat while Black skulked around the hospital.

The door was plain white, no viewing window, no sign, and locked from the outside with a bolt and padlock. The high-tech approach. I found padlocks even easier to pick than regular door locks, so I was inside before anyone asked me what the hell I was doing.

Jackpot. Well, sort of. Rows and rows of filing cabinets stretched away from me, filling almost the entire room. The only bit of space was at the far end, where a scarred wooden desk identical to those in the main office sat in front of the window. Each of the filing cabinets had a sticker on the front denoting an Arabic letter. I only had to hope that the filing clerk knew the alphabet better than whoever had fucked up the computer system.

"Mack, gimme the first name."

Half an hour later, I'd found four of the files, but none of the serial numbers matched our victim. Two to go—Reem Younes and Malgorzata Kaminski—but as I approached the Y cabinet, I heard more footsteps in the corridor. Two sets, and coming in my direction. Keep going. *Keep going.*

But it seemed my luck had run out tonight.

"Why is the door unlocked?" a male voice asked. Not an Egyptian. He sounded French.

"Who cares?" a woman asked, followed by a giggle. "Just get inside."

Ah, shit.

CHAPTER 17 - EMMY

THE LIGHT CAME on as I crawled under the desk, thankful for the modesty panel across the front. Once designed to stop perverts from looking up their secretaries' skirts, now it was the only thing between me and a very awkward conversation. What were the pair doing in the filing room so late at night anyway? I hazarded a guess that it had nothing to do with paperwork, and I was right.

The man's belt buckle hit the tiled floor with a *clunk* alongside his stethoscope as he dropped his trousers. The woman was wearing scrubs. A nurse? Now I knew why the admin office had a *no fraternisation* sign on the wall. Seriously, who had time for this shit? These assholes were supposed to be downstairs fixing car crash victims, not screwing over a desk, because that was surely what was about to happen.

Another giggle, followed by, "Ooh, Dr. B. You're so big."

Jeez... She'd been watching too many adult movies.

A condom landed next to me, and the woman's manicured hand groped around to retrieve it an inch from my knee. I flicked it towards her, thoroughly cheesed off. At midnight on my vacation, *I* was the one who should've been getting screwed, not some nurse who had better things to do. Mack's laughter in my ear didn't help either.

As the woman started moaning, porn-star-style, I pulled out my phone and fired off an email to my beloved colleague.

Next time, you can do the hard work and I'll sit behind a keyboard.

She typed faster than I did, and her reply came almost instantly.

Oh, please. You think Python's a kind of snake.

The only saving grace was that Dr. Grunts-a-lot didn't last long. Two minutes of sweaty balls slapping flesh, and it was all over, for them at least. They hurried out, still breathing hard.

"Well, that was fun."

"If it's any consolation," Black said, "a dog pissed on my boot while I was waiting."

"Couldn't you have gotten rid of it?" Mack asked as I snorted.

"Not when there was a trio of doctors smoking three feet away."

We were clearly in the wrong jobs here. And speaking of jobs, I still had work to do. Two sets of patient records left to find, and I'd better do it fast because I didn't fancy hiding under the desk again.

As Sod's Law dictated, the file I wanted was the last one I checked. Malgorzata Kaminski, a thirty-three-year-old Polish national who'd had her arm pinned two years ago after a fall. She'd listed an address in Assalah.

"Got it," I told the others. "I deserve a glass of wine

after this."

Actually, make that a bottle, because when I checked the door, the doctor and his lady friend had carefully bolted it afterwards.

"Uh, we have a small technical problem."

"Don't tell me problems; tell me solutions."

If I had a dollar for every time Black had said those words...

"Fine, I have a solution. I'm coming out the window. If I fall, you'd better fucking catch me."

"I'll always catch you, Diamond."

And that was why I loved him.

Three floors up, and thank goodness we were around the back of the building because the last thing I needed was a crowd of onlookers seeing me climb out onto the windowsill in my scrubs. Knowing my luck, or rather the lack of it, they'd try to talk a suicidal "doctor" out of jumping.

Slowly, slowly, I inched my way down, clinging onto whatever I could—stonework, window frames, a sign proclaiming the Dahab International Medical Center to be the "No. 1 hospital in Egypt." By the time I landed in Black's arms, my nails looked as though I'd filed them with power tools.

"I called the hotel," he murmured in my ear. "The wine's waiting in the villa."

"Gimme a second. I just need to pop inside and ask that horny nurse where she got her manicure done."

"Want me to fly Bradley over?"

"No, I want to go to bed."

"That sounds like the best idea I've heard all day."

When I crawled out of bed in the morning, Black was already pottering around in the kitchen. Glass clinked as I staggered in his direction.

"Tell me you're making coffee."

The counter came into view, and I took in the bottle of drain cleaner, the hydrogen peroxide, the nail polish remover... If he was making coffee, I'd changed my mind. I didn't want any.

"No, I'm making luminol. I want to find out for sure whether it's blood on that cord we found with the second heart scarab."

"Where did you get all this stuff?"

"Borrowed it from the hospital. I grudgingly admit that Bradley's bag has a practical use after all."

He turned the burner on under a conical flask, poured in some chemicals that bubbled and fizzed, then watched as acrid fumes drifted across the kitchen.

"Is this safe?" I asked.

"More or less."

"More or less?"

"I haven't done this for a while."

"Fucking hell."

"Don't worry, I got good grades in chemistry."

"James told me you set fire to the lab building."

"James has got a big fucking mouth."

"So it's true?"

"There was never any proof of that, and in any case, my parents kindly donated a new one."

We did have a fire extinguisher in the villa, didn't we? Yes, by the back door. I checked it was pressurised, then threw on a pair of shorts and a T-shirt and went in search of coffee. No way was I dealing with an explosion before I'd loaded up on caffeine.

By the time I got back with a family-sized cafetière and a plateful of pastries, Black was scraping white powder out of a beaker, and the whole villa stank. Just another day in paradise.

"Well?"

"Almost done. Is there any fruit?"

"I brought you a banana." The catch on the kitchen window was stuck, so I jimmied it open with a knife to let in some much-needed fresh air. "I'll be on the terrace."

Information was already coming in on Malgorzata Kaminski, also known as Gosia. The basics weren't difficult to find—she even had a website with a blog attached. And the logo looked familiar.

Love Life, Love Dahab, the same slogan that had been on Carmela's bag.

A coincidence? Or had they connected with each other in the past? I scrolled through the pictures of Dahab, of Gosia's life and friends, but I didn't see Carmela in any of them.

"Hmm," Black said, peering over my shoulder.

The other notable thing about the website was the "Missing" poster splashed across the home page, together with an appeal for information on Gosia's whereabouts. She'd vanished on June twenty-seventh, just over three months ago. The picture showed a brunette with a tanned face and plaits hanging down over either shoulder, smiling for the camera with her arm around somebody out of shot. The mountains formed a backdrop, and she was carrying a backpack.

"Last seen walking in town," Black said. "What if she decided to carry on walking farther?"

"You mean into the mountains?"

In Dahab, people liked to explore. To take pictures, to get fit, or simply to get some peace alone. A lot of people claimed to have had spiritual experiences in those hills.

Black scrolled farther down the page. "She's wearing hiking boots in this photo. If she meandered into the mountains and fell and hit her head, it's not inconceivable we're looking at an accident."

"If it wasn't for the two scarab beetles and now the logo, I might just believe that. Is the luminol done yet?"

"Assuming I've remembered the recipe right, yes."

"Then let's find out if we're on the right track with this." I glanced at the screen again. "You know, if you squint, Gosia looks a bit like Carmela. Same face shape, same hair colour, similar smile. You could mistake her for a sister."

Inside, I closed the shutters in the bedroom, leaving us in darkness apart from Black's flashlight. He'd put his concoction into the spray bottle Bradley had bought for the houseplants that died about five years ago.

Moment of truth...

I got ready with the camera as Black sprayed luminol at the necklace. The thing lit up like a damn Christmas tree, splodges on the cord fluorescing blue, and when Black turned it around, the spell on the back of the scarab glowed eerily in the gloom.

Sure, luminol could give false positives, most commonly if it touched bleach, but with the colour of the stains on the cord and the circumstances, it was pretty clear we were looking at foul play.

Gosia hadn't died of natural causes.

I clicked on Gosia's Facebook profile, having logged in with a fake name I used on the internet. No way did I want details of the real me sitting on a server somewhere to be sold to the highest bidder. Every so often, I clicked on a bunch of random adverts just to keep the data trolls nicely confused—internet Emmy was a thirty-seven-year-old spinster who enjoyed quilting, skydiving, heavy metal music, plumbing, and collecting Christmas ornaments. She also had a pet snail and may or may not have had a fungal toenail infection.

Gosia's life was more clear-cut. Once I scrolled past all the "Have you seen this woman?" posts, a picture of a dedicated eco-warrior emerged. She promoted vegan food, organised litter collections, and was a fierce advocate for animal rights. Her latest initiative, *Sixty Seconds to Save the Planet*, aimed to install recycling points within a minute's walk of anywhere in Dahab.

"Didn't Aurelie say that Carmela met Youssef while they were cleaning up the beach?" Black asked. "I wonder if Gosia was involved in organising that?"

"It's possible." I scrolled through pictures of teams traipsing along the shoreline carrying sacks of rubbish, but I couldn't spot Carmela or Youssef in any of them. "I bet Aurelie would know."

"Then let's ask her."

"Can I come?" Zena asked from the open patio door that led onto the terrace. "I'm bored."

Were we ever going to get a moment to ourselves?

"Don't you have bridesmaid stuff to do?"

"Mom and Chris are talking to the caterers this morning, and I'm not invited. Please? I'll stay really quiet. There's nothing else to do around here."

"What about going to the beach? There must be ten different kinds of water sports you could try."

"Mom won't let me. She says it's dangerous."

"What, even paddleboarding?"

"I might die of boredom if I go paddleboarding."

Okay, I had to give her that one. I looked at Black, and Black looked at me, then he shrugged as if to say "she's your responsibility." Aurelie wouldn't mind if an extra person came, right? Letting Zena tag along was easier than trying to win an argument with a teenager.

"Fine. But you let us do the talking."

Zena mimed zipping up her mouth and throwing away the key, then immediately started speaking again. "I won't say a word. Promise. I'll be back in two minutes. I just need to go and change my shoes. These flip-flops are rubbing."

"Meet us out front, okay?"

On the way to the lobby, we saw Captain Bob striding towards us, his back ramrod straight as always. Why did he look so serious?

"Have you seen Zena?" he asked.

"She went to change her shoes. Why?"

"Lynn called. They drove into town to meet the tailor for their final dress fittings, but while Lynn was getting changed, Zena disappeared. She's back here?"

That little minx. She'd lied, or at least bent the truth, although I had to give her credit for doing so with a perfect poker face.

"Yeah, she's here. Guess she must've walked back."

"Damn. I was almost hoping she wasn't. Now I'll have to talk to her. What am I supposed to say to a young lady who hates everything?"

"She doesn't hate my rabbit."

"That's true. She's actually been easier to deal with since you arrived with the bunny. I thought we might have turned a corner, but now this happens... Lynn's at the end of her tether, and I don't know what to do to help. I know Zena's not keen on Chris, but he makes Lynn happy, and...and... Give me a platoon of SEALs and a war zone over a teenager any day."

From the stories Black had told me, Bob had spent much of his military career overseas, so he hadn't been around for his own daughter's childhood either. No wonder he didn't know how to deal with Zena.

"What does Sondra say?"

A shrug. "We never had any of this trouble with Lynn."

"Zena mentioned she wanted to live with her father." Might as well be honest. "Has anybody asked him for some input?"

Bob's face clouded over. "The man's an asshole. He sends Zena expensive gifts and says the right things on the phone, but when Lynn spoke to him about taking her for a while to see if that'd help, he refused to let her stay even for a weekend."

"Does Zena know that?"

"Lynn didn't want to hurt her any more than she's been hurt already."

A difficult conundrum. By sparing Zena's feelings, Lynn had caused a different kind of pain. And I knew what it was like to be rejected by a parent. Both of them, in fact. My father didn't stick around for long enough to know my mother was pregnant, and as for the woman who'd borne me, I'd taken second place to just about everything in her life—drink, drugs, boyfriends, you name it.

Over the last decade, I'd gone out of my way to help teenagers who'd ended up in similar situations. As well as Blackwood Security, we ran a charitable foundation to fund our pet projects, and mine was a scheme to help street kids in London and Richmond find work and a place to live. I even mentored some of them myself when I had the time, so Zena's antics weren't the first time I'd had to deal with teenage angst.

"Maybe Lynn has good intentions, but Zena feels like a spare part at the moment. Is it true that Chris made her get rid of her pets?"

"They moved house, and he said there wasn't room for them at the new place."

"She said they lived in her bedroom, so surely if she wanted them to share her space, that was up to her?"

"Between you and me, I agree with her about the pets. But although Chris has his faults, Lynn's come out of her depression since they've been together, so I have to support her decision to marry him."

His grimace said he didn't care much for Chris either, and I felt sorry for Captain Bob too. It couldn't be easy watching his family fight.

"We're going into town to ask Carmela's friend some more questions. How about we take Zena with us and go to the tailor for the dress fitting afterwards?"

"You don't mind?" Bob looked to Black when he asked. "Aren't you supposed to be on vacation?"

"The vacation isn't really happening," he said. "Too many dead bodies. And Zena's oddly enthusiastic about helping—does that bother you?"

"If she's with you two, no harm's going to come to her," Bob said, reminding me I needed to have a chat with Zena about the dangers of wandering around town alone. Although we weren't yet sure whether Gosia's death was murder, it seemed wise not to take chances. "Zena always did have a morbid curiosity about death, but so long as she's not causing it, I won't lose any sleep."

"What about Lynn?"

"Lynn's more of a hearts-and-flowers girl."

"I meant will she mind Zena tagging along with us?"

"Oh, I'll talk to her. Tell her not to worry. Right now, I think she's just grateful to avoid some of the tantrums. She says Zena's going through a phase."

The girl herself came running along the path, but her footsteps slowed when she saw her grandfather. Busted.

"Uh, I can explain."

"You don't have to," I told her. "We're going into town, and you're going to try on your bridesmaid's dress while you're there."

"But—"

"If you don't like that idea, you're welcome to stay here and help your grandpa unblock the toilets by the dive centre. Right, Bob?"

He looked puzzled for a second, then nodded. "Right."

"Car door's unlocked. I suggest you get inside it."

"It's a horrible dress."

"You only have to wear it for a few hours. Then you can ceremoniously burn it on the beach and scatter the ashes at sea if you like, but you're going to be a good bridesmaid and make your mom happy, okay?"

"Mom's never happy."

"Okay, then make her less unhappy. Car. Off you go."

Zena slunk away in the right direction, and I grinned at Bob. "There. Now we understand each other."

CHAPTER 18 - BLACK

"I REMEMBER HER," Aurelie said when Black showed her the picture of Gosia on his tablet. "Gosia, right? She's one of those militant environmentalists. When we first got here, she was running a campaign to ban plastic bags, and then it was the recycling."

"Was she friends with Carmela?"

"I don't think so. Why?"

"Did you know she'd gone missing?"

"Everyone knew. There were posters all over town for weeks, then it kind of died off. Did she ever turn up?"

"A body was found in the mountains yesterday morning, and we believe it could be Gosia. It's possible the two deaths are connected."

The colour drained out of Aurelie's face, and for a second, Black thought she might keel over sideways. Not that there was very far to fall. To say the furnishings in Aurelie's apartment were sparse was an understatement, and the four of them were sitting cross-legged on cushions on the floor. Minimalist tastes or a lack of money? If Black had to guess, he'd go for the latter. Teaching a handful of yoga classes each week in Dahab probably didn't pay much.

The only nod to decoration was the frogs. Ornaments littered the side table, and Black recognised the signature of a local artist on a picture above the TV. The guy sat at his stall in the high street every evening, brush in hand, and Emmy had half a dozen of his paintings hanging on the walls back home in Virginia.

"Really?" Aurelie choked out once she'd swallowed a few times. "Connected how?"

"We found a stone scarab beetle with Carmela, and there was a similar amulet near Gosia."

"A scarab beetle? That's it?"

"For the moment, yes. Nothing's certain at this stage, and the body's identity hasn't been confirmed, so this information needs to stay between the four of us."

"Okay."

"Do you remember Carmela owning a scarab beetle? A heart scarab? About this size..." He held his thumb and finger an inch apart. "Carved from black stone, maybe onyx."

"Yuck, no. Carmela hated creepy-crawlies. A little while ago, one of the restaurants was giving out scarab charms with the bill instead of mints, but they were much smaller. Carmela refused to take ours. I didn't want it either, so we left it on the table."

Seemed they'd eliminated any possibility of the first scarab belonging to their victim. Plus Bob had asked the groups who'd been out on the *Blue Tang* in the week before Carmela's body was found, and they'd denied all knowledge, and Khaled had no idea why one of his colleagues might have brought a tchotchke like that to a crime scene. It seemed more likely that the killer had left it with Carmela, but why?

Should they be looking for a historian with an interest in death?

"Even if they weren't close friends, do you recall

seeing Gosia talk to Carmela?"

"I can't... It's really true? Two people dead? In Dahab? I mean, that's crazy," Aurelie said, still processing. "It's always been such a safe town, and now..." She held out a trembling hand. "Look—I'm so nervous I can't even hold a drink without spilling it. Every time someone goes past outside, I break out in a cold sweat."

"I'm sure there's nothing to worry about," Emmy said.

"Somebody knocked on the door last night, and I nearly had a heart attack."

"Who was it?"

"You think I opened it? Are you insane? My best friend was *murdered*."

Black knew exactly what Aurelie was thinking. *What if the killer comes back for me?*

Statistically, it was unlikely, and the best way they could eliminate the possibility completely was by finding the fucker. Which meant he needed to steer the conversation back on track.

"Gosia and Carmela—do you remember seeing them talk to each other?"

"Uh... Once or twice, they said hello to each other in town. And on the beach. Gosia and her boyfriend would organise people to pick up the rubbish, and we went along a couple of times."

"And that was when Carmela met Youssef?"

"Yes. Wait! I think Gosia and Youssef might have had an argument that day."

"What makes you say that?"

"Carmela came over with Youssef and said one of the organisers had laid into him for selling chickens. In the beginning, she just felt sorry for him for getting shouted at, but by the end of the day, they'd gotten to know each other and he invited her out for dinner."

"Did either of them go into any more detail about what happened?"

"No, I think they both got distracted."

"I'm surprised Youssef stuck around if he got rebuked like that."

"He was only there because he'd brought his little sister, and she wanted to stay with her friends."

So there had been a possible conflict with one of the organisers, but which one? Gosia or her boyfriend? And they'd also established that Youssef knew both women. Definitely a point to follow up on.

"Do you know who Gosia's boyfriend was?"

"Sorry, I don't. A Bedouin, I think, but I don't know his name."

Never mind. Black knew a man who would: Khaled. Black would bet his new Porsche that the police hadn't identified Gosia yet, which meant he could trade that little snippet of information for the name and address of Gosia's significant other.

"Don't worry; we can find out. Another question—the bag we found with Carmela was purple with the slogan 'Love Life, Love Dahab' on it. Do you know where she got it from?"

"No, but when we first came to Dahab, they were in every shop. I think they were part of Gosia's scheme to reduce plastic waste, which is such an important cause, don't you think? Why do you ask? Is that another connection?"

"It seems unlikely if they were widely sold."

An apparent dead end. Black hated dead ends, but

they were an unavoidable frustration in every investigator's life.

A tear rolled down Aurelie's cheek. "I just want this person caught."

"We'll do our best to make sure that happens."

With just over a week of their "vacation" left, it seemed unlikely Emmy and Black would find a resolution themselves, especially with the limited resources available to them in Dahab, but they could train Khaled in the basics and pass over any information they gathered before they flew back to the US. *You can't win 'em all.* Black had been trying to persuade himself of that fact for years, but leaving unfinished business still irked him to no end.

Zena, who'd kept her word and stayed quiet since they'd arrived, fished around in her pocket and passed Aurelie a tissue.

"It'll be okay. My grandpa says Black never gives up." She pointed at a ceramic frog perched on top of a stack of well-read paperbacks. "Is that a Malagasy Rainbow Frog?"

"I'm not sure."

"Did you know they've got claws on their front feet that let them climb vertical walls?"

"I love frogs, but I don't know much about all the different species."

"I've always wanted a pet frog. Either a Green Frog or a Fire-Bellied Toad, but my mom won't let me have either at the moment."

"Are they difficult to keep?"

And so started the frog discussion. While Zena and Aurelie talked amphibians, Black let his mind wander across the clues they'd found. On paper, Youssef was still the most likely culprit so far. Black didn't like the man, but was he a killer? He seemed almost too obvious, too easy a candidate. And he hadn't struck Black as all that smart.

The person they were after had been careful, with few clues left behind and only luck leading to the discovery of both bodies. This case was shaping up to be a challenge, and Black never shied away from one of those. But this time, he had two adversaries—a killer, and the ticking clock.

CHAPTER **19** - EMMY

"SHE WAS STABBED," Khaled told Black and me over a meal at the villa the following morning. Was it a late breakfast? Brunch? An early lunch? Toast, fruit, pastries, juice... "The second victim," Khaled elaborated, poking the air with a butter knife for emphasis. "The doctor said the bones on the mountain belonged to a female, and she was stabbed."

One piece of information we already knew, and one we didn't. Stabbing, huh? Messy. I avoided it wherever possible. A silenced double-tap to the head was the way to go, preferably with a .22 so the bullets ricocheted around inside the skull and mushed everything up. Quick, easy, and clean.

"How did the doctor ascertain the cause of death?" Black asked, spreading honey on his toast. Good shout. With all this talk of death, my strawberry jam didn't look so appetising anymore.

"There were knife marks on the ribs. The doctor says she was stabbed at least six times."

"What about Carmela? Any luck with that autopsy report?"

Khaled gave a helpless shrug. He seemed to do that a lot, probably had it ingrained through years of practice or passed down from his father along with his name and his nervous attitude. Ten bucks said he'd have ulcers by the time he hit thirty.

"When I went to the station this morning, the captain was in his office. I'll try again this evening if he doesn't stay late. Her dental records arrived from Italy, though, so her identity has been confirmed. Now we just need to find out who the other woman is. The captain told me to go through the reports of missing people, but my computer in the office is broken. That's what I'm supposed to be doing right now—arranging for it to be fixed."

"Broken? In what way?"

"The screen won't turn on. I stopped at the repair shop on the way here, and somebody will come tomorrow, maybe the day after, *inshallah*."

"The hotel has a spare screen you can borrow. We need to get that list of missing women."

But not for the reason Khaled thought. Black and I had spoken about the case this morning, lying in bed, my sweaty body draped over his as we discussed tactics in some weird form of afterplay. Still, Black was happy —two of his favourite things were sex and solving murders.

Two deaths in Dahab within such a short space of time—what if this was just the beginning?

The dead women shared certain characteristics— both foreigners, brunettes, and young-looking. While Carmela had habitually worn make-up and came across older than her nineteen years in photos, Gosia had been blessed with one of those ageless faces. Someone could have told you she was twenty or forty and you'd have believed them either way.

"Do you think she will be on the list?" Khaled asked. "So many people come and go in Dahab, it's hard to keep track of them."

"She was a long-term resident," Black said, tipping our hand. "And yes, she'll be on the list. But the main reason we want the names is to see if any other dead bodies are likely to turn up."

Khaled's hand paused halfway to his mouth, and a lump of almond flaked off the Danish he was holding and landed on the tiles. Did rabbits eat almonds? What we needed there was a dog. Back in Virginia, my Doberman, Lucy, hoovered up any stray pieces of food as soon as they hit the floor.

"You know who the second victim is?"

"Malgorzata Kaminski, also known as Gosia. An environmental activist from Poland."

"What...? How? How do you know this?"

"She had a metal plate in her arm from the repair of an old injury. The plate had a serial number, and the number was registered to her."

We'd expected questions on how exactly we knew that little detail, but Khaled betrayed his inexperience by skipping ahead.

"Gosia. I think I know her. *Knew* her. The recycling bins, yes? She organised the recycling bins?"

"That's right. What else can you tell us about her?"

"I can't remember when she came to Dahab, but it was a long time ago. Many foreigners, they visit for a month, two months, then they find it is too quiet or too hot or too isolated and they go home. But Gosia, she stayed, and some people didn't like that."

"What do you mean?"

"She was an outsider, but she tried to change the town."

"How?" I asked. "With her environmentalism?"

That was a word, right?

"Yes."

"Why would recycling and cutting back on plastic make people upset?"

"Because her views were extreme—all or nothing. She didn't just want to cut back on plastic, she wanted to eliminate it completely. She named and shamed shopkeepers on the internet if they didn't switch to paper carrier bags, and snatched straws out of tourists' drinks. And last summer, she tried to stop the Bedouins from fishing off the coast. They've been doing that for hundreds of years, and many of them weren't happy that their way of life was being questioned."

"Wasn't she dating a Bedouin?"

Khaled nodded. "Selmi, who runs the organic garden. She did have plenty of friends. People either loved her or hated her."

Love or hate—that jibed with what Aurelie had told us about the vibe between Gosia and Youssef. They'd argued, but at the same time, Gosia *had* managed to inspire a whole group of people to clean up the beach with her that day.

Now we had two victims, one with plenty of enemies and one who didn't seem to have any at all. The only solid links so far? Two heart scarabs and the aforementioned chicken-meister. But it was interesting that Gosia had pissed off a bunch of fishermen, firstly because they'd know how to tie a surgeon's knot, and secondly because like divers, they'd know the sea wall dropped off sharply at the spot where Carmela's body was found.

I quickly did the math. Two people, one week of vacation left, and probably a hundred Bedouin fishermen in town. Black and I would need help to question that many people. Either we could fly men here from Blackwood's Cairo office or Khaled would have to step up. Our people were better trained but already stretched thin, and they didn't have the benefit of local knowledge. Khaled seemed keen, but there was only one of him and his competence was questionable.

And that wasn't our biggest problem. Until the police identified Gosia themselves and notified her family of her death, we couldn't admit we were investigating her murder either.

Decisions, decisions…

Black cut his eyes to me, then glanced at Khaled, and I knew he was going through the same thought process. Seventeen years, fifteen of them married, and we were on the same wavelength. I gave the tiniest nod. On balance, local knowledge and a police badge won out. We'd just have to get creative with our questioning.

"The first task is to ensure your colleagues are aware of the body's identity, which means you'll have to follow a similar process to us—take the details of the orthopaedic device to the hospitals in Dahab and ask them if they can link it to a patient. I'd *strongly* suggest starting with the Dahab International Medical Center. Will there be any problems getting the captain to authorise that?"

"I don't think so. He wants to find out who the victim is, but if I suggest the death was anything but an accident, he will be unhappy."

"Then you'll have to tread carefully, and so will we until somebody speaks to Gosia's next of kin. For the moment, we'll have to frame this as a follow-up to her disappearance."

"But we hardly have any clues," Khaled said. "Where do we start?"

"With circumstantial evidence. We need to make three lists—one with Carmela's acquaintances, one with Gosia's, and a third with anyone in town you suspect might be capable of the murders."

"How do we know who to put on the lists?"

We'd gone from lock-picking 101 to investigations 101, but Black stayed patient. "Local knowledge and profiling."

"Ah, profiling! I have seen that on—"

"*CSI*," I said. "We know."

"Offenders can be divided into two basic categories —organised and disorganised," Black told him. "Organised offenders tend to be smarter, and they're also more likely to have a job and a spouse. They plan out their crimes and maintain enough control to avoid being impulsive. They also target their victims carefully, bring the tools they need with them— weapons, restraints, cleaning materials—and tend to hide the bodies when they're done with them. Disorganised offenders are the opposite—they often live alone, have lower-than-average intelligence, and may be unemployed. They don't have a lot of control over their actions, and the crime scene's more likely to be a mess."

"I need my notepad," Khaled muttered, fishing around for it in his pocket and frantically scribbling away the instant he got to a blank page. "So which type are we dealing with?"

"Which do you think?"

Khaled chewed on his bottom lip as he thought. "Organised?"

"That's my conclusion too. Yes, the killer improvised when he used Carmela's own bag to sink her, but the rest of the job was quite tidy. Although remember, we don't have a crime scene for either victim yet, just two dump sites. I don't believe the girls were killed where we found them."

I agreed with that. What kind of idiot would stab a girl to death on the seashore? Granted, the track past the caves wasn't busy, but just dumping the body was risky enough without her screaming bloody murder first. And when we'd been hunting for Gosia's bones, I'd scanned the surroundings. Nothing that resembled a bloodstain had graced the granite and sandstone rocks nearby.

"So we are looking for somebody smart, employed, maybe married," Khaled said.

"Yes. Although we're not quite in serial killer territory, it wouldn't surprise me if there was another victim out there that we haven't found." Khaled paled a shade at Black's words. "Most serial killers are male and in their twenties or thirties. They don't tend to cross racial lines, and most kill close to home, especially for their first few victims. Call it a comfort zone. It's unlikely our perpetrator's travelling from Sharm el-Sheikh or Nuweiba to kill these girls."

"There are hundreds of men in Dahab. Most of them have jobs and families."

"We found scarab amulets with both bodies. Start by looking at anyone with an interest in Ancient Egyptian customs, maybe a foreigner. And the cord on Carmela's body was tied with a surgeon's knot, which raises the possibility of a fisherman or a doctor being involved. Then we have to consider how the killer picked the victim. How they gained access. What about Gosia and Carmela attracted him? Start with your own knowledge—you've lived here in Dahab your whole life. Ask your colleagues and go through police files. Speak to Carmela's friends and Gosia's associates. Hopefully, we'll start to see some patterns emerge as the lists grow. Does everyone in the police department share the captain's attitude?"

"About three-quarters."

"Then enlist the help of the cops who *do* want to see a murderer behind bars. We also need to establish whether there could be any bodies we haven't found yet. Can you send us the missing persons list once your computer's working?"

"I don't think it's a list. Just separate reports."

"Then somebody needs to go through them. Reckon you can handle that?"

Khaled's Adam's apple bobbed as he swallowed. He didn't seem particularly confident, but he nodded anyway. I was worried he might just be telling us what we wanted to hear.

"Good. I'll drop you off in town with the computer screen, and once you've got the reports, we can go to the organic garden and talk to Selmi."

"What about me?" I asked.

Three of us versus one witness could come across as intimidating. Plus, although Dahab wasn't as bad as many places in the Middle East, sexism was still alive and kicking in that part of the world. Selmi might be more forthcoming with a couple of men.

"Don't you have a bridesmaid's dress to pick up?" Black was trying not to smirk, the asshole. "And you need to get a rabbit hutch from somewhere. That fucking bunny's chewed halfway through one of the bed legs, and she's gonna go for the door if we don't do something fast."

Bunny wrangler and errand girl? Well, I *was* on vacation, after all.

CHAPTER 20 - BLACK

MASRA'A SAIDA, OR Happy Gardens, clung to the edge of Dahab, hidden behind high walls built from mud bricks. The construction didn't look particularly stable, as if a stiff breeze could send the whole lot tumbling into an ugly brown pile. But the front gates were open, potted plants covered in fragrant pink blooms lined up either side. Bradley would have called the shade flamingo or wild orchid or cotton candy or some other bullshit, but that didn't change the fact that it was still fucking pink.

Pink that matched the current colour of Black's bathroom at Riverley Hall. Did he sound bitter? That's because he was. Bradley had deliberately waited until Black flew to Argentina for a job before he redecorated, and for the last two months, he'd been "too busy" to change it back to a more appropriate colour. White. Grey. Blue at a push. Anything that didn't look as though a bottle of Pepto Bismol had thrown up in there.

The man they'd come to meet was Selmi Mohammed, Gosia's significant other and an expert in organic gardening, according to Masra'a Saida's website. Inside, neat rows of plants grew in sandy soil, bordered by shallow channels for irrigation. In the distance, a rattly old pump started up, and water began to flow. Presumably there was somebody around, then.

"*Ahlan*?" Khaled called, and a man emerged from a hut on the far side of the compound. Tall and wiry, he wore the flowing white robes of a Bedouin, and Black put him in his early thirties. Was this the man they were looking for?

"Is that Selmi?" he asked Khaled, and the younger man nodded.

The plan had called for Khaled to take the lead, but he seemed kinda frozen as Selmi strode towards them.

"Is there any news about Gosia? Is that why you're here?"

Selmi's body was stiff with tension, his eyes bloodshot. Allergies? A lack of sleep? A pharmaceutical problem?

"I... Uh... There was... We found... Uh, this is Charles Black. He's, uh...."

"A consultant from the United States," Black filled in, because Khaled was never going to finish that sentence otherwise. "I'm helping the Dahab PD to review some of the older cases on their books."

"And Gosia's disappearance is one of them?"

"Yes."

"So there are no new developments?"

"Two days ago, a member of the public found some bones near a hiking trail in the mountains. At the moment, they're unidentified, but—"

"A hiking trail?" Selmi's shoulders dropped an inch. "That's not Gosia. She doesn't hike in the mountains alone anymore."

"Are you sure?"

"A while ago, she fell in a canyon and broke her arm. There was no phone signal, and afterwards, she realised that if it had been her leg, she would have been stuck there. It scared her. So now she only hikes if she is with somebody."

That little snippet of information blew away the last slim hope that she'd just gone for a long walk and died all by herself. For the moment, Black refrained from mentioning that somebody could've dumped her there and focused on the facts surrounding her disappearance.

"As I said, I'm helping Khaled here to take another look at some of Dahab's cold cases. Do you have a few minutes to go over what happened before she went missing?"

"Of course. I'll do anything to find her. Do you want tea?"

Rule number one: always accept a drink if offered—it made the subject feel at ease.

"Thank you."

Black and Khaled followed Selmi over to a house in the nearest corner. Built from the same rough bricks as the rest of the structures, it didn't look like much from the outside, but inside, someone had gone out of their way to make it comfortable with colourful pictures on the white walls, plants on every surface, and a floor covered in those woven rugs that were stacked outside every souvenir shop on the high street. Gosia's influence, no doubt. No self-respecting man would have bought that many cushions.

In the three months that had passed since Gosia's disappearance-slash-death, it didn't look as though Selmi had changed anything at all. A dog-eared romance novel with a Polish title still lay on the coffee table with a bookmark halfway through. A woman's sweater hung over the back of a chair. Pink flip-flops adorned with fabric flowers sat next to the front door.

He still expected her to come home.

Khaled fidgeted beside Black on one of the low sofas until Selmi returned with a silver tray. The glass of sweet herbal tea looked like a thimble in Black's hands and had the usual layer of sludge at the bottom. He was more of a coffee man, but he swallowed it down anyway.

"I expect you've read the police file…" Selmi started.

Nope. "I'd rather hear you tell the story again, in your own words."

Khaled got out his notepad as usual, ballpoint pen at the ready. Black would rather pay attention to a subject's facial expressions and body language than stare at a page, and thankfully he had a good memory, so he rarely bothered taking notes until afterwards. Besides, he was recording the whole conversation on his phone, as always, and that file would automatically upload to Blackwood's server back in Virginia should further analysis be needed.

"It began like any other day. We got up and watered half the plants, then Gosia updated our Facebook page and website while I went into town to pick up breakfast."

"How did you get there? Did you drive?"

"No, I cycled."

"Do you have a vehicle?"

"Yes, but that week, the engine was being repaired. We hired a driver to help with deliveries, but he wasn't working that day."

"So you cycled. How long were you gone for?"

"About half an hour. I also stopped at the

supermarket to pick up more rice on the way back."

"Do you know if Gosia spoke to anybody while you were out?"

"Just Slonko and Annie. Our goats. Gosia cleaned out their pen while I was gone, and she didn't mention any visitors."

"Interesting names."

"Slonko means 'sunshine' in Polish, and Annie's short for Aniolku, which means 'angel.'" Selmi's breath hitched. "Gosia named them."

"Could anyone have phoned?"

"It's possible, but she didn't mention it. The police didn't check?"

Khaled gave a quick shake of his head. Boy, that was a thorough investigation they'd done.

"I'll make sure it gets looked into," Black said. Another job for Mack. "What happened after you got back?"

"We ate breakfast, then I planted melon seeds while Gosia went into town to take the weekly orders. We send some of our produce to the markets at El Tur and Suez, but mostly, we sell in Dahab to shops, restaurants, and private homes. Last year, we started a box scheme, and it took off better than we ever hoped. That was Gosia's idea too. Without her, it's...it's hard."

"What does taking the orders involve?"

"We have a list of customers, and each Monday, she visits to ask what fruit and vegetables they want that week. We grow everything ourselves, so the produce is seasonal, always different. Once we know what to harvest, we pack everything into the boxes and deliver it on Thursdays."

It didn't escape Black's notice that Selmi spoke

about Gosia in the present tense, and it sounded natural rather than forced. Black wasn't a bad judge of character, and either Selmi deserved an Oscar or he was telling the truth about Gosia's disappearance.

"Why don't you just call people?"

"We've found people order more produce if we speak to them in person."

"Do you have the customer list?"

Silently, Selmi rose and walked to a messy desk on the far side of the room. An ancient laptop took up most of the space, but there was a drawer underneath stuffed with paper. He extracted a sheet and brought it over.

There had to be fifty names on it, each one highlighted in either yellow, blue, or pink. Some had notes scribbled next to them, times and locations, phrases like "before prayers" and "at Dolphin restaurant."

"What do the colours mean?"

"Pink means Gosia visited to take an order, yellow means she didn't, and the blue people, I couldn't find to speak to." There were only two of those. "I wrote down where the people lived or worked, and if they remembered the time she came, I put that too."

Roughly two-thirds of the list was pink, which meant Gosia had gotten through most of her day without incident.

"Did she take a particular route?"

"No, she'd go back and forth because people weren't always in. Or she sometimes had to look for them in more than one place, like at their business or at home, or visit at a particular time."

"Who was the last person she visited?"

"I think Misha Ivanova." A Russian name, which made sense when Selmi pointed at a spot by the sea on el-Melal Street. Russians had bought up a lot of the beachfront property in Assalah. "Unless she saw one of the people I couldn't find."

"Did you speak to Misha?"

"She said Gosia visited, took her order, and left as usual."

"Which direction did she head in?"

"Nobody saw her after that."

"Misha didn't see her go?"

Selmi shrugged helplessly and shook his head. "No. Her baby was crying, and she didn't see Gosia after she walked out the door."

Black understood his frustration. Khaled hadn't mentioned any of this, probably because he didn't know. And that most likely meant that the police had left Selmi to do his own investigation while they carried out vital tasks like ogling snorkelers in the bay and snacking on baklava.

"We'll follow up on that. The blue names—what can you tell me about them?"

Loose ends... Black hated loose ends...

Javier Martinez was a Spanish freediver who'd rented an apartment in Masbat for the six months prior to Gosia's disappearance. When Selmi went to speak to him, he found the place empty. According to the landlord, Javier had paid a month's rent in lieu of notice and flown back to Spain in a hurry, ostensibly to deal with a family emergency.

Missing customer number two was noted simply as "Marten B—Assalah." A new customer, one Gosia had spoken to on the phone and promised to add to her weekly rounds. Selmi had never managed to track the man down. Black thought the name sounded Scandinavian.

"Was Youssef al-Masri ever a customer?"

"From the chicken shop?"

"Yes."

Selmi shook his head. "Gosia wouldn't have sold our produce to him even if he'd wanted to buy it."

"They didn't get on?"

"When a man is wilfully cruel to animals, he can't expect people to like him. Why do you ask these questions?" Selmi's posture stiffened. "Do you think Youssef made Gosia leave?"

"There's no evidence to indicate that. We just heard that they may have had a disagreement on the beach one day, and we need to follow up every lead."

"Yes, they did. He came to pick up rubbish, and she told him he should go and feed his chickens instead. Did you know he leaves them for the whole day without food and water?"

"I'm aware of that. How did he react?"

"As he always does—he just ignored her. He never accepts that what he does is cruel."

That sounded like the Youssef Black had met—slightly selfish, reluctant to engage in conflict, but all too willing to bury his head in the sand. But did his shortcomings extend to murder?

"Can I take a picture of the list?" Black asked. Wordlessly, Selmi slid it in Black's direction, and soon, a high-resolution copy was safely stored on Blackwood's network. "I may have follow-up questions at some point."

"Anything. I'll do anything that'll help to find her.

I'm not a rich man, but...but..." Selmi's voice cracked. "I'd give everything I have to get her home."

Fuck. People accused Black of not having a heart, and at times, he was inclined to agree with them. Over two decades of seeing the worst of human nature had left that spot in his chest ice cold, and although events in Colombia two and a half years ago had led to him thawing a little, feeling love and empathy the way other people did was still foreign to him except where Emmy was concerned. His darling wife had fought her way inside every barrier he'd thrown up.

But today? Today, Black wanted to tell Selmi the truth so the man could start healing, and then he wanted to find whoever killed Gosia and put a bullet through their head.

"Leave it with me," he said. "I'll see what I can do. One more thing—did Gosia ever wear a scarab amulet on a blue cord?"

"How did you know?"

Fuck. "Somebody mentioned it. Said it was a nice one. Do you know where she got it?"

"We took a trip to Luxor three years ago. No, four years now. We visited the temple of Hatshepsut, and a Bedouin outside told her the necklace belonged to a pharaoh, that it would protect her in this life and beyond." Selmi choked up. "I said it was too expensive, but Gosia bought it anyway. I hope it is working."

"She was wearing it when she disappeared?"

"I think so. I haven't seen it since that day."

Black forced those damned emotions back into the dark hole where they belonged, and once again did what he was best at. He lied.

"We're still treating this as a disappearance. Don't

give up hope."

"I will never give up hope."

Out in the sunshine, Black took a deep breath, kissed goodbye to the last remnants of his vacation, and turned to Khaled.

"Tomorrow morning, you need to round up every cop in the Dahab Police Department who has an interest in seeing this case closed and organise them to canvas the people on this list. We need to build up a full picture of Gosia's last day. Then we have to cross-reference the names to a list of Carmela's known acquaintances, paying particular attention to fishermen and anybody with medical experience. And talk to her neighbours. Someone must have seen something."

"That'll take weeks."

"There are six days until we leave."

Khaled swallowed hard. "I'll call people this evening. Is there anything else?"

"Yes. It's important to be discreet. I can't imagine Captain al-Busari being overjoyed that we haven't gone through him to question Selmi, which means we need to go around him for the next stage too."

"Uh..."

"And we've got to get ahold of that autopsy report."

"Tonight?"

"Yes, tonight." Black bleeped open the doors on Bob's truck. "Let's go."

"How was your day, dear?" Emmy asked.

Better now, since she was lying on the bed in her underwear.

"The good news is that we have a new list of people to question. The bad news is there are forty-seven of them. I've just spent an hour briefing Khaled and half a dozen of his buddies on exactly what questions to ask. We've got two names to follow up on ourselves."

"Two? That's doable."

"And the other bad news is that the scarab amulet we found in the mountains belonged to Gosia. She was wearing it when she died. Which means—"

"The killer didn't bring it with him, and any link between the two deaths is purely circumstantial. Two dead girls, one small town."

"Exactly."

The historians were now at the bottom of the suspect list.

Speaking of historians, Miles had emailed again, insisting that if the amulet was a genuine ancient Egyptian funerary offering, it belonged in a museum. In his eyes, the fact that it was evidence in a murder investigation was a mere triviality. Trying to placate a militant archaeologist was something Black could do without in a week when everything else had gone wrong already.

Was one day off really too much to ask for?

Emmy paused for a moment, turning the news over in her mind. Then her mouth set into a hard line, an expression Black had seen on her many times in the past. Determination. He loved that look. She hated to lose almost as much as he did.

"Doesn't change much. We've still got two murders to solve. What about the autopsy report? Did you get that?"

"No, because Captain al-Busari's still at his desk."

"Bit keen, isn't he?"

"I gather his wife doesn't like him very much. And he wasn't working on a case, he was updating the police department's website. When he saw Khaled had stuck around, he made him help with Twitter. Seems he's better at PR than policing."

"So rather than actually doing the work, he just makes people think he's doing the work?"

"Exactly."

"Hmm... Maybe we should try that, then I could do you instead."

"Nice try, Diamond."

Emmy ran the tip of her tongue over her top lip, and all thoughts of interviews and searches and incompetent law-enforcement officials vanished. Dammit, she did this on purpose. *Focus, man.*

"Did you get a rabbit hutch?" he managed to utter.

"I'm lying here in Victoria's Secret's finest, and you're asking me about a rabbit hutch?"

Oh, fuck it. What was the point? Black's cock was already hardening, and he deserved a little fun after the evening he'd had. His belt buckle clinked as his pants hit the floor, and the knife from his pocket skittered across the tiles. He was about to hide it somewhere safe —to say Emmy was unpredictable in her sleep was like saying a nuclear weapon could be a bit dangerous—but then he had a better idea.

"What the hell are you doing?" Emmy gasped.

"This." He held up the remains of her tattered underwear, and before she could knee him in the balls, he flipped her over and bound her hands above her head, looping the bra through the slats of the headboard. She tensed, then relaxed and crawled up the bed so her ass was in the air. He smacked it, hard, but she just giggled.

"Control freak."

Yes, he was. And he knew that secretly, she didn't want it any other way.

CHAPTER 21 - EMMY

MY LAPTOP WHIRRED away as I sipped my coffee on Wednesday morning. Had I drawn the long straw or the short straw? I wasn't sure.

On the plus side, I'd been well-used last night, and an hour or two of downtime wasn't a bad idea. But on the minus side, I had to research two missing targets online and pick up a rabbit hutch while Black was out *doing* something, even if that something involved "borrowing" an autopsy report then wrangling a bunch of wet-behind-the-ears police recruits into some semblance of a team. Khaled and his buddies may have forgotten to mention their plans to the captain and were now looking to Black as their de facto leader. Some people got all the fun.

Still, I had my trusty sidekick.

"We need to get more carrots," Zena called from the rabbit's bedroom. *The rabbit's freaking bedroom.* "What time are we picking up the hutch?"

"Ten o'clock. That hasn't changed since yesterday."

"Hear that, Crash? You're gonna get your own house. No more eating the furniture."

At first, the carpenter on el-Fanaar Street had told me it'd take a week to build a hutch, but when I offered him a thousand bucks, he'd promised to work through the night and have it ready this morning. I'd left Zena to hash out the specs while I went to the bakery, so all in all, it hadn't been a bad trip into town. For me, at least. We'd picked up Zena's dress too, and yeah... It wasn't as bad as the first one, which was freaking crocheted, but if it was yours truly who had to wear that abomination, I'd be drinking the tap water and eating uncooked chicken in a desperate attempt to avoid the ceremony. Those wedding photos would haunt the poor girl for the rest of her life.

Although when we got to the carpenter's place and he proudly unveiled the rabbit hutch, I nearly stuffed her into the revolting outfit myself.

"What the actual fuck?"

Zena walked around it, reaching out to touch the wood reverently. "Isn't it amazing? It turned out even better than I hoped."

"It's... It's..." Three fucking storeys high. A mesh run took up the whole of the bottom, and on top of that sat a split-level rabbit mansion accessed by a ramp. It even had shutters on the damn windows and a tiny domed roof. "Zena, it's bigger than the bedroom she's in at the moment. It won't even fit in the truck."

The carpenter beamed at me. "Yes, yes, it comes apart. Like IKEA."

Good grief. "We only have one rabbit."

"I thought we could get her a friend," Zena said. "In case she gets lonely."

Holy shitballs, what had I done? "No. No more rabbits. We're only here for another week, and fuck knows what we're gonna do with her after that."

"But they should live in pairs. I checked."

"I don't even know what I'm going to do with one rabbit yet."

"Grandpa can look after her. I'll leave him instructions."

Oh, Bob would be just thrilled to hear that, I was sure. And what was Black gonna say when he came home and realised the entire lawn was covered by the Playboy fricking mansion? I'd have a *lot* of sucking up to do, and my jaw still hurt from last night.

"Let me think about it, yeah?"

The carpenter was grinning like a lunatic as he handed me an invoice. "My brother will help me to put the rabbit house into your vehicle. Do you want us to make it at the other end? That will be another fifty dollars."

The only thing worse than them coming with us would be having to reassemble the damn thing myself, although if I kept busy, that might stop me from strangling Zena.

"Thirty dollars."

"Okay, thirty dollars."

"Deal." I'd have paid a hundred.

As they were loading the monstrosity into the truck, I heard laughter and turned to see a white pickup had pulled up alongside. Gunther from the Happy Fish restaurant leaned out the window, chuckling. Omar, Carmela's waiter friend, was in the passenger seat, and his mouth was doing that twitchy thing like he was trying to keep a straight face. All I needed was for NorthernGrrrl from the hotel to put pictures of the farce on Twitter and my mortification would be complete.

"What on earth is that?" Gunther asked.

"Would you believe it's a rabbit hutch?"

"*Scheisse*, you'd better have a big yard."

As if I didn't know that.

He drove off in a cloud of smoke before I could beg for a ride out of there. Was this destined to be my life? People laughing at me for making bad decisions? A man in a white shirt and black trousers walked past on the other side of the street, smirking, and I recognised him as one of the porters from the Black Diamond. Did anyone else I knew want to show up?

"Are you mad at me?" Zena asked when we were halfway to the hotel with the carpenter and his brother following in the carpenter's cousin's taxi.

"Whatever gives you that idea?"

"I'm sorry, okay? Awad said he'd make whatever I liked, and I didn't think it'd turn out quite that big. I just want Crash to be happy."

Please, somebody shoot me. I'd do it myself if I hadn't left my semi-automatic back in the villa.

"Black's gonna lose his shit when he comes home, so you'd better make yourself scarce when he arrives. But in the meantime, the only words I want to hear out of your mouth are 'How can I help?'"

"Now you sound like my mom."

"I'm not old enough to be..." I trailed off as I realised with no small amount of horror that, technically, I *was* old enough to be Zena's mother. Boy, that made a sobering thought. Her smirk said she'd done the math too.

"Actually, you—"

"Shut it."

"Perhaps if we painted it?" Zena suggested two hours

later. "Green to blend in with the bushes? White to match the buildings?"

"White. It reflects the heat." Why was I even having this conversation? "But I'm not sure we have enough time."

When would Black be back? I hadn't heard a peep out of him, and although we generally worked on the premise that no news was good news, that didn't help much in our current situation. I tapped out a quick text.

Me: How's it going?

CB: Al-Busari's updating the PD's Facebook page. Khaled's filing and making lists. The others are out asking questions.

Zena breathed hot air all over me as she leaned over my shoulder. "The police have a Facebook page? What do they put on it? Pictures of checkpoints? Stats on the number of times they've fallen asleep on duty?"

"Who knows? But we might have enough time to paint this anathema."

Another call to Awad, the carpenter, saw him on his way back, this time with a bunch of nieces and nephews in tow, all willing to pitch in as long as I bought them candy and let them use the hotel swimming pool afterwards. Perhaps I should've felt guilty for employing child labour, but I was desperate, okay?

"Drones," Zena said.

"I'm sorry?"

"Drones. Captain al-Busari really hates drones. Apparently, the Egyptian government's banned them, and according to Facebook, if he catches whoever keeps flying one around Dahab, they'll be 'severely punished.'"

"So that's what they're doing instead of

investigating real crimes? Chasing drones?"

"According to Google Translate, they wasted fifty man-hours trying to find the culprit last week. It buzzed a police vehicle, and the captain went out personally to command the search."

"Really?" Hmm... I kind of wanted my husband back at some point, and who knew how much longer he'd have to sit outside the police station waiting for al-Busari to leave. "If only we had a drone."

But where the hell could I get a drone in a country where they were illegal? It wasn't as if I could nip down to the shops and buy one.

"Someone's definitely trolling the captain," Zena said, oblivious to the plan forming in my mind. "Look. They've linked to YouTube footage of the chase in the comments."

"Let me see that."

When Zena said "footage," I thought she meant a video of the drone, not *from* the drone. Wow. Whoever was flying the thing had balls, I'd give them that. They'd hovered it three feet above al-Busari's balding head while he leapt about like a demented marionette below.

But how could I find the pilot?

Possibilities flew through my mind. I could get Mack to hack into the YouTube account and find the owner's IP address, then cross-reference that to either an address or a phone number, then track down the location and pay the owner a visit. Or I could isolate the people in the background and use facial-recognition software to identify them, then find out where they lived and see if any of them saw the drone operator. Or... Or I could simply send the person a message.

I quickly switched over to a covert browser, set up a new YouTube account, and commented under the video.

IHeartMischief79341: Are you available for private parties?

I added a throwaway email address, then turned back to the more immediate problem—Crash's crash pad. At least if Black kicked me out, it was big enough for me to live in too.

I'd just texted Bradley for further advice on the colour scheme when my phone pinged with an email.

DaredevilDork: What kind of party?

IHeartMischief79341: I'd like to cause a small distraction in Dahab ASAP. Are you interested in making a few bucks?

DaredevilDork: For doing what?

How much did drones cost? A quick internet search gave me a ballpark figure of two thousand quid for a high-end personal drone. Three hundred dollars seemed like a reasonable amount to pay the guy.

IHeartMischief79341: A fly-by at the police station. The captain spends too long sitting at his desk.

DaredevilDork: Captain al-Busari? He's a lazy arse. Even if you go to the station with witnesses, he refuses to take a report.

Did I detect a hint of bitterness? Another victim of al-Busari's complacency, perhaps?

IHeartMischief79341: I figure he could do with stretching his legs. Will you help?

DaredevilDork: How do I know you're not the cops?

IHeartMischief79341: You don't. But if you have confidence in your skills, that shouldn't matter. I'll wire you $100 bucks as a deposit and another $100 upon completion.

DaredevilDork: Make it $150 on completion and we have a deal.

IHeartMischief79341: Agreed. We have a deal.

DaredevilDork: Pay the money to this email address by PayPal and give me half an hour.

"Is it time for lunch yet?" Zena asked.

"Nope." I stuck a spare paintbrush in her hand and consulted the text that had just arrived from Bradley. "The window trims need to be Baker-Miller Pink." He swore that would have a calming effect on Black. "Find out what that is and paint them."

Chapter 22 - Emmy

"HOW'S IT GOING?" I asked Black when he phoned mid-afternoon.

I'd been waiting for the call ever since my new favourite dork sent me a video of his antics half an hour ago. He—or possibly she, who knew—had flown the damn drone right up to the police station and tapped on al-Busari's office window. Two minutes later, a dozen cops ran out and gave chase, led by the captain, but I hadn't spotted Khaled in the group.

"Better than I hoped."

"Oh?"

"We got the reports. And they're...interesting."

"Oh?"

"I'm on my way back. We can discuss it then."

"Oh."

"Everything okay, Diamond?"

"Couldn't be better."

"Liar. Did you pick up the rabbit hutch? Tell me you picked up the rabbit hutch."

"We picked up the rabbit hutch."

"Good. Then whatever else you're not telling me can wait. Have you eaten? Do you want me to bring lunch?"

Fantastic—a way to prolong the inevitable by another five minutes at least.

"I'm starving. Could you get me a cheese twist from

the German Bakery?"

"I'm nowhere near the German Bakery."

Yes, I was well aware of that. I'd considered asking him to go to the koshary place on the other side of Assalah Square, five minutes farther away than the bakery, but ultimately, I'd decided that might be pushing my luck.

"But I've got this craving..."

"Why are your cravings always for carbs?"

"Cheese isn't a carb."

Black sighed. "Just one cheese twist?"

"Maybe two."

"Fine. Do me a favour—find me paper, pens, and tape while I'm gone. I need to start a link chart when I get back. More information's coming, and I want to organise my thoughts."

By my calculations, we had roughly twenty minutes. Twenty minutes until Black did that thing where his face went all stony and he looked like he was about to explode.

"Zena, paint faster."

I needed to swap out my underwear for something fancier.

"What the fuck?"

Black stopped in front of Casa Crash, and his hands twitched at his sides, itching to ball into fists. Where was Zena? Well, she'd crawled up the ramp and hidden inside with the rabbit, leaving me to deal with one severely pissed-off husband.

Where should I start? "Uh—"

"Why has the kiddies' play area been extended into our garden?"

"It's not a kiddies' play area." Although granted, the wire mesh at the bottom would have kept them nicely contained. "It's the rabbit hutch."

Uh-oh. His eyes had turned into two chips of granite, flat, glittery, and hard.

"The *rabbit hutch*?"

"Yup, the rabbit hutch." I leaned in closer and whispered, "I'm not wearing any knickers."

All things considered, that had seemed like the best option.

His gaze lost its focus, just for a second, and I fought a smile. Men were so predictable, even my cyborg of a husband. I angled my body to block Zena's view if she got brave and peeped out the window, then cupped Black's rapidly growing bulge.

"Forget the rabbit and show me what you got, Chuck."

"Bitch," he murmured in my ear, but he meant it as a term of affection. "I won't forget this, but I will let you suck my dick while I think up an appropriate punishment."

"Ooh, make it hard."

He threw me over his shoulder in a fireman's hold, one hand inching under my shorts to check whether I'd lied about the underwear. Of course I hadn't. This was a win-win situation for me. My ass cheek stung when he gave it a hard smack.

"Shh. Zena's in Crash's lounge."

Black spun back to check, but Zena was still hiding. "What the...? On second thought, perhaps temporary amnesia isn't a bad idea after all."

An hour later, I sat naked in bed next to Black, who had the photocopied pages of Carmela's autopsy report propped against his knees, covering up the good bits. One of us was sitting in the wet patch, and after the bunny hutch fiasco, I figured it was only fair that it should be me. Bits of pastry flaked off the cheese twist and landed on my bare tits as I munched. Just another day in the life of a pair of jet-setting billionaires.

"Carmela had marks on her ribs," Black said. "Although the doctor couldn't be sure whether they were from a knife or from whatever ate her afterwards. Looks as if her abdomen took the brunt from the barracudas. They got everything but her upper lungs, bladder, and part of her large intestine. There wasn't enough left of her vagina and anus to tell whether or not she'd been sexually assaulted."

"You know I'm eating, right?"

He just grinned and waved one of the autopsy photos in my face. "Horrifying what a fish can do, isn't it?" His smile faded. "Hmm."

"What?"

"There were marks scored on her vertebrae too. L1 and L2."

Top of the lumbar spine. "Teeth marks?"

"Possibly, although they don't look like it." He passed me another picture, this time out of need rather than a desire to put me off my breakfast. "What do you think?"

I thought it was a miracle the Dahab Police Department had invested in a decent photocopier. The close-up showed two shallow lines slashing across both vertebrae. But while barracudas had strong jaws and teeth that could shear through bone, there was something wrong with the picture.

"It's not a fish. These two lines together? They're not parallel. They converge at the bottom. If it was a barracuda, the lines would be equidistant all the way down."

"Agreed."

"So they're more likely to be knife marks, meaning the two deaths probably *are* connected."

"Again, agreed."

"And if the marks came from a knife, whoever used it must've gone to some effort to cut into the bone on both Carmela's back and her front. Maybe he was angry?" Which was worrying—anyone who could exercise that degree of fury had a serious problem. "What does the report say?"

"The ME drew no conclusions. Interestingly, he doesn't say she drowned either, which means al-Busari came up with that on his own. And the ME *did* send samples for a toxicology test, which means Khaled's got more work to do." Black huffed. "We need those results. Hope that doesn't waste another day—we got lucky this afternoon."

"Lucky?"

"A drone flew past at exactly the right moment. Al-Busari ran out of the station after it and didn't even bother to lock his desk. Khaled tells me the man's had a problem with drones ever since one distracted him into crashing his car."

"Luck? That wasn't luck. That was minutes of careful planning and a two-hundred-and-fifty-dollar bribe."

"You did that?"

"Don't sound so surprised. I'm not just a pretty face, Chuck."

Black took my left hand and brought it to his lips. Kissed my wedding rings.

"No, Mrs. Black. You're everything."

CHAPTER 23 - EMMY

TURNED OUT GETTING the toxicology report wasn't as tricky as we thought. The ME had noted the name of the lab on the autopsy report, and while Khaled was in al-Busari's office, Black had got him to stick one of Mack's special USB drives into the captain's computer. Now that Mack had access to the captain's email, all Khaled had to do was call the lab and issue a kick up the backside on the captain's behalf. An administrator assured us the report would be sent over later that day.

Meanwhile, Black papered one wall of the living room and started writing. He always said he thought better with a pen in his hand, no matter how many fancy programs were available to organise his notes, and left to his own devices, he'd soon create a network of messy lines and scrawled ideas.

That left me to carry on where I'd left off this morning—with the hunt for Javier Martinez and Marten B. In between rabbit duties, I'd searched online, checking freediving forums and Dahab noticeboards for our two mystery men, but the only Javier Martinez I'd found was based in the Maldives and denied ever having been to Dahab. Now I needed to head into town. A quick freshen-up—life was too short to waste messing around with my hair, and I'd mastered the art of the three-minute shower years ago

—and I was ready to go.

"Laters, Chuck."

He pulled me in for a searing kiss, and I nearly didn't make it out the door. His shorts rode low on his hips, and I wanted to stay and run my tongue down that deep V of muscle, not visit every freediving centre in town in search of a man who might once have bought organic vegetables.

But Black read my mind and opened the door for me.

"Break a leg, Diamond. And if you come back with any more pets, I'll break your damn neck too."

"Okay, okay. No more pets."

Right at that moment, I only wanted to find the animal who'd murdered two young women and castrate him.

"Hey!" Zena ran up to me as I headed for the car. "Where are we going?"

"I'm going into town. You're going to keep out of Black's way and feed the rabbit."

"But—"

If I'd just been going shopping, I'd have let her tag along, but having to keep an eye on a teenager while I asked questions and concentrated on people's body language would only slow me down.

"You should spend some time with your family. Why don't you ask Bob if there's anything you can help with?"

"That's so boring."

"Not everything in life is fun. I'll see you later, okay?"

I started from the north end of town, near Assalah, calling at each freediving centre on the list I'd put together—eleven of them in total. I stuck reasonably close to the truth with my story—that I was a private investigator hired by a grieving family to investigate Gosia Kaminski's disappearance, and we thought she may have visited a freediver named Javier Martinez on the last day she was seen. And, by the way, did they happen to have heard of Marten B, spelled the Scandinavian way?

All I got from the first ten centres were shakes of the head and shrugs of the shoulders. Nobody seemed particularly evasive, just clueless. What if I couldn't find the guy? Should I start trying the scuba centres? Because there were three times the number of those.

And as I trekked down the side streets around the lighthouse, I began to notice an increase in activity. People out in their yards moving patio furniture, restaurant staff stacking chairs and tables and carrying cushions inside.

"What's happening?" I asked a waiter carrying an electric fan.

"It's going to rain tonight." He seemed kind of nervous, breathless, barely pausing as he hurried past.

For a Brit, rain was an everyday occurrence. I'd grown up under a grey sky, splashing through puddles on my way to school in London's East End. The English weather had been a metaphor for my life at that time. Cold, miserable, and all-around depressing. But here in Dahab, it only rained once or twice a year, and when I say rained, I mean *rained*. I'd never been there for a storm, but I'd seen the videos, and even weeks later, the aftermath had still been evident—damaged roads, a fine layer of sand everywhere, rubbish spread over the bottom of the bay. On one dive, Black and I had come back with a carpet.

I crossed the bridge in the middle of the high street, a local landmark built purely for the run-off water to flow underneath. Behind the bridge lay a clear expanse of tarmac that looked as though it should've been a parking lot, but cars were banned, the entrance guarded by a pair of Khaled's colleagues. From there, it was a clear run across the desert to the mountains, where rain would torrent down the old wadis in a few hours if the weather forecast was right, searching for the quickest path to the sea.

I needed to get back to the hotel. The local restaurants weren't the only businesses that had to prepare for an impending deluge.

The Into the Blue dive centre appeared on my right-hand side, hidden down a narrow alley between a spice shop and an art gallery. Might as well tick off the last centre on my list before I headed back to the Black Diamond to help carry things. The rabbit would have to sleep inside again tonight. Black would be thrilled.

Inside Into the Blue, a young blonde girl was struggling to drag a couch under an overhanging roof on the edge of a small courtyard.

"Here, let me help."

I grabbed one end, and together we hauled the couch undercover. The girl almost tripped over when one flip-flop got hooked under a tree root, but she managed to right herself before she ended up flattened by what was a hideous piece of furniture. Didn't orange velvet go out of fashion in the seventies?

"Thanks so much." Her accent was British, her breath coming in short pants. "My boss asked me to move all this stuff, but..." She trailed off as she looked around at a collection of sunloungers and wooden tables, a rack full of souvenir merchandise, and a small bookshelf.

"I'll lend you a hand. It won't take long."

"Really?"

Helping a fellow Brit in need? It was practically my civic duty. "Sure. Grab the other end of this table."

It only took ten minutes to get everything stowed away undercover, and my new friend collapsed into one of the relocated chairs.

"Phew. Thought I'd never get that done. The boss said last time it rained here, the water came up to people's ankles in the high street. Uh, why are you here? Are you looking for diving lessons? Sorry I didn't ask before."

"Actually, I was hoping you could help me."

"Help you? With what?"

I gave her a brief summary of the hunt for Gosia. "So I'm looking for two missing people who are possible witnesses. I don't suppose you know either of them?"

"Sorry. I've only been working here for two months, and before that, I was in Hurghada. But there's a group of Spaniards arriving tomorrow afternoon for a holiday. Perhaps they'd know Javier?"

"Any chance you could ask them?"

"Sure, no problem. Can you leave your number? I'll ask around too, just in case anyone else has heard of him or Marten."

"You're a star. Good luck with the storm."

"You too. I'm hoping the weather forecast's wrong, but it feels kinda gloomy."

Yes, it did. When I got back to the hotel, the staff

were scurrying around carrying everything from gazebos to massage tables to a freaking electric stove. Black walked past with a chair in each hand, and Zena ran behind him with the cushions.

He raised one dark eyebrow, and I shook my head. He did the same in return. No major breakthroughs for either of us, but we had a storm coming through and dealing with that took precedence for now.

"Grandpa says it's gonna be real windy," Zena told me.

That I could believe—the breeze was already whipping up into something ominous as black clouds scudded overhead.

"Sure looks like it."

"Do you think Crash's house'll be okay?"

"It's built like a fort, but she can stay inside tonight just in case. Have you put all of your own stuff somewhere safe?"

"Yes," she said, but she looked away. Really? Sometimes, her fibbing skills let her down.

"Okay, what have you left out?"

"Nothing important."

Hmm. "I think you should give your bridesmaid dress to me for safekeeping, don't you?"

She let out a noise that was half growl, half screech. "How do you always know what I'm thinking?"

"I was a teenager once too."

"Were you? Because I think you skipped that for extra time training with Aunt Lydia."

"Who?"

"From *A Handmaid's Tale*? The TV show?"

"Didn't see that one." I rarely found time to watch much TV, and apart from Disney movies, which

Bradley insisted on having on in the background every damn day, my viewing habits tended towards sci-fi movies. Or sometimes action thrillers, but I spent most of the time picking apart the plots. "Just give me the bloody dress, Zena."

The first drops of rain fell at dusk as Black and I retreated to the villa with a hasty dinner of rice, chicken, and vegetables prepared by the hotel chef. Drizzle quickly turned into a torrent, and I kept an eye on the ceiling for leaks as we ate.

"Looks like you got a lot done," I said, studying the living room wall in between mouthfuls. Photos and notes surrounded a large-scale laminated map of Dahab pinned in the centre, and that had been annotated too. There were two lists of names. One I recognised as being from Selmi, and another was titled *Khaled's suggestions*, divided into two sections. Eight fishermen and seven doctors. Only two men were on both lists, and both had the word *alibi* written next to them in green.

"Khaled and his team have got through half of Selmi's list so far. All but one person either confirmed Selmi's account or claimed they couldn't remember that far back."

"All but one?"

"According to the manager of the White Cat restaurant, Gosia looked out of sorts that day, and when the woman asked what was wrong, Gosia said she'd had a disagreement with her boyfriend."

"Did she say what about?"

"No. When the witness asked the question, Gosia brushed it off and said everything would be fine, that they both just needed some time to cool down."

"And Selmi didn't mention this?"

"He didn't. I think I need to have another talk with him tomorrow, assuming we don't all drown in the meantime."

"You'll be okay—you're basically an amphibian." I should have ordered fries instead of rice. This meal was entirely too healthy. "What's with the map? Are you plotting her route?"

"Yes."

"It doesn't look very direct. What do the different colours mean?"

Some of the blobs were red, and some were blue. Green lines connected them in a spiderweb.

"Red times are confirmed with the witness, and the blue ones are taken from Selmi's list. Right now, there seem to be a few anomalies, although those might shake out when we get the rest of the data in."

"Anomalies? You mean the route she took? It's not very direct."

"Exactly." He traced the green line with a finger. "Here, she travelled from Assalah to Masbat and back again, and later, she went from Dahab City to Assalah and back."

Assalah and Masbat were at opposite ends of the high street. Not a huge distance—maybe fifteen minutes on foot—but why waste half an hour when she didn't need to? And Dahab City was even farther away.

"Who did she speak to on those visits? The ones she travelled a distance for?"

"In Masbat, she took an order from a French girl.

Khaled described her as dishy, but I think he meant ditzy. Said her house was full of crystals and smelled like hash, and when he mentioned Gosia, the girl burst into tears."

"A bit of a space cadet. So it wouldn't have been inconceivable for her to be wrong?"

"No. The next visit on the list is unconfirmed but more interesting. The Happy Fish restaurant."

"Where Carmela worked?"

"I'm going to speak to Gunther myself tomorrow morning."

A jagged fork of lightning in the distance drew me to the window, and as I pressed my nose to the glass, a rumble of thunder rolled overhead. I loved storms, unless I was on a boat. Storms at sea could get messy.

When I first started this job, I'd struggled with my emotions. I used to lock too much shit up inside, where it leaked out in my nightmares before one particular incident tipped me over the edge. Back then, I'd been a machine, and I used to walk outside in the rain because the sting of the raindrops was one of the few things that made me feel alive. And also because I figured getting struck by lightning wouldn't be a bad way to go, all things considered.

It had taken a full-on breakdown for me to realise that my soul wasn't dead but sleeping, nearly dying to make me want to live. Now that I had a healthier relationship with both my emotions and my husband, I didn't need the rain so much, but old habits died hard.

"Where the hell are you going?" he asked as I pulled the door open. Wind scattered his papers, and he made a grab for the pile.

"Outside."

"Are you insane?"

"Probably. I used to do this a lot when you weren't around."

"What, lose your mind?"

"No, walk in the rain. Dance, sometimes. It helped to wash away all the dirt that stuck to my insides." I held out a hand. "Join me?"

He stared for a moment, then rose to his feet with a grace that belied his size.

"I must be crazy," he muttered.

"You can share my room at the funny farm."

The deluge soaked me to the skin almost as soon as I stepped outside the door. The security light came on, illuminating the terrace and the white-and-pink bunny house beside it, which was holding its own against the howling wind. Branches whipped around, casting shadows that jumped and swayed. I grasped Black's left hand with my right and rested my other hand on his shoulder.

"Now what?" he asked.

"You can lead."

"You really want to dance?"

"Why not? We're on vacation."

For a moment I thought he'd refuse, but instead, he fumbled in his pocket for his phone. The faint strains of "Por Una Cabeza" were just loud enough to be heard over the storm as he led me in a tango. A nice, dirty tango that may have involved some lips and a bit of tongue too. Black tore off his shirt, then mine. Water dripped down his abs, and when he dipped me backwards, I couldn't resist running the tip of my tongue over his pecs on the way back up.

Are you surprised we knew how to dance? Don't be.

When we had to bump off oligarchs and politicians, a few social skills made blending in at their fancy parties easier.

"This is more fun than I thought," Black said with a rare grin.

"I'm all about the good times, Chuck."

He lifted me, and I wrapped my legs around his waist. Did I mention that we had a ballroom back home at Riverley Hall? We'd fucked against every wall of it. And the floor-to-ceiling windows, although Bradley got really snippy when I accidentally pulled down a curtain.

"Speaking of good times... How strong do you think that rabbit cage is?"

"Uh, I think it's fairly solid."

Just like Black's cock. Thank goodness the hedge around our terrace had grown nice and tall, or some of the guests would be getting an eyeful.

"Then let's— Fuck."

The music stopped as Black's phone rang, and I recognised Mack's ringtone. He quickly answered on speaker.

"Toxicology report's on its way," she said. "I'm no expert, but y'all're gonna want to take a look at it."

Dammit. We'd have to take a rain check on the fun stuff.

Chapter 24 - Black

"HALOTHANE?" EMMY SAID. "Isn't that an anaesthetic?"

Seemed they'd had a slow day at the lab because they'd tested for everything. And Carmela Conti's blood had contained enough halothane to knock her out twice over.

"Yes, it is, although it's fallen out of favour in recent years."

Black had expected alcohol, or perhaps hash, not a general anaesthetic. But it made sense. One good whiff of that, and she'd have been oblivious to whatever came next.

"So who would have access to it? Doctors? Because that would fit with the surgeon's knot."

"Yes, it would. Halothane's still widely used in hospitals in the developing world, but not in the US or Europe. And veterinarians use it too."

"There's a vet in Assalah Square—the one who checked the rabbit over. Perhaps others too. We should ask Bob."

"And three hospitals—one government and two private." Black had driven past them all on his trips around town. "But you know the problem here?"

"Everything's for sale if you've got enough cash?"

"Precisely." And if a hospital employee had been

selling drugs for a few extra bucks, they were hardly likely to admit it. This case had too many questions and not enough answers. "We need to make a list of everyone with hospital or veterinary connections and cross-reference it with everything else."

"Carmela and Gosia both had hospital connections, remember?" Emmy said. "Gosia had her arm pinned, and didn't Carmela have her cheek X-rayed after the door incident? They were both pretty. Any chance they could have caught the eye of the same rogue doctor?"

A possibility, although Gosia's broken arm was an old injury. "Something else to check."

Khaled and his buddies would have a busy week, and so would Black. The young private was keen but green, and without supervision, the methodical approach went out the window. Still, if it got them closer to catching a murderer, the effort would be worth it.

He carried Emmy to bed and pulled her close, her back to his front, her wet blonde hair spread out across a towel on the pillow.

"Love you, Diamond," he whispered as his eyes closed.

"Love you too, Chuck."

If only Black had known what the morning had in store for them, perhaps he wouldn't have slept quite so soundly that night.

A ringing phone woke Black, and for a moment, he considered turning it off and going back to sleep. Then it stopped and started again straight away.

"Tell them to get lost," Emmy murmured.

"It might be important."

"Sleep is important. Your dick is important. Breakfast is important."

He kissed her on the temple and rolled out of bed to take the call in the living room. This had better be good.

"Bones! There are bones!" Khaled half shouted. "Everywhere there are bones!"

What was he talking about?

"You're going to have to explain."

Black heard the cop suck in a breath. "From the mountains. They came with the water."

"The rain washed bones down from the mountains?"

"Yes!"

"What kind of bones? Animal or human?"

"The doctor from the government hospital is coming, but some of them look like the bones we found before."

"Have you got photos?"

"Yes, yes, I will send them. I have to go—Captain al-Busari has just arrived."

There were plenty of mammals in the mountains—goats, foxes, the odd camel—but would Khaled get their bones confused with a human's? Black had a bad feeling about this.

"What's up?" Emmy called from the bedroom.

"It's possible more bones have washed down from the mountains. Want to go take a look?"

"Why not? Hold on a second..." A second turned out to be long enough for Black to fill the coffee machine and set it going. "Yup, the pictures are already on

Twitter."

Of course they were. Social media worked faster than the police these days. "Let's see."

Three femurs, a skull, part of a pelvis... Since they'd found both of Gosia's femurs—or at least, he'd assumed they'd both belonged to Gosia, something he was kicking himself for now considering the number of times he'd warned his team never to assume anything— that meant at least two more victims. Four bodies. And a good chance they had a serial killer on the loose.

Fuck.

"How long has this been going on for?" Emmy muttered, echoing Black's thoughts.

"When did it last rain this heavily? And if this is all the work of the same person, why did they change their method of disposal between Gosia and Carmela?" There he was, assuming again. "We need to review the missing persons list and see if there could've been another victim in between."

"This is getting out of control."

An epic understatement. By the time they got into town, there were cops everywhere, most of them wandering aimlessly. Captain al-Busari was standing on the bridge, shouting orders at a group of scuba divers who seemed to have been co-opted into searching the bay. Their tanks bore the logo of a local dive school. So much for bringing in a specialist team from Alexandria.

"Go! Go now!"

"Visibility's terrible. The water's full of silt, and we can only see a foot in front of our faces."

"Then you will have to go down again!"

There didn't seem to be much point in trying to

explain the rules about bottom time and nitrogen narcosis to the captain at that moment, and judging by the roll of the divemaster's eyes, he shared the same thought. Better to get out of the way, then have the argument later. He signalled to his team, and they descended beneath the waves.

Yellow tape cordoned off the evidence, fluttering in the breeze, strung between lampposts and signs advertising desert safaris and snorkelling trips. At first, Black thought it was crime scene tape, but on closer examination, he realised it said "Happy Birthday!" Talk about being under-equipped for the job.

"He's not happy, is he?" Emmy said under her breath. No prizes for guessing who she meant.

"Because he can't sweep this under the carpet anymore. Two bodies, he could write off as an accident and a suicide, but four? That's stretching the bounds of believability."

"Twitter's blown up, and it's all over Facebook. Mack's sending me updates. Oh, and she said nobody apart from Selmi called Gosia on the twenty-seventh and you'd know what that means?"

"That was always a slim hope."

"Plus Dan's consulting with a forensic anthropologist about today's bones to see if she can give us any information that'd help to identify their former owners."

"Good."

Black spotted Khaled standing on the steps of the supermarket with a colleague and went over to see if there was any more news.

"How's it going?"

"The captain is very angry. It's his daughter's

birthday today, and she's supposed to be having a party."

"What about the case?"

"We have found eleven bones near the bridge, but more could have fallen into the sea. Or washed along the street. The water was up to people's knees late last night."

As if on cue, a small boy walked up, palm held out. "Is this a bone you're looking for?"

"Where did you find that?" Khaled asked.

"By the Mexican restaurant."

The Mexican restaurant that Black still hadn't gotten around to taking Emmy to. There and then, he vowed to take her on a proper vacation in the near future to make up for this one.

"Are there any more?"

The kid shrugged. "Maybe. There is mud everywhere."

"This is mental," Emmy whispered. "People are gonna start taking bones home as souvenirs if the police aren't careful."

"I'd offer our help again, but I'm not sure the captain would be receptive to that."

"What do you call that colour he's gone? Crimson? Scarlet?"

"Puce. I doubt we'll get much help from Khaled today."

"Yeah, he's too busy guarding... Is that a scapula?"

"Looks like it. I need to talk to Gunther. Are you coming?"

Emmy opened her mouth to reply, but her phone rang before she could speak. She answered it instead.

"Really? I thought they weren't coming until the

afternoon? ... Okay, I'm nearby, so I'll pop over. See you in ten minutes."

Black raised an eyebrow expectantly.

"The Spanish freedivers have arrived. They caught an early flight."

"You speak to them, and I'll find Gunther. Then we can regroup. I want to get a good look at the state of the hotel too. See if there's any damage."

"Sure." Emmy stood on tiptoe to kiss him on the cheek. "See you in a bit."

CHAPTER 25 - BLACK

DEBRIS LITTERED THE high street from one end to the other, but people were already out with brooms, buckets, and hoses to clean up the mess. Around the corner known as the lighthouse, where a pair of derelict hotels bordered the promenade—victims of an inheritance dispute, Black had heard—the walkway was still covered with shit. Quite literally in some places, judging by the smell of it. The sewers didn't cope too well with the storm either. Good thing he'd worn a pair of hiking boots.

Gunther was outside Happy Fish, sweeping as he directed a trio of staff to put trash into bags. He smiled when he saw Black. Seemed genuine, but it wouldn't be the first time Black had come face-to-face with a liar.

"Much damage?" he asked.

Gunther paused, leaning on his broom. "It's mostly cosmetic. Everything needs cleaning, but in this heat, it should dry out quickly."

"No more rain forecast?"

Black already knew the answer, of course. He'd checked on three different weather apps before he left the villa.

"Not in the near future, thank goodness. Are you looking for something to eat? Because we won't be opening the restaurant until the evening."

"Actually, I have a couple of questions."

"About Carmela?"

"About Gosia Kaminski, actually." Black watched Gunther's expression carefully, but it didn't change. "I appreciate the timing isn't the best, but we're keen to follow up any leads relating to her disappearance, especially in light of this morning's events."

"What events?"

"You haven't heard? A bunch of bones washed up near the bridge last night, and it looks as if some of them are human. Gosia's still missing, so..."

Black let Gunther fill in the blanks, and this time, the man paled a shade or two. Shock at the possibility that more of his fellow townspeople had lost their lives? Or was it guilt? Surprise that the bodies had been discovered? Black only trusted two people in this town —his wife and Bob Stewart.

"You think the bones might be hers?"

"I think we need to keep an open mind. Questions are certainly going to be asked, so it's good to stay ahead of the curve."

"Well, I knew she was missing, obviously. Everyone did. Most people just assumed her boyfriend had something to do with it."

"Really? Why's that?"

"Gosia could be somewhat domineering, and Selmi was... What's the word? Henpecked. *Ja*, that's it. And when she vanished, he took over the business. It seems to be doing well. We still buy produce from him. Perhaps we shouldn't have, but I've always believed in the premise of innocent until proven guilty."

Sowing the seeds of a man's guilt in one breath, then proclaiming his innocence in the next.

Intentional?

"Nobody wants to see an innocent man go to jail, but at the same time, folks don't want a murderer on the loose, do they? And we can't ignore the fact that two young women have disappeared from a small town in a relatively short space of time."

"And that's why you're here? In case the two deaths are connected?"

"Precisely. Which brings me to my questions. I'm trying to firm up the timeline of the last day Gosia was seen alive, and I understand she came to take an order for the restaurant."

"I recall Selmi asking the same thing a few months ago. *Ja*, she did. It was a Tuesday, wasn't it?"

Black pretended to check a note on his phone, even though he knew the details by heart. "Yes, a Tuesday. At a quarter past ten, you said."

"That's what Carmela told me."

"Carmela?"

"Tuesdays are usually quiet, so Carmela looked after the place until the evening that day. When Selmi came over looking for Gosia, I asked Carmela, and that's what she told me—that she spoke to Gosia and gave her the order around a quarter past ten. Although Carmela's timekeeping was never so good. More than once, I had to speak to her about her lateness."

"Was anyone apart from Carmela around at that time? What about the other waiters? Omar?"

"Omar didn't work here back then. There was only the chef, but he was in the kitchen and he said he didn't see her."

It struck Black that this was all very convenient. The only witness to Gosia's visit to Happy Fish was dead. There were two ways to look at it—firstly, Gunther could be lying, or secondly, there was another possible link between Gosia and Carmela.

"What time does the restaurant open?"

"Noon."

"So Carmela was here early that day?"

"Once or twice a week, she came in beforehand to tidy. The new waitress isn't so conscientious." Gunther waved at the nearest table. "See? This salt shaker is almost empty."

"I see. I'll need to speak to the chef to confirm."

For a moment, Gunther's eyebrows pinched together in a frown, but he quickly nodded. "Of course. You're right—nobody wants a murderer walking the streets of Dahab."

"Where were you on that day?"

"Does it matter?"

"I'm just wondering whether you might have seen Gosia in town."

"I wasn't in town—my sister and her husband were staying with me, and we took a trip to Coloured Canyon. Maggie likes to take pictures of the wildlife in the desert."

"Did you have a guide for this trip?"

"No, I drove. I've been there many times."

Again, no witnesses. But then again, if Gunther had family staying, it would have been more difficult for him to commit murder unnoticed.

"How long did your sister and her husband spend in Dahab?"

"Actually, they're still here. They fell in love with the place and decided to stay until spring. Winters in Europe can get so cold. Did you know it snowed in

Germany last week?"

Yes. "Can't say I did."

"Do you want to speak to my sister as well?"

"Is she around?"

"Not today—she and Stefan went to Sharm el-Sheikh to renew their visas, and they couldn't come back yesterday evening because of the rain. Apparently, there's some damage to the road by the middle checkpoint."

"I'd appreciate a call when she gets back."

"*Ja*, of course. Was there anything else?"

Black handed over a business card with his number. "You mentioned taking Carmela to the hospital before she died. After she walked into a door?"

"*Ja*, for X-rays."

"Can you recall who treated her? The doctor's name?"

"Sorry, but *nein*. I waited for her outside in the car."

"Why didn't you go in?"

Gunther shuddered. "I don't like hospitals. The smell of them makes me feel ill."

What kind of lily-livered asshole left an injured woman to deal with a hospital visit by herself?

"Which hospital was it?"

"The Dahab International Medical Center."

The same place that had treated Gosia. So many puzzle pieces, but how did they all fit together?

"Interesting. Any chance I can speak to your chef now?"

The chef knew who Gosia was, but had no recollection of seeing her at the restaurant at the end of June. Black bade the pair of them goodbye and went to find his wife. She hadn't called with any news, good or bad, so he headed for the Into the Blue Dive Centre. He'd always enjoyed freediving himself, although in his version of the sport, he didn't go hand over hand down a rope in a sleek wetsuit and monofin like Dahab's freediving cohort. No, in the Navy SEALs, freediving had consisted of trying not to die after jumping off a boat into a freezing sea. Just call him a masochist. It was character building, okay? He'd also made friends for life in the teams, and although he didn't miss the bureaucracy one bit, he still sometimes wished he could relive those days again.

Although right at that moment, he'd have settled for a quick scuba trip or even a swim. No such luck, though.

He found Emmy in the dive centre, drinking coffee as she laughed and chatted in Spanish with a group of younger men. It didn't escape Black's notice that all four of the assholes had their gazes fixed on her chest, and he was tempted to remove their eyeballs, especially those belonging to the plumpest of the quartet, who was practically salivating.

"Hey!" She waved at him from her seat. "Do you want coffee? This is Mateo, David, Rodrigo, and Juan. Rodrigo reckons he knows Javier Martinez."

Black squashed onto the seat beside Emmy and wrapped an arm around her shoulders. Held each of the men's gazes in turn as he kissed Emmy on the temple. Every one of them looked away.

"Tell me more. Which one of you is Rodrigo?"

The chubby guy gave a nervous cough. "I am."

"How do you know Javier?"

"I met him here. Earlier in the year?" The prick seemed nervous. Black couldn't think why. "We dived together, but Javier's father died suddenly and he had to go back to Madrid."

"Do you have contact details for him?"

"A number. I gave it to your girlfriend."

"My wife."

The guy swallowed hard. "Your wife, *lo siento*."

Emmy snorted, then pasted on a perky grin. "Rodrigo's been *very* helpful, and he makes a great cup of coffee as well."

"I'm not thirsty."

"Oh, too bad. The guys have been telling me all about their trip to the Bahamas. Apparently, freediving at the Dean's Blue Hole is to die for." She clapped a hand over her mouth and giggled. "Oops. Perhaps we shouldn't mention dying. Mateo's a doctor, and he swears he just saw a metatarsal by the Jasmine restaurant."

"If you want to go to the Bahamas, I'll take you to the Bahamas."

Emmy reached up to squeeze Black's hand, taking a moment to loosen his grip on her shoulder. Shit. He shouldn't have dug his fingers in like that.

"See?" she said to her new "friends." "Isn't he a treasure?"

The four Spaniards didn't seem to agree, and Black gave them a cold smile. "We should go and help with the clean-up at the hotel."

"We totally should." She drained her cup and stood, shrugging Black's arm away. "It was lovely to meet you guys."

Black made a conscious effort to unclench his teeth while Emmy kissed each man on both cheeks, European style. She did this on purpose to wind him up. He knew she did, and it still got to him.

"Stop glowering, Chuck," she chided, laughing as they walked back to the high street. "We were just talking."

"I know that."

But those words tapped into Black's greatest fear, and his greatest fear was losing Emmy. While he might remain coldly rational in every other facet of his life, where his wife was concerned, his blood ran hot.

"I'm wearing your ring."

"I know that too."

She leaned in closer. "Does this mean I'll get fucked by the green-eyed monster when we get back? Because if so, putting up with Juan's halitosis was worth it."

Black barked out a laugh and lifted her against him for a stride. "I'm getting hard already."

CHAPTER 26 - BLACK

EMMY SAT ON the edge of the bed, her phone pressed to her ear. Black's eyes had turned from green back to their regular dark brown, and she'd reminded him once more why a little jealousy mightn't be a bad thing.

"Hi, my name's Emerson Black," she said in Spanish. "I'm a private investigator working in Dahab, Egypt, and I understand you visited back in June? This is a long shot, but I'm trying to trace the whereabouts of Gosia Kaminski. She sold organic fruit and vegetables, and I'm speaking to everyone she might have come into contact with around the time of her disappearance. Your name was on her list of customers, and I'm interested in finding out when you last saw her, and whether she said anything that might have a bearing on our investigation. If you could call me when you get a moment, I'd be grateful." She reeled off her number and lay back on the bed. "Voicemail."

"I figured that. Ready to help with the clean-up? The eyesore on the lawn survived, so the bunny can go outside again."

"Do I look ready?"

No, she didn't. She looked edible, and it was all Black could do to stop himself from having another taste.

"You need clothes. And I want to visit Aurelie

before dinner. She might be able to confirm or deny parts of the story Gunther told me earlier."

"Mexican?"

"Whatever you want, Diamond."

"Who is it?" Aurelie's voice sounded shrill, shaky following Black's knock.

"Emmy and Black," Emmy said. "Are you okay?"

The door swung open, and Aurelie stood there, pale, arms wrapped around her body.

"I guess so. Just nervous, that's all. Did you hear about the bones they found earlier?"

"The whole town's heard about them now."

According to Khaled, reporters were camped outside the police station, and Captain al-Busari was upset he couldn't keep the whole mess buried anymore. Still, that wasn't Black's problem.

"It's all linked, isn't it? Carmela and Gosia and this new body." *Bodies.* "Gosia was found up in the mountains too."

Very likely. "It's possible."

"Why did Carmela get put in the sea?"

Khaled had a theory about that, one he'd tried out on Black earlier, and Black was inclined to think it might be correct. The man was starting to act like a detective now.

"Between Gosia's disappearance and Carmela's death, a new quad-bike safari company opened, and their tours go farther up into the mountains than any other provider." It was their riders who'd found Gosia's remains, in fact. "Whoever dumped the other bodies up there probably got twitchy and decided to try somewhere new."

"I guess that makes sense." She gave her head a little shake. "Where are my manners? Come in. Do you want a drink?"

"I'd love a coffee," Emmy said. No surprises there. Caffeine ran through her veins, although she never drank it late in the evening because it made her nightmares worse.

"I've only got instant."

"Instant's fine."

"Make that two," Black said.

He didn't miss the tremble in Aurelie's hands as she prepared the drinks, or the way her head snapped around every time she heard a sound outside. The woman was scared.

"Nervous?" he asked.

"How can I not be? People keep dying. I've had to reschedule tomorrow evening's yoga class because none of my pupils want to go out after dark."

The coffee was terrible, but Black took a sip anyway. "There may be a silver lining. There's no way the police can deny there's a problem now. If more people are working on the case, there's a better chance of solving it."

"Is that why you're here? The case?"

It was hardly likely to be a social visit, was it? Unless the person in question was a close friend, Black avoided those whenever possible.

"Yes. What can you tell me about Carmela's timekeeping?"

"Her timekeeping?" Aurelie gave a high-pitched laugh. "Well, it was terrible. She arrived late for everything."

"Including work?"

"Gunther hated it. He kept trying to get her to wear a watch—he even bought her one—but she always took it off because she hated the tan lines and then forgot to put it back on again."

So Gunther had been telling the truth on that point at least. "That ties in with other information. What about her recent hospital visit? Did she mention that?"

"For her cheek? Uh, she was relieved it wasn't fractured."

"Do you know which doctor she saw?"

"Which doctor? You think there's a *doctor* involved in this?"

"It's just one line of inquiry. Did she tell you anything about him? Or her?"

Because women could kill too. Emmy was a case in point.

"No, nothing. She might have said something to Youssef, but I doubt it. They didn't discuss stuff like that. That was another reason she turned down his proposal—because she wanted a soulmate, somebody she could talk to about anything and who'd actually listen."

"That's a goal worth holding out for."

"Really? Because I want that too, but sometimes I think I've been watching too many Hallmark movies."

"Wait," Emmy said. "You won't regret it, I promise."

Black smiled. Caught himself. Blanked his expression again. "We'll ask Youssef, just in case."

"Hold on, I just thought of something." Aurelie hurried into the living room and began rummaging through a box in the corner. "Youssef brought some of Carmela's things back. Her mom wants her personal items, and I offered to send them. If we left it to Youssef, it'd never get done. I'm sure I saw paperwork from the hospital in here."

Sure enough, there was a bill for Carmela's treatment. Examination, X-ray, blood test, painkillers, miscellaneous consumables. Treated by Dr. Faisal Abdullah. Another name to check out, and not one that had appeared on Khaled's suspect list. Why not?

Bracelets jangled on Aurelie's wrist, and Black caught sight of the staff of Asclepius engraved on one of them—the emblem of the American Medical Association. He reached out and held her wrist steady to take a closer look.

"How about you? Have you ever been to the hospital here?"

Aurelie realised what he was looking at. "No, thank goodness. But I'm allergic to gummy bears, and a friend from high school got me the bracelet as a birthday present."

"Gummy bears?" Emmy asked. "That sucks."

"Doesn't it? I've got an EpiPen and everything. Believe me, I'm not going anywhere near the candy aisle until whoever killed Carmela's been caught."

"We'll do our best to make that happen."

On the way to the Mexican restaurant, Black caught Emmy glancing towards the supermarket.

"You want gummy bears, don't you?"

"How did you know that?"

"Because I'm your fucking soulmate, Diamond."

There was only one woman for him. There'd only ever be one woman for him.

Chapter 27 - Emmy

BLACK'S PHONE RANG at—what the hell was the time?—right, at eight o'clock in the morning. With hindsight, perhaps washing down half a dozen tacos with a pitcher of margaritas last night hadn't been the best idea. And Black wasn't moving. I flicked the sombrero off his face.

"Are you gonna answer that?"

"Urgh."

According to Nate, Black used to drink plenty in the SEALs, but when he moved to the private sector, he'd started on a health kick that had lasted over a decade. He indulged in the occasional beer, red wine with dinner, and good Scotch, offset by smoothies and gallons of water. Benders were few and far between. But last night, he'd drunk me under the fucking table. Quite literally. I'd slithered off my stool sometime around midnight, and he'd slung me over his shoulder and carried me to a taxi.

Yes, there were dead people all over the place, but we were still on fucking vacation, okay?

"It might be important."

"Then you answer it."

"It's your phone."

He rolled over, and I shuffled my backside up the bed. Why the hell was I wearing a poncho? My mouth tasted like six-month-old huitlacoche, but crawling to the bathroom for a toothbrush was distinctly unappealing. Did I leave any paracetamol in the nightstand?

Black finally picked up the phone and put it on speaker. "Yes?"

"Mr. Black?"

"Who's this?"

"My name's Maggie. Gunther is my brother."

Gunther... Gunther... Ah, right. Restaurant dude. No paracetamol, and no water either. Dammit, I'd have to get up. And I needed coffee.

"Maggie. Yes, this is Charles Black. Thanks for getting back to me."

"Gunther said you wanted to talk to me about a girl who went missing several months ago?"

"That's right. On the..." Black laid his head back on the pillow and screwed up his eyes, thinking. "On the twenty-seventh of June."

"I checked my calendar, and my husband and I went sightseeing with Gunther to a canyon on the other side of Nuweiba that day, then ate a late lunch at an oasis nearby. As I recall, the rocks had the most unusual colours and patterns. Have you been there?"

"No, I haven't."

"If you're looking for a day out, I'd recommend it, but not if you're claustrophobic. Some of the paths were so narrow I had to take my backpack off and carry it above my head."

"I'll bear that in mind."

"Is there anything else?"

"Not right now. Have a good day."

"You too."

Black tossed the phone back onto the nightstand and groaned. "My liver hates me."

"Perhaps we should go back to the restaurant and see if they serve menudo?"

The best hangover cure money could buy, according to Carmen, who was Nate's wife and one of my best friends. Although I'd nearly revoked our friendship the day she tried feeding me that vile concoction. Of course, she didn't tell me it contained chilli and cow's stomach until I'd taken a mouthful.

"Nice try, Diamond. I'll settle for orange juice."

"And you expect me to fetch it?"

He smiled at me, and it was my turn to groan as I crawled out of bed, tore off the poncho, and stumbled to the kitchen in a pair of shorts and a camisole. I always slept clothed because the only thing worse than trying to kill someone while sleepwalking was trying to kill someone while sleepwalking naked. Been there, done that.

"Gunther's story checks out?" I asked as I rummaged through the fridge.

"Seems that way. Which means Gosia spoke to Carmela right before she died."

"And you think there's a connection? Could she have seen something she shouldn't have?"

"If she did, why wait three months to shut her up?"

I didn't have an answer for that. Or the capacity for thinking one up at that particular moment in time—not before my first cup of coffee.

"Who knows? Maybe the boyfriend can shed some light?"

"He's on my list to talk to again. And Youssef. I want to ask him about Gosia."

"What about the doctor? The one who treated Carmela?"

"I thought I'd pass him to Khaled to do the preliminaries."

"Good idea. Do you want an espresso? Americano? Cappuccino?"

"All of the above."

"Fuck."

One tiny word from Black's lips, and I abandoned my fight with the bed in my old room—now nibbled on every leg—and walked into the lounge. Sadly, I didn't think he was talking in the carnal sense.

"What's up?"

"Khaled called. The captain finally listened to our second-hand advice and they've identified Gosia."

"Surely that's a good thing?"

"An hour later, he arrested Selmi."

Ah, shit. And we hadn't had a chance to talk to Selmi again yet either. "On what grounds?"

"Khaled was hazy on that. But after yesterday's Twitter storm, al-Busari's boss called to ask what the hell was going on. From the sounds of it, the captain thought he'd better be seen to be doing something, and locking up Gosia's boyfriend seemed like a good option."

"What's he gonna do with no evidence? Beat a confession out of him?"

"Let's hope not."

"How long can they hold him for without charge?"

"This is Egypt, Diamond. I don't think rules like

that matter."

Okay, that was a dumb question. "So where does that leave us? With Youssef? What about the doctor?"

"Khaled actually knows him. Apparently, Dr. Abdullah's a big soccer fan, and they watch the games at the same café. Or at least, they have done for the last month. Dr. Abdullah moved here from Cairo at the end of August when his predecessor retired. That's why he wasn't on Khaled's list—because he didn't live in Dahab when Gosia died."

"How about the previous guy? Is he still around?"

"Apparently so, but he's in his sixties and suffers from arthritis. Khaled said there's no way he could've manhandled bodies around the mountains. Some days, he can barely even walk. And he doesn't have his own vehicle, he hires a driver instead."

One clue after another flittered away. All this reminded me why I ran the Special Projects department at Blackwood rather than beavering away on the investigations team. It was far less frustrating to plan and execute a mission to remove a person from the planet than to work out why someone else had done so.

"What about the other doctors?"

"We've moved them to the top of the list."

My phone pinged.

Zena: Have you seen this?

Oh, hurrah. The news about Selmi had hit Twitter. I had a feeling this would be a really long day, not least for him. If he was innocent, he shouldn't be in jail. And if he was guilty, how were we going to prove it?

"I already told you, I didn't do anything," was Youssef's opening argument. Neither of us had said a word. What if we'd just wanted to buy a chicken?

"We aren't suggesting that," Black said. "But we do have a few questions."

"Can't you see I'm busy?"

He wasn't kidding. It looked as though the whole roof of the chicken shop had caved in. Broken planks lay in a pile out the front, together with palm fronds and a rusty satellite dish.

"The rain?"

"I told my father many times that it needed to be fixed, but he refused to listen. We've been working since dawn."

"Then it's probably time to take a break. Want us to get some drinks?"

Youssef's pissed-off expression softened a touch. "We would like drinks. Thank you."

There was a tiny supermarket opposite, and Black loaded bottles of soft drinks and cartons of juice into bags while I paid. Five bucks. Cheapest bribe ever. Back at the chicken shop, Youssef and his three friends were sitting on the kerb, sweating in the midday heat.

"What are your questions?" Youssef asked, opening a Coke.

I let Black do the talking while I focused on watching the men. Body language said a lot that words didn't.

"Do you know Gosia Kaminski?"

"Who?"

One of Youssef's friends helped him out. "The foreign woman who tries to stop the fishing."

"Oh, her. What has that *majnoon alkaliba* said about me now?" Unlike Black, Youssef didn't use *crazy bitch* as a term of endearment.

"Nothing. She's dead."

From the way his jaw dropped, I'd have bet money on him not knowing Gosia's fate. Either that or he was a better liar than me, which was unlikely.

"I didn't mean what I said about her being a *majnoon alkaliba*. It's just... I... She always tries—*tried* —to get the shop closed. And the fishing boats. She cared more for octopuses than people."

"There's a rumour you used to argue with her."

"Everyone in town argued with her! She kept poking her nose into business that didn't concern her."

"Can you give me an example?"

Youssef stayed quiet, but his friends spoke up. "She lay down in the entrance of the gas station to protest about pollution."

"She let a herd of camels loose one night."

"She handcuffed herself to the mayor's gate after he complained about stray dogs."

Boy, she really knew how to make friends with the locals.

"Did Carmela know her?" Black asked.

"Why does that matter?"

"Because Carmela's dead too."

Youssef put his drink down, his mouth drooping at the corners as he deflated. "You think they are connected?"

Black shrugged. "One small town, two girls dying within three months? We have to consider the possibility, don't you think?"

"I suppose. But I don't think they were friends. They might have spoken sometimes, but that was all."

"Gosia went missing, didn't she?" one of the friends said. In my head, I christened him Alvin because his front teeth stuck out like a chipmunk's. "There were posters."

"The posters disappeared," Youssef said. "I thought she must've come back."

"Well, she didn't," I told him. "And a witness said she talked to Carmela on the day she vanished."

"What witness?"

"Carmela's boss."

"Gunther? Yes, he knows a lot of people."

"How well do you know him?"

"He buys chickens. I see him every week, two or three times."

"Does he pick them up? Or do you deliver?"

"I take the chickens to the chef at the restaurant. Gunther calls the day before to say how many."

"Did Gunther and Carmela get on well?"

"Most days. Sometimes, she complained he made her do too much work. When his sister came to stay, he started taking days off to visit places. Carmela was happy to have the job, though."

"I understand Gunther took her to the hospital just before she died?"

"*Hal hu*?" Did he? So Carmela hadn't discussed her accident with Youssef. "Why?"

"She hit her face on a door."

"But that was just a bruise."

What a dick.

"Are you aware of her visiting the hospital in Dahab

at any other time?"

Youssef shook his head. "Hospitals are too expensive. My uncle has herbs to fix illness."

If my experience with Bedouin herbs was anything to go by, then no wonder she'd kept quiet and gone to the medical centre. I'd felt a tiny bit squiffy one day and declined lunch, whereupon a helpful dude had mixed me up a glass of green stuff that smelled repulsive and tasted worse. A minor stomachache turned into a night on the loo, and even now, I still got the phantom bitterness of that goop on my tongue whenever I thought about it. I grabbed a carton of pineapple juice and sucked half of it down.

Black glanced at me with the faintest of smirks, and I knew he was remembering that night too. Nothing said "I love you" like running to the supermarket at eleven p.m. for more bog roll.

"Why do you have all these questions?" the skinniest guy asked. "I heard the police already arrested somebody."

"Because it's possible they've arrested the wrong person. Didn't you hear what happened in Fidda Hilal a while back?"

"Yes, but—"

Black's phone rang. Saved by the bell. He glanced at the screen and answered.

"Sir?"

There were few people to whom Black would grant that courtesy. He even called the president by his first name. My money was on the caller being Captain Bob.

"How long ago? ... Have you tried calling her? ... Did anyone see her leave? ... Okay, we're on our way."

I raised an eyebrow.

"Zena's disappeared. Apparently, there was some sort of argument with Lynn and Chris, and now she's turned her phone off and nobody can find her." He turned to Youssef and co., holding out a business card. "We need to go. If you happen to see a teenage girl, white with dark blonde hair, around Emmy's height, do me a favour and call."

Chapter 28 - Emmy

"NO WAY WERE we bringing the mutt back with us. It was probably rabid."

Chris had one of those voices that earplugs were made for. Shrill, whiny, and it got louder whenever he wanted to get his point across. Bob was right—he and Lynn really were a great match in some respects.

"Actually, rabies is—" Sondra started.

"And fleas! All of those creatures have fleas too. Mangy things, filthy and—"

"Can we get back to the topic at hand?" Bob asked. "Your daughter?"

"Technically, she's not my daughter."

Lynn looked as if she was about to cry. "Be quiet, Chris. We need to find her."

"When did anybody last see her?" Black asked.

"About—"

Chris took over again, cutting Lynn off.

"We went into the village to get pastries because the waiters here at the hotel don't understand a word I say." Really? Faced with Chris, I'd be tempted to pretend I didn't speak English either. "Crazy there's no McDonald's here! What kind of third-rate town doesn't have a McDonald's?"

"Zena?" Black prompted.

"Oh. Yeah. Zena wandered off and came back with

some scruffy dog. Wanted to keep him. Can you believe that?"

Yes, I totally could. And while the logistics of keeping a stray dog at the hotel would be tricky, a part of me wanted to round up half a dozen hounds and bring them back just to piss off Chris.

I smiled sweetly. "Aw, what a lovely idea."

"Don't even think about it," Bob growled.

Spoilsport.

"And then?" Black asked.

"We told her no, of course, and then we came back here."

"She was a bit upset," Lynn put in. "She said the dog was too skinny. After we got back, she ran off to her room, and when I went to check on her a half hour later, she was gone."

"Presumably to look for the dog. Whereabouts was it?"

"We don't know where it came from, and it ran off when Chris yelled at it."

What an absolute treasure that man was. Beyond the Rolex and the fact that he admittedly wasn't pig ugly, I couldn't understand what Lynn saw in him.

"Can you describe it?"

Bob was already one step ahead. "Brown and white, medium sized, gangly. I got one of our drivers to take Lynn and Chris around the streets by the bakery, but there was no sign of Zena or the dog. I've got a dozen men in town still searching, but there are so many places she could hide. And I'm also wary of the situation at the moment."

"What situation?" Chris asked.

Bob ignored him. "We need to find Zena and bring

her back here."

"What area do you want us to take?"

"Can you start at the lighthouse and work your way towards Assalah?"

"We're on our way."

As Black drove back into town, I called anyone I thought might be able to help. On the plus side, I'd gained quite a few contacts over the last day or two, and soon we had everyone on the lookout, from my new freediving buddies to Aurelie to the guy who ran the Mexican restaurant, who promised to send a spare waiter out to assist with the search. Khaled and his team had been dispatched up into the mountains to hunt for more bones. He sounded about as happy with the situation as I felt.

"Isn't this fun?" I muttered as Black boosted me over the fence around an abandoned house. "Just think, we could have been planning Anton Ludovich's trip to the afterlife right now."

"And instead, we're chasing stray dogs in the sunshine. Don't say I never take you anywhere exciting."

"If I was Lynn, I'd have kept the dog and ditched Chris. I know people have different tastes, but the man's about as yummy as Ebola virus."

A flash of a brown tail disappeared around the corner of the building, and I jogged after it, pausing to peer through cracked windows as I went. Although this search was horribly inconvenient, it struck me that it gave us a great excuse for snooping around. Carmela and Gosia had been killed somewhere, and we hadn't yet found their murderer's hidey-hole.

But it didn't appear to be this place. There was

nothing inside but an old chair and a pile of dusty plastic bottles, and when I finally caught up with the dog, it was definitely more black than brown.

By the time the sun dipped behind the mountains, we must've searched fifty buildings. No Zena, and no killing room. My hands were scratched, I needed to pee, and I was in desperate need of something cold and wet that wasn't a dog's nose. If nothing else, I'd gotten to practise my parkour skills, which had grown somewhat rusty over a couple of months filled with more meetings than gym time.

Then my phone rang. Aurelie calling.

"Are you still looking for Zena?"

"Unfortunately."

"I think she might be behind my building. I only caught a quick glimpse, but there was a dog with her too."

"We'll come over right now."

"Should I go and check it's her? It's just that it's getting dark..."

"No, you stay put. We're only five minutes away."

We found Zena behind a dumpster, feeding bread rolls to a fluffy brown-and-white dog that was sitting in her lap.

"What the hell are you playing at? Your grandfather's sent out search parties all over Dahab."

"I know. When I went to the bakery, the guy at the counter asked me if I was Zena Tovey because everyone was out looking for me, and I said I wasn't."

Good grief. *Don't murder the teenager, Emmy.*

"You've wasted hours of people's time. We've all been worried about you."

"I bet Chris hasn't. He's probably driven to Sharm el-Sheikh to find a McDonald's."

Okay, I had to give her that one.

"Well, everyone else has been worried about you. Why'd you run away?"

"Because Chris is an asshole. He wouldn't let me feed her." She motioned towards the dog. "And she's so hungry. Look—you can see her ribs."

"Is everything okay?" Aurelie asked from behind me. I'd seen her approaching out of the corner of my eye, and she was hesitant, nervous, her arms wrapped around her waist. "I saw you from the window."

"Zena here decided to cause an international incident because a dog was hungry."

"No, because my mom's boyfriend is a heartless dick," she corrected.

"Now isn't the time to be having this argument. You lost the opportunity to take the moral high ground when you scared the shit out of your family. It's time to go home and apologise."

"Not without Patch." A tear rolled down her cheek and plopped onto the dog's fur.

Privately, I was on her side. The dog was kinda cute, just skin and bone, but if we walked in with her tonight, Chris would have a fit and everyone would take his side. Including Bob.

"This isn't how you negotiate, Zena. You can't do something shitty, then start making demands. There has to be give and take."

"You took Crash home and put her in the bedroom."

"That was different."

"How?"

Black came to my rescue. "Emmy's earned the right to make her own decisions, and she's got a lifetime of favours banked to fall back on. You haven't built up that cushion yet."

"But—"

"You've pissed everyone off today," I told her bluntly. "Your mom was supposed to be doing a seating chart for the wedding, your grandfather and his staff should've been cleaning up storm damage, and Black and I were meant to be investigating two girls' deaths. Instead, we've been hunting for you. And, just in case you've forgotten, there's a murderer running around. Your family's been frightened out of their minds."

Her face fell, and she sniffed a bit. I felt like a bitch for making her cry, but that needed to be said.

"I'm sorry I worried people. But Patch'll starve."

"I could feed her," Aurelie offered. "If she stays nearby, I can put out food in the mornings."

"Do you have any kibble? She needs a proper diet."

"How about a compromise?" I suggested. "We'll go and buy a bag of dog food and give it to Aurelie. And if you manage to follow your mom down the aisle with a smile on your face, we'll put in a good word for you with Bob."

"Two bags of kibble."

Now she was starting to get it. "Two bags of kibble, and you have to help your mom with her table decorations."

She folded her arms. "Fine."

I turned to Aurelie. "Thanks for doing this. Do you want anything else from the supermarket while we're there?"

"Some chocolate? I could really use some chocolate."

"We'll be right back."

As we walked along the promenade, twenty people must've stopped us to ask if that was Zena with us. Bob really had got the whole town out hunting for her. This time, she couldn't lie, and people seemed genuinely happy to see her safe. Black called Khaled with an update too.

"Good news, buddy. We've found the missing girl. You can get some sleep now."

I didn't hear Khaled's answer, but Black barked out a laugh. "Well, good luck with that."

"What happened?" I asked.

"A herd of horses got free from a trekking stable on the edge of town. The captain heard a rumour it's some sort of 'free the oppressed' tribute from Gosia's supporters, and so he's taken Khaled's team off crime scene duty to help round them up."

"Free the oppressed? Are they crazy?" Zena asked. "Horses are flight animals. They'll get scared and run into traffic or something."

"There are times when people have the best intentions, but they don't quite think things through, do they?"

"Was that a dig at me?"

"Yes."

Black snorted.

"I said I was sorry, okay? Sometimes, I don't like you very much."

Chapter 29 - Emmy

THE NEXT MORNING, Black's phone rang right after sunrise. Khaled was calling. What was this hell we'd fallen into? Never again was I going to mention the word "vacation."

"What does he want?" I groaned. "Tell me it's not more bloody bones."

Black put the phone to his ear and listened a moment, then a smile spread over his face.

"Good news, Diamond."

"Really?"

"It's not more bones. It's another body. Well, part of one. Get dressed."

"*Part* of one? Where?"

"By the water treatment plant."

Black already had a pair of cargo pants on, and I looked longingly at the coffee machine as I struggled into a pair of running tights.

"No time," he said, reading my mind. "I told Khaled to secure the scene, but he didn't even have any tape."

"Nobody's got a birthday today?"

"Don't. Just don't. The last thing we need is another montage on Twitter."

"True, but I feel like a zombie."

"You can eat me later. Where's the good camera? Next time we go on vacation, remind me to bring my field kit." He held up a bag. "I've put together what I can find here, but it's woefully inadequate."

"I can't believe you just said that."

"What, that it's woefully inadequate?"

"No, before that."

"It wouldn't be the first time you've sucked my cock, Diamond."

"I meant the part where you used the words 'vacation' and 'field kit' in the same sentence."

If I felt like a zombie, I looked positively perky beside Khaled. The black circles under his eyes could've been drawn on with charcoal.

"When did you last sleep?" I asked him.

"Uh, yesterday? The day before? I spent the whole night catching animals. After the horses, they let out some camels and a group of donkeys. What day is it?"

"Saturday."

"Where's the body?" Black asked. "Who found it?"

"Over by the oxidation ponds. I found it with Gamal."

Black started walking in the direction Khaled pointed. A hundred or so yards away, I saw a gaggle of men standing near a police car, surrounded by a ring of what looked like tied-together plastic bags flapping in the morning breeze.

"Tell us what happened."

"Captain al-Busari ordered us to chase down all the escaped animals before they caused an accident, and he also wanted the people who let them out arrested."

"Did you catch them?"

"Only two people we found by the Canyon dive site. There were probably more because the horses by Three Pools and the camels by the Blue Hole got loose at the same time, but they said they were alone."

"And you found the body while you were looking for the animals?"

"We were chasing a donkey. It ran over here, and when we got close, a vehicle drove off ahead of us at high speed. Then Gamal fell over the bag with the body in it."

As Black had said, it wasn't a whole body, just a torso, and even parts of that were missing. What was left was in a black plastic bag, and somebody had slit it open to reveal the grisly contents. A pool of vomit seeped into the sand next to where the remains lay, and I honestly couldn't blame whoever had horked it up.

"Ick."

On first impressions, there were two things that interested me apart from the obvious gore. The first was the shark tattoo that covered the left shoulder, its tail disappearing into a tattered fringe of flesh and skin where the arm had been hacked off. The second was the pecs. Yes, this body was male.

"Not what I expected," Black murmured.

"It doesn't fit."

"No, it doesn't. Both of the other victims were female, and serial killers rarely deviate from their chosen type."

"What's the chances that there are two homicidal maniacs in Dahab?"

Black snapped on a pair of nitrile gloves— presumably he'd raided the first aid kit at the villa—and crouched down to take a closer look. Rather him than me. The body was already starting to smell, and beetles crawled over the exposed flesh.

"I'd say the chances are slim. See?"

He angled the top of the bag towards me, and I saw a length of red cord tied around it. And—you've guessed it—it was tied with a surgeon's knot.

Ah, shit.

We were now firmly in serial killer territory, and with the discovery of this new victim, so different from the rest both in the sex and in the method of disposal, the waters were now so muddy that the next step was a mystery.

"At least we've eliminated one suspect," I said, trying to look on the bright side. "It wasn't Selmi. He's still locked up at the police station, right?"

Khaled nodded.

"Excuse me, excuse me, coming through."

A small Egyptian man ducked under the makeshift rope and strode towards us, carrying a black leather briefcase almost as big as he was. None of the cops stopped him, so I figured he was somebody they knew.

"The medical examiner?" Black guessed.

"Yes, Dr. Ibrahim." Khaled nodded, bleary-eyed. "From the government hospital."

"Who are these people?" the doctor asked Khaled. "Foreigners? Why are they here?"

"I'm an American detective consulting on the case," Black told him.

"Good, good. Captain al-Busari needs all the help he can get." The old guy's knees cracked as he bent to examine the body. "*Na'am*, he's definitely dead. Somebody has made a mess."

"How long has he been dead?" Khaled asked.

"There's no significant decay. I will take the liver temperature. Air temperature is twenty-one degrees."

When the doctor started fishing around the dead guy's abdomen, I was kind of glad I'd skipped breakfast. I might have spent years causing death, but that didn't mean I enjoyed looking at the aftermath. Not at all. The squelching noises put me off lunch too.

"Hmm..." The doctor's curious expression turned to confusion. "There is no liver."

Black raised an eyebrow. "No *liver*?"

"Here is the stomach, the spleen, the diaphragm... No liver. It's not here."

"Maybe our killer cooked it up with fava beans and a nice chianti?" I suggested.

Black opened his mouth. Closed it again, then spoke. "You know, I was about to come up with a pithy comeback, but you could actually be right."

"What does that mean?" Khaled asked. "Fava beans and chianti?"

How could he have missed that masterpiece? "You never saw *The Silence of the Lambs*?"

"I do not like sheep."

I burst out laughing, and everybody stared at me. "Uh, cannibalism. Hannibal Lecter, the guy from the movie, he ate his victims."

And also had a sense of humour. My friend Sofia, who knew more about drugs than most doctors, had explained it to me once. Lecter's antisocial personality disorder could have been treated with monoamine oxidase inhibitors, or MAOIs. And what three food groups couldn't you eat with MAOIs? Meat, alcohol, and high-protein produce. Not only was Lecter cracking a joke, but he was also admitting he hadn't been taking his meds.

But I didn't think Khaled would appreciate that little snippet of information. In fact, he'd gone quite pale.

"You think there's a cannibal in Dahab?"

"We have to consider everything when it comes to motive."

"That could be right," the doctor said. "The victims were all young. Tender meat."

One of the privates standing behind Khaled ran off, doubled over, and retched. Wasn't this a fun morning?

"We need to keep pushing forward with the investigation. When we're done here, we'll go over the statements you've taken so far. And you said you saw a vehicle—can you describe it?"

"It was dark, and I didn't see it very well."

"But you probably saw more than you think. Was it a dark colour or a light colour?"

"Dark. It did not stand out against the night."

"And what shape was it? A pickup? An SUV? A sedan?"

"Not a pickup. It was taller than that."

"Did you see anybody behind the wheel?"

"No, it was driving away from us."

"Who else saw it? Gamal?"

Khaled waved over the kid who'd just heaved his guts up. "They want to know about the car we saw last night."

"The SUV?"

"Did you get a good look at it?" Black asked.

"I only saw the back."

"What can you tell us?"

"It was an SUV." Duh. Gamal glanced sideways at

Khaled, who nodded encouragingly. "A Jeep, perhaps? Or a Kia? Something like that. There was a white sticker in the back window. That is all I saw."

Black asked a few more questions, but that really was it. Still, at least we had one more clue than we'd had before.

"Right, we need to cross-reference the people on our list with the vehicles they have access to. Does anyone know what Youssef drives?"

"A white pickup," Gamal supplied. "But it was not him last night. Gosia's group set his chickens free, and he spent all evening trying to catch them."

One step forward, two steps back. If that was true, we'd lost our two main suspects.

And we were supposed to fly home in three days.

CHAPTER 30 - EMMY

I YAWNED AS Black sent a sleep-deprived Khaled home to get some rest, and then listened in as he began educating the remaining gaggle of privates in the rudiments of searching and documenting a crime scene. A sketch. Photographs. A careful fingertip search, noting the location of any items of interest. And keep an eye on observers—it wasn't unusual for the perpetrators to stop by to admire their handiwork.

While he focused on the what, I wondered about the why. Why here? I put elastic bands from Black's makeshift field kit around my shoes so my footprints could be differentiated from any already there and took a look around the wider area. The previous bodies had been well-hidden, one underwater and one high in the mountains. This torso had been abandoned in plain sight, although that could have been because Khaled and Gamal disturbed the killer. Had he taken the rest of it home with him? Or... Or...

My gaze landed on the chain-link fence around the water treatment plant and the oxidation ponds beyond. If I was going to hide a body, and I couldn't get into the mountains because the police were searching them and there were animal rights protesters running around at each end of town...

The flutter of plastic caught my eye, a black ribbon

snagged on top of the fence.

"Black! Over here. The scene goes up to the ponds. Fifty bucks says the rest of him's in there."

The question was, how the hell were we going to get him out? No way was I diving in there with all that sludge and fuck knows what bacteria.

In Khaled's absence, Gamal seemed to have become the de facto leader of our motley bunch of helpers. According to Khaled, the department's officers preferred either desk jobs or checkpoint duty because then they got to sit down all day. The legwork fell to the privates, and most of the investigation too, it seemed.

At least until a cloud of dust announced the arrival of Captain al-Busari. Took his time, didn't he? What was it today? A housewarming party? Somebody's anniversary celebration?

"We should go," Black said to Gamal. "Remember everything I've told you. Work slowly and methodically, and don't let the captain or anybody else trample over the scene before you've finished with it."

By that point, the ME had removed the body with a promise to carry out the autopsy that day and email the preliminary results to Gamal and Khaled by the following morning, so we made ourselves scarce. Why didn't we confront the captain? Because we were only in town for a few more days, and if he kicked us off the case, there'd be even less chance of solving it. Not trying to brag, just stating a fact. Under al-Busari's leadership, the Dahab Police Department was a useless hive of bureaucracy, even though he had some good men working there. And not only that, he could make Captain Bob's life very difficult if we pissed him off before we left.

Retreat didn't come easily to either of us, but Black played war like a game of chess. He thought strategically and always stayed two moves ahead. If he said back off, we'd back off.

But we'd be ready to attack at the perfect moment.

"What now?" I asked when we got back to the villa.

"First, I'm going to give Dan the good news—today, she gets to learn all about oxidation ponds so we can work out how to search them. And we need to identify this morning's victim. He wasn't local judging by the colour of his skin, and then there's the shark tattoo. In this town, there's a fifty-fifty chance he's a diver. We need to visit the dive centres."

"Ooh, yay! I can go see Rodrigo and his buddies again."

"Or you can go to the scuba centres while I take the freediving schools."

"Sure, that's fine too. Did I mention Mateo's gay? And also single?"

"Shut up, Emmy."

"And he's into muscular physiques."

"Keep that up and you're walking."

Well played, Emmy, well played. The first of the scuba centres happened to be right next door to an ice cream stand, which meant I got to have a delicious three-scoop lunch while I asked my questions. According to the girl behind the counter, only one of their customers had a shark tattoo, and it was on his ass. I didn't ask how she knew that.

My joy was short-lived, though. At the fifth centre I went to, our mystery man's picture was taped to the front of the counter, the words *Have you seen Duncan Sumner?* written across the top in red marker. Blond hair, blue eyes, his smile wide as he held a surfboard on a faraway beach. Something about him looked familiar, and I racked my brains as to what.

"Can I help?" the guy behind the counter asked. An Irishman in his late thirties, but he'd been in Egypt for a while judging by his weathered skin.

"I'm here from the UK for a week, and I thought I might try scuba diving. How would I go about that?"

The worst part? As with Gosia, I couldn't tell anyone the full story. Not before Duncan had been formally identified by the police.

"We offer the full range of PADI courses, but if you've never tried scuba before, it'd be best to start with an intro dive."

I pretended to look interested, nodding along while he explained the details. "Awesome. I've got a camel safari this afternoon, but I'll see what I can fit in later in the week. Hey, who's this guy? Is he missing? I'm sure I saw him in a restaurant earlier in the week."

"You probably did—he's been living in Dahab for three months now. But he only went missing last night. He went out to help search for that girl who ran off— Zara or something, her name was—and just never came back home. His wife's getting worried. Says it's not like him to disappear without calling."

That was where I'd seen him. He was one of the people who'd stopped us on the promenade to ask if

Zena was the girl everyone was looking for. He'd been heading towards the high street at the time. How the hell had he ended up in the desert?

His wife was right to be worried.

"Do you have a spare flyer? I'll ask around at my hotel."

"Sure, I can print one off."

Outside, I fished my phone out of my pocket to call Black, but before I could dial, it rang in my hand. Sloane, my office assistant in Richmond, was calling.

"Emmy? There's a Spanish man on the phone for you. Javier Martinez? He says you left him a message about organic food?"

"Yes! I did. Can you put him through?"

The line was crackly, and I ducked into an alley to get out of the wind. The waves were crashing onto the shore just a few metres away too, which made it difficult to hear.

"Javier?"

"Emerson Black? I received your voicemail."

"Thanks for getting back to me, and apologies for contacting you out of the blue."

"It's okay. This is about Gosia? You say she's gone missing?"

"I'm sorry to say that her body was found in the mountains behind Dahab this week. She's been identified now." Javier's gasp told me his feelings on the matter. "You knew her well?"

"No, I mean, not really. But she was such a kind soul. Always helping the animals."

"Yes, I've heard that. We're trying to reconstruct her movements on June twenty-seventh, which is the last day she was seen alive. We understand she went out to take orders for vegetable boxes. Do you recall seeing her?"

"No, I didn't see her."

That was a quick answer. "You're sure?"

"Certain. You see, the twenty-seventh of June was the day my father died, and when I got the call in the morning, I packed and took a taxi straight to the airport in Sharm el-Sheikh. The only people I spoke to before I left were my sister in Madrid and the driver. I left money in the apartment for my landlord and called him later that week from Spain to explain what had happened."

"I'm sorry for your loss." I'd get our Madrid office to check his father really had died, but assuming Javier was telling the truth, we'd hit another dead end. "When was the last time you saw Gosia?"

"The week before, as far as I remember. Whatever day she came to take the orders."

"Did you see anyone with her? That day or any other day?"

"No, it was only ever her. She came to the apartment to ask what I wanted, then a man delivered the food in a truck a few days later and collected the money. Her husband, I think? He said they ran the market garden together."

Selmi. "I don't suppose you know a man called Marten, spelled M-A-R-T-E-N, who was in Dahab at around the same time as you? His surname begins with a B. He's the only other person on Gosia's list we haven't managed to trace."

"Marten? You're sure it's a man?"

"I don't know of any women called Marten. Why do you ask that?"

"Because my neighbour in Dahab was called Beatrice Marten. I suggested she order boxes from Gosia too, but I'm not sure whether she ever did. She's a vegan, and she used to make the best katsu curry. We spent— You don't need to know this, do you?"

"You were close to Beatrice?"

"We both moved into our apartments on the same day, so we became friends. But I haven't seen her since I left. She went back to Holland soon after."

"I don't suppose you've got a phone number for her?"

"No, but I have an email address. Would that help?"

"Definitely." He read it out, and I scribbled it onto the back of Duncan's picture. "Thank you."

"I wish you the best of luck with finding the person who killed Gosia. Please, if there is anything more I can help with, just call."

"It's three a.m. What are you doing?"

Black had been asleep earlier, but now he was sitting up in bed, staring at his tablet. I rolled over to look, rubbing my nose where my iPad had hit it earlier when I fell asleep reading a biography of Jeffrey Dahmer.

"The autopsy report's arrived. Dr. Ibrahim must've worked all evening."

"Did they find any teeth marks?"

"I've only read the first paragraph." And judging by the squiggles, it was in Arabic. "What's *klawi*?"

"Uh, kidneys, I think?"

"Right. They're missing."

"Shit. The liver and the kidneys are both missing?"

"And the heart."

"Dahmer ate the hearts and livers of his victims, but not the kidneys. Hardly surprising, since they stink." Of urine. That was what they made, after all. "What about the spleen? Is that there? Did you know spleen sandwiches are a Sicilian delicacy? Some mafia guy Sofia 'dated' made her eat one, and she puked up after."

"The spleen was still there. And Dr. Ibrahim found the same cut-marks on the ribs again. Plus there's a note in the email to say the marks were also on one of the bones found by the bridge."

"If we're not careful, there's gonna be a mass exodus. So many of the residents are only here temporarily, and who wants to wait around to become a victim? At least Twitter hasn't mentioned cannibalism yet, although I imagine it's only a question of time."

Black wrapped an arm around me as I leaned in closer to read the rest of the report, and despite the warmth, I couldn't help shuddering. The dismemberment hadn't been a particularly professional job. Somebody had cut both femurs and both humeruses right through, close to where they joined the torso. Dr. Ibrahim's best guess was a hacksaw, although he still had to run more tests on that.

And the dismemberment was a new thing—Carmela's skeleton had been intact, and all the other bones that'd turned up had been whole.

"Why start chopping up corpses now? Ease of disposal?"

"Ease of disposal would make sense. The fence around the oxidation ponds is six feet high. It'd be difficult to haul a whole body over. And smaller pieces would be easier to hide."

"They'd also fit better in a stock pot."

"I'm not sure about cannibalism. It's rare. A tabloid money spinner."

"Do you have a better idea?"

Black fell silent, staring at a sliver of moonlight that fell across his notes on the wall opposite. He was wearing his thinking face. What was going on in his brain? I'd learned to read him quite well over the years, but parts of his psyche were still a mystery to me.

Finally, he smiled. "As it happens, I do."

CHAPTER 31 - BLACK

"WELL?" EMMY ASKED, and Black suppressed a chuckle at his wife's impatience. How long should he make her wait?

She turned the bedside lamp on, and he blinked as light flared against his retinas. "It's just a theory."

But one that made sense and slotted so many of the puzzle pieces together. In fact, he was kicking himself for not having thought of it sooner. The sun had turned his brain soft while Emmy turned other parts of his body hard, neither of which was conducive to running an efficient investigation. He wouldn't change his new life with her for the world, but sometimes, just sometimes, he missed the ease with which he used to be able to focus twenty-four-seven rather than a mere twenty-three-and-a-half.

"Tell me already."

Rather than answer, Black got up, turned on the ceiling light, and studied his wall of notes. Yes, it *did* fit.

"What are the three main motives for murder?"

"Money, sex, and revenge. But don't discount the occasional lunatic."

"I'm not discounting it, just saying that it's statistically unlikely." *A money spinner.* "What do kidneys, hearts, and livers have in common?"

"Uh, they're all vital for life? Although a stab wound to the liver is reasonably survivable, and a stab to a kidney needs a follow-up wound to be effective too."

"Go back to the first part. Vital for life. Kidneys, hearts, and livers are transplantable. They've got an aftermarket value, if you like."

"You think someone's stealing organs for transplant?"

"It's more likely than a freak making offal pie. Think about it—all the victims were young and healthy, taken from an area with a transient population and a lax police force where their disappearance would be unlikely to cause a ripple. We know Duncan had organs missing, and the damage to Carmela's abdomen was worse than to the rest of her body. Those knife marks weren't from stab wounds; they were from organ removal."

"Hence the halothane. They couldn't have risked stabbing a victim in case it damaged the goods."

"And we've got other medical connections—there's the surgeon's knot, and we know that Gosia and Carmela visited the same hospital. Want to make a bet that Duncan got treated there too?"

"But where are they doing these transplants?" Emmy asked. "Surely if people were coming on holiday to Dahab and going home with new kidneys, there would've been rumours of a black market? And the Dahab International Medical Center might be okay for minor injuries, but we've snooped around it, remember? The security's crap, and unless they're hiding a world-class transplant team in the basement, they're not equipped to switch out a heart."

"The transplants wouldn't necessarily have to be

carried out in Dahab. Sharm airport's an hour away, and we already know the officials there'll land private planes for a backhander, no searches, no questions asked. Or they could transport the organs by boat. Israel, Saudi Arabia, and Jordan border the Gulf of Aqaba, and they've all got money."

"Fuck. It *does* fit."

"We need to focus back on that hospital."

"They must be stealing to order. I mean, if they killed someone, harvested the organs, and then they weren't a match for the recipient, it'd be a waste of time, wouldn't it? And they wouldn't get paid."

"No, they wouldn't. We've got a rogue organ broker with access to inside information."

The question was, what information did they need to obtain? How did organs get matched to recipients? Black needed to do some research. What time was it? Just after eight p.m. in Virginia. He picked up the phone.

"Dan, I need you to find me a transplant surgeon."

This was the worst part. That point in an investigation when you knew where you were going, but getting there was like crossing a minefield—slow, tedious, and liable to cause harm if you made the wrong move. The perpetrator had to be unsettled, and if they acted too quickly, they could scare him off. And Black considered it was more likely than not that the suspect was male. Few women could manhandle an uncooperative body into a vehicle, let alone drag one over a reef.

Thanks to Emmy loading a backdoor into the

network on her visit to the medical centre, Mack had got them a list of employees. Fifty-three names. Only one appeared on Gosia's customer list, a man named Timo Bergeron, and he would take priority. Black had tasked Khaled with finding background on the rest, and the young cop was also primed to notify him when Duncan's wife had been informed of his death, which was supposed to happen this morning thanks to Black passing on details of the man's identity yesterday evening. Then they'd ask her whether he'd visited the medical centre.

Mack had gotten ahold of Bergeron's schedule, and he'd been rostered onto the late shift today—four p.m. to midnight. She'd found his address too, and Google Earth showed a single-storey villa with a small garden not too far from the Black Diamond Hotel. Perhaps they should've brought that stray home after all? Walking a dog was a good way to surveil a property without attracting attention. In that neighbourhood, they'd get some strange looks if they sat outside in a vehicle.

"How do you feel about jogging?" Black asked Emmy.

"In general, or today specifically?"

"I want to take a look at Timo Bergeron's place."

"I'll get my trainers." Emmy paused a moment at the door to the bedroom. "Dr. Bergeron. Dr. B. The guy with no stamina in the filing room was called Dr. B. Reckon it's the same person?"

"The only other doctor who might fit is Dr. Badawy."

"That sounds Egyptian, and our Dr. B didn't. If it *is* the same guy, it could explain how he's been able to lure the female victims into his lair, wherever that is."

"Generous equipment?" Black recalled the nurse's comment about the man's size that he'd overheard. No, size wasn't everything, but Emmy certainly seemed to appreciate it.

Except his wife doubled over laughing. "No! I just meant that if he can charm a nurse into the filing room when they're meant to be working, he wouldn't have much trouble convincing a woman to go for a drive with him."

"Yes, of course. You're right."

As Emmy got changed, Black mused about Gosia's travels on her last day. One of the anomalous routes had her going from Timo Bergeron in Dahab City to see Carmela at Happy Fish, then back to Dahab City. At least, that's what they'd assumed. *Assumed.* There was that dirty word again. Gunther said Gosia had spoken to Carmela, but he hadn't said where. Nobody saw Gosia at the restaurant, and what was more, nobody had seen Carmela either. What if Carmela had run into Gosia in Dahab City and given her the order there?

A possibility, and one he was annoyed at himself for not thinking of before. And if it was true, it raised the question of what Carmela was doing in Dahab City in the first place. Could she have known Bergeron?

While Emmy hunted for her tennis shoes, he called Aurelie.

"It's Black. Do you recall Carmela mentioning a man named Timo Bergeron?" No preamble. He didn't have time for that today.

"Uh, no? Who is he?"

"A doctor at the Dahab International Medical Center. Ring any bells?"

"No. I mean, I'm thinking, but I honestly don't recall her mentioning the name or a doctor."

"Did she spend much time in Dahab City?"

"There's a pottery shop over there she liked. Youssef used to complain about her buying too much of it, but he still kept it all after she died." Aurelie choked softly. "I honestly can't believe she's gone."

"A pottery shop? That's it?"

"Does that help?"

"Maybe. I'm not sure yet."

His next call was to Gunther.

"It's Charles Black."

"Ah, Mr. Black. How are you and your wife?"

"We're fine." Why did people bother with small talk? "When you asked Carmela about the final order she made for vegetables with Gosia, did she specify where she was when they spoke?"

"Why? Is it important?"

"I'd appreciate if you could just answer the question."

A moment of silence, and Black waited the man out. Sometimes, people needed time to think.

"No, I don't believe she did say. I just assumed Gosia came to the restaurant as usual."

Assume. That nasty little word. "Thank you."

"Do you have any more questions?"

"That's it for now."

Dahab City was as far from being a city as you could get—comparing it to a city block was generous, and the place was a rabbit warren of unnamed streets and alleyways. Many of the homes there were surrounded by high walls, and Bergeron's was no exception. Fragrant jasmine perfumed the air as Emmy and Black stopped outside, Emmy gasping for breath convincingly with her hands on her knees. There were advantages to being over six and a half feet tall—when Black stood on tiptoes, he could see into Bergeron's yard.

"Somebody's home."

A shadow had just walked past the kitchen window. The figure carried on into the next room, and as the man passed a set of patio doors, Black got a better look at him. Middle-aged, balding with a slight paunch, Bergeron came across as unremarkable upon first glance. But so many monsters did.

"Is it him?" Emmy asked.

"It's a male."

Did a woman live there? Any children? The washing line held lightweight men's pants, collared shirts, and boxer shorts. No mess in the tiled yard that could indicate a dog. He scanned the roofline but didn't see any security cameras or an alarm box. The locks looked like generic mass-produced shit, the type that could be opened in seconds by anyone proficient with a set of picks.

"I'd say on first impressions that he lives alone, but we should talk to a neighbour to make sure. And when I say 'we,' I mean 'you.'"

This was another occasion when Black's size and gender both worked against him. Men were intimidated, and while women ordinarily fell over themselves to flirt, especially if they found out the size of his wallet, they'd be understandably wary in this climate of fear.

He didn't need to explain that to Emmy. They'd been together for long enough that they followed each other's thought processes even if they didn't necessarily agree with them.

"Sure. Now?"

"Why not? We're supposed to be leaving in two days."

"Don't remind me."

Alleys bordered Bergeron's villa on three sides in this maze of an enclave, but the fourth side backed onto another property, a smaller home that didn't appear to be so well kept. Paint peeled off the metal gate, and it let out an ear-splitting screech as Emmy pushed it open.

"Wish me luck."

Emmy didn't need luck. She had training and experience on her side.

Black listened from the sidewalk as she spun a story to the lady who answered the door about wanting to find a property to stay in long-term and taking a fancy to her neighbour's place. Did the woman know whether it was a rental? Oh, it was? Any chance it would be available soon?

A cat leapt onto the gatepost and mewled at Black just as the call of the muezzin rang out from a nearby mosque. Almost midday, and time for prayers. A group of Egyptians walked past, and Black pretended to pet the animal for a moment, but when another half-dozen men meandered in his direction, he decided to go for a jog around the block until Emmy was finished. No point in drawing attention to himself.

On his second circuit, Emmy slipped out of the gate and joined him.

"Fucking hell, she's got seventeen cats. If I'd stayed any longer, she would've forced me into adopting one."

"No more pets. What did she say about Bergeron?"

"He's lived there alone for the last two years. No girlfriend or wife, but occasionally she sees women arriving."

"Does she see them leaving?"

Emmy snorted out a laugh. "Not often. Apparently, they stay until late and she sleeps like the dead. Should I try talking to Bergeron?"

"Not yet. I'd rather stay off his radar until we've got more information."

Chapter 32 - Black

MORE INFORMATION CAME through right after lunch. Emmy and Black had raided the hotel buffet and carried plates of food to their terrace to discuss the latest developments when Black's phone rang.

Did Dan have good news?

"It's me. I've got a colleague of Dr. Beech's here. Gavin Newby—he's a transplant scientist."

Colin Beech was a doctor at Richmond General, their local hospital back home in Virginia. He'd do anything for a donation to the hospital's charitable fund, and through the years, Emmy and Black had handed over so much cash that the new paediatric wing was named after them. Finding a tame transplant expert to answer their questions at seven a.m. was nothing for Colin.

"Great. Can you put him through?"

Once the introductions had been made, Black started with his questions. "Hypothetically speaking, if I wanted to provide body parts to order for transplant, what tests would need to be done in order to establish a donor was suitable?"

"That's an easy one. You'd need to ensure the blood types match. If they don't, the organ'll turn black and die within days no matter what you do."

"That's it? Blood type?"

"Careful tissue matching can help the organ to last longer, but the risk of rejection can be controlled with drugs. You'd want to ensure your donor was healthy, but basically, the answer is yes. As long as the blood types match, the transplant can go ahead."

That was more straightforward than Black had imagined. And what had been on Carmela's invoice from the hospital? That's right—a fee for a blood test. Black glanced at the glass beside him and wished he hadn't poured karkade to have with his lunch. The dark red colour was a ghoulish reminder of the case.

"Okay, so let's say a match has been made—what happens next?"

"A surgeon would need to remove the appropriate organs under sterile conditions, and if the donor and recipients weren't in the same hospital, which is the most common scenario because organs travel easier than sick people do, those organs would need to be packaged for transport."

"How would you package them? Do you need a specialised container?"

"Not at all. You store the organ in a thick plastic bag, then place that inside another bag filled with melting ice. Anything colder damages the organ. Then you just need to secure the whole lot in an insulated container. When I worked in London, I'd ride across the city on the Tube carrying organs in a picnic cooler. Nobody batted an eyelid. Of course, the bureaucrats have put more rules in place now, but that's how we used to do it."

"How long will an organ survive outside the body?"

"You're talking six to eight hours for a heart or liver, but kidneys can go seventy-two hours. We fly a bunch of our leftover kidneys to the UK."

"How about the Middle East? Do you ever send any there?"

"No, they play by their own rules. The Egyptians provide a lot of living kidney donors."

And most likely dead ones, judging by what they were currently dealing with.

"Who do they provide them to?"

"It used to be the Israelis. They had a thriving market for organ tourism until the government banned it. Of course, it hasn't disappeared completely, just gone underground. And the Saudis have problems with renal failure due to poor immune systems, so it wouldn't surprise me to find some of the Israeli outfits have moved across the Gulf. The Arabs have plenty of money."

They sure did. Blackwood had run a training program for a contingent of Saudi troops two years ago, and their men were less competent than the Egyptians. They turned up late, did the bare minimum, and then fucked off again. Plus they couldn't shoot for shit. When Blackwood declined to extend the contract, they offered to double the fee, then triple it. The answer was still no.

"Do you have any specific information on brokers or surgeons who might be involved in the black market?"

"Oh, no, we're strictly above board here."

"I wasn't suggesting for a moment that you weren't. But sometimes people hear rumours."

"The Israeli government's crackdown was well-documented. Other than that, it's just talk at conferences. Friend of a friend, that sort of thing. I could ask around if it would help?"

"We'd be grateful. And please give my regards to Colin."

"I'll do that. He asked whether you'd be willing to consider a donation to the charity raffle at the staff Christmas party?"

"No problem—just get him to call my assistant, and she'll arrange it."

Emmy shoved a forkful of salad into her mouth. "After that conversation, I'm glad I picked the vegetarian option for lunch."

"It's me, Khaled."

Black knew that from his phone screen.

"Why are you whispering?"

"There is a problem."

"What kind of a problem? Did you speak to Duncan's wife?"

"Captain al-Busari has found out you're working on the investigation. I think Dr. Ibrahim accidentally told him you were at the water farm yesterday. He is not happy."

It wouldn't be the first time Black and Emmy had upset local law enforcement, and it wouldn't be the last.

"We'll keep out of his way."

"He said he's coming to your hotel, and he's banned any of us from speaking to you. Gamal heard him say he would make you leave town."

They'd be leaving soon anyway, but Black didn't appreciate being told what to do by a jumped-up asshole with the investigative abilities of a cheeseburger. Which left them two main options—stay and argue it out, or give al-Busari the slip for the next couple of days. In light of the guy's incompetence, option two shouldn't be too difficult, and it was easier than having a row in the middle of the Black Diamond Hotel. There was also the possibility of phoning a friend—Black had accumulated plenty of favours with the Egyptian government over the years—but that would take time they didn't have.

"Emmy, we need to get out of here."

Now Emmy's phone rang too. "Hey, Bob ... He's where? ... Okay, we're leaving." She hung up. "Captain Couch Potato's in the lobby, and Bob says he's pissed."

At least they'd finished lunch. Emmy grabbed the bag they kept packed and ready in the cupboard beside the front door for this very purpose, one that contained enough cash, food, and clothing for the two of them to survive until the heat died down and also some extras for those little emergencies.

"Tell me again how this is a vacation?" Emmy said as they strolled along the beach, arm in arm.

"We're together, and we're on a beach."

"Tenuous, Chuck, but I'll go with it."

CHAPTER 33 - EMMY

WE HAD ONE small piece of luck on our side that Sunday. Louise Sumner, Duncan's wife, didn't like Captain al-Busari any more than we did. Apparently, he'd waltzed into her rented home in Assalah, interrogated her about Duncan's tattoo, then announced he was dead while their young daughter cried in the next room. Louise was a pretty girl in her mid-twenties with dark blonde hair and a thick Scottish accent, who clenched her fists while she talked about the captain's visit, her hazel eyes flashing with anger.

When a nervous Khaled had called Black with her address, we'd worried she might not speak to us, but there I was, crouched on the floor handing her tissues as she sobbed her heart out. Black was outside, keeping watch for any of al-Busari's men. According to Khaled, three-quarters of the department was still loyal to him, too nervous of missing a paycheck to step out of line.

"I-I-I can't believe it. They won't even let me see his body."

I squeezed her hand. "Honestly, it's not a good idea. I saw it yesterday, and that isn't how you want to remember him."

"But what if they've got it wrong?"

"Under the circumstances, it's unlikely, but you could ask for a DNA test. I know that's not what you want to hear."

"I always thought we'd grow old together. What am I supposed to tell Katie?"

That left me stumped. Kids confused the hell out of me, especially the tiny ones. "How old is she?"

"Two and a half. This was supposed to be the experience of a lifetime for all of us. You know, living in a foreign country for six months to experience a different culture. Duncan wanted to go to St. Lucia, but it was too expensive, so I convinced him to come here." She burst into a fresh round of tears. "This was all my fault."

"No, it wasn't. The only person to blame was the person who took his life."

"And you said you're trying to find them?"

I'd stuck fairly close to the truth this time. That we were two investigators who'd come to Dahab on vacation and got sucked into a mystery when we found Carmela's body. Luckily, I'd had business cards and ID in the go-bag we'd grabbed from the villa. Well, not so much by luck, more by planning.

"We're trying. Can you talk me through what you remember about the day Duncan disappeared?"

"We went on a boat ride in the morning. You know, the yellow submarine?"

I did. It was definitely yellow, but it wasn't a submarine, just a big glass-bottomed boat that took tourists out to look under the water.

"I bet Katie loved that."

"She did. We all did. Those are the last photos I'll ever have of Duncan."

"Who was on the trip with you? Anybody you've seen before?"

"The boat was nearly empty. Just us and two other families. Katie played with the English kids, but I think the others were Russian and they just kept to themselves."

I jotted down names and descriptions just in case, but I didn't think that would help us. Nobody else had mentioned the yellow submarine. Plus the police had a checkpoint at the jetty, and people arriving and leaving were carefully monitored.

"Where did you go after that?"

"Into town to get lunch."

"How did you get there?" It was a long walk, too far with a toddler in the midday heat.

"By taxi."

"Do you have a regular driver? Or did someone just pick you up on the road?" In Dahab, every vehicle was a taxi for the right price, especially if you weren't fussy about riding in the back of a truck.

"We called the guy who always picks us up. He's a bit more expensive, but reliable."

"How much more expensive?"

She named a figure double the going rate. Ouch. "I'll need his details."

"Uh, I've got his card in my purse. I'll find it."

No, that name hadn't cropped up anywhere either.

"Which restaurant did you go to?"

"The Flying Carpet. They do small portions for Katie, and the waiters are so friendly."

She was right, and we knew the owner. He had business interests in the UK too, and we often stopped to chat when he was in town. Either Black or Bob would have his number, and we could get a list of staff. But again, it didn't feel right.

"And then?"

"While we were eating, somebody came in to ask if we'd seen a girl with blonde hair going past. Apparently she'd gone missing from a hotel by the lagoon, and people were out searching for her. Katie was getting tired, so I took her home, and Duncan went to help look." Louise choked up. "That was the last time I saw him. He said he'd pick up dessert on the way home, but he never arrived. It got later and later, and he hated eating after nine because it messed with his metabolism."

"We were out looking for the girl too. I'm ninety percent sure we actually spoke to Duncan that evening."

"Really? Where? What did he say?"

"Along the promenade between Assalah and the lighthouse. We'd found the girl by then, and he asked if it was her with us."

"*You* found her."

"We got a tip-off from someone we knew."

Louise's shoulders dropped an inch. "That gives me hope. If you found her, you can find the person who killed Duncan."

"We'll do everything we can. At that point, he was heading in this direction by the looks of it, and he wasn't carrying anything. Which means he might have stopped at one of the restaurants along the way. That gives us somewhere to start."

Only one of those restaurants had been on our radar before—Happy Fish. Black had dropped Gunther down to the "unlikely" column once his sister confirmed his alibi for Gosia's disappearance, plus he drove the wrong vehicle—I'd seen him behind the wheel of a white pickup. But this was yet another piece of circumstantial evidence. What if his sister had gotten her dates confused? Or he'd borrowed the white pickup from someone? Should we take another look? It couldn't hurt.

Carmela would have been familiar with the other restauranteurs nearby too, and if I recalled correctly, several of them had ordered produce from Gosia. But so far, none of them had a medical connection. At least, not one that we knew of.

Hmm... The scenario could fit. Snatching a grown man off the street would have been tricky, even in the dark, and the only way I could see it happening was if he got shoved straight into a vehicle. But if a friendly waiter invited him into a quiet restaurant? Most people along that strip sat at the tables on the beach, not inside where the heat from the kitchen made your clothes stick to your skin. Who would notice a struggle?

"You'll speak to them?" Louise asked. "The people at the restaurants?"

"Tomorrow morning."

Maybe even this evening, but if we were going to take a closer look at Bergeron, it'd have to be tonight while he was at work. *Tick, tick, tick.* We didn't have much time left.

"One more question. While you were in Dahab, did Duncan ever visit a hospital?"

Louise gave me a curious look but nodded. "How did you know? He got scratched by a cat, and it turned septic."

"When was that?"

"Right after we got here—around two and a half months ago."

"I don't suppose you've still got the paperwork?"

"I never throw anything away. Duncan complains—complained—about it all the time." Louise gave another hiccupping sob. "But I've got a filing system. Hold on a second." She got up, and the sound of paper shuffling came from the kitchen before she returned. "Here you go."

On another day, in another town, nobody would have given the invoice a second glance. But two things stuck out. Firstly, the blood test. Why was that necessary for a cat scratch? Secondly, the name of the doctor who'd treated Duncan: T Bergeron.

CHAPTER 34 - BLACK

DECISIONS, DECISIONS...

THE lead on the restaurants along the promenade was a promising one, but if they didn't check out Bergeron tonight, they'd lost twenty-four hours. And with the speed this case was moving, that could be a fatal mistake.

Which was why Black found himself standing outside the man's villa late on Sunday night with Emmy at his side. She'd act as sentry while he took a look around inside. He glanced both ways down the alley. Nothing. Two steps and a jump, and he was over the wall into the garden—all that time in the gym paid off on occasion, and truthfully, he much preferred being out in the field to being stuck behind his desk.

The place was in darkness as he approached, drapes drawn tightly across every window and a dim bulb glowing over the front door. So he went around the back and picked the lock by feel. If one practised enough, light was unnecessary.

Inside, he paused in the living room to let his eyes adjust to the gloom, then turned on a flashlight with a red filter over the lens. Red light didn't have the same devastating effect on night vision as white.

Black started with a cursory glance around each room, and on first impressions, the house was neat and clean. No bloodstains, no stink of bleach. No hacksaw sitting out on the coffee table. No handy copy of *Gray's Anatomy* for reference. The bathroom smelled of roses. *Roses?*

That was the first indication Black had that something was wrong.

The second was the quiet snuffle as he paused outside the bedroom door. *He wasn't alone.*

Shit.

This was what happened when things got rushed. He *hated* operating with half a fucking plan. Still, he couldn't back out now. He tiptoed forward, careful not to let his rubber soles squeak on the tile, and peered around the doorjamb. In the gloom, he could just make out the silhouette of a woman, her dark hair splayed across the pillow. Guess that was why the woman next door rarely saw Bergeron's visitors leave—because they didn't. They stayed there. On the plus side, at least she was alive.

And he'd seen enough. If Bergeron was dismembering women, he wasn't doing it in his house. The next step would be to get Khaled or one of his buddies to run surveillance, but fuck knows how that would work with Captain Cantankerous clamping down on any actual police work.

Black retreated the way he'd come, swiftly, silently, his gloved hands leaving no evidence of his visit. Emmy was pretending to talk on the phone when he reached the garden wall.

"Clear?" he asked softly.

"One minute... Okay."

Black vaulted the wall again and landed on bent knees with barely a sound. Paused to kiss his wife, then started walking.

"Well?" she asked, as she always did.

"Nothing. Unless you count the female asleep in Bergeron's bed, that is."

A normal person might have gasped. Emmy merely laughed. "Sleeping? At least you didn't have to keep passing her tissues."

According to Bob, al-Busari had stationed one man beside the gatehouse at the Black Diamond and another in front of Emmy and Black's villa. Al-Busari had also sworn Bob to secrecy, but the man clearly didn't understand the SEAL brotherhood and Bob had messaged Black the instant the asshole left.

Bob: Villa's out of bounds, as is the front entrance. I've left the north gate unlocked, and you're in room 206 tonight. The manager of the Sinai Dreams Resort next door says you can use their parking lot.

They were in Bob's truck again, just one more ubiquitous white pickup amongst hundreds. The SUV was still parked outside the villa, and there it would stay until the captain admitted defeat.

"Dinner, Diamond? It'll have to be room service, but at least we don't need to eat the rations you packed."

"Damn, I was really looking forward to a protein bar."

"Save your appetite for tomorrow morning. You'll be eating at every restaurant on the promenade."

Because now that they were the subject of a manhunt, Black's size made him stick out too much to be running around town asking questions. Emmy, on the other hand, was a chameleon, so she'd have to carry the load tomorrow while Black played getaway driver.

In their temporary lodgings, Emmy grabbed a packet of hair dye from the bag and disappeared into the bathroom. Black preferred her as a blonde, but needs must. Bradley could fix whatever she did when they got back to Virginia.

"Any preference for dinner?" he called.

"Chicken and vegetables. But get them to leave it half an hour because I want to do a few circuits first."

Emmy might mess around during her downtime, but when there was the prospect of some action, she ditched the junk food and took care of herself. She'd sleep well tonight too. Her brain seemed to have an inbuilt defence mechanism that stopped her from sleepwalking when it was essential she get some rest. Which meant Black could relax too, or as close to it as possible with a pair of cops skulking around the property. He stretched his legs and did a set of burpees before calling the kitchen. Better. The burn of well-used muscles was his second greatest addiction after his wife.

"What do you think?" she asked, stepping back into the bedroom with damp hair.

Dark brown. She'd gone dark brown, almost black, and she'd dyed her eyebrows too. With a pair of non-prescription glasses, she wouldn't be instantly recognisable.

Quite literally, Captain al-Busari wouldn't know what hit him.

CHAPTER 35 - EMMY

"IS THAT SUPPOSED to be...whistling?" Black asked on Monday morning.

I couldn't whistle. I couldn't sing either, but thankfully my shooting skills more than made up for my lack of musical ability.

"Shut up. This is gonna be a good day—I can feel it in my bones. What's the plan, kemosabe?"

"First, I need to get ahold of Bob and ask him to get my good camera from the villa. If we come across anything interesting, a phone camera won't cut it."

"No need. I'll go."

"There's most likely still a cop sitting outside, who may or may not be awake."

"Then I'll just wear my handy burka. Trust me, Chuck, I'm good at this."

"You have a burka?"

"We're in the Middle East, and *I* packed the go-bag. Of course I have a burka. Won't be long. Do me a favour and order breakfast, yeah?"

Two days left in Egypt, and we were so fucking close I could taste it. Duncan's murder had felt rushed, careless. The killer was rattled, and when people were rattled, they made mistakes. We just had to keep pushing. Bergeron, Gunther, or someone else? Before Black's shenanigans last night, I'd have said Bergeron, but now I was leaning towards Gunther. Right now, Mack and Dan were digging into their lives from afar, hunting for anything that could either finger them as a suspect or give us leverage in our questioning.

The cleaning cart outside room 104 was unattended, so I borrowed it and pushed it slowly through the hotel grounds, hunched over the handle. Most of the hotel staff wore a uniform, but we had a few Muslim women working there who preferred to wear traditional dress which included covering their faces, and we respected it as long as they were in non-customer-facing roles. My name badge said I was Menat, the goddess of fate, which seemed quite appropriate today. Although I strived to create my own path, there was always an element of unpredictability on any job.

"*Sabah al-khair*," I muttered to the cop slouched on my sunlounger. At least Zena had fed Crash. The run beneath the hutch was full of salad.

"*Sabah al-noor*," the guy replied, then focused on his phone again.

Inside, I fetched Black's camera and the battery charger that went with it, then raided the floor safe in the bedroom for goodies. My gun, a spare knife, enough cash to buy off a stable of informants...

The cop didn't even glance up as I trundled the cart past him again. Nope, he just sat there. A coiled fucking spring.

Down on the beach, the wedding preparations were well underway. Lynn and Chris would tie the knot tomorrow in a gazebo by the water, and a florist was busy securing flowers to every inch of the framework. The gauzy curtains reminded me of Zena's second dress.

Poor girl.

The prospect of taking an hour out of the case to watch Lynn and some jackass from Seattle commit to each other until their inevitable divorce didn't exactly fill me with glee. What if that hour meant the difference between solving the case and handing it over to a man who couldn't find his dick with two hands and a hooker helping?

Think positive, Emmy. We had two reasonable suspects.

"What did you get?" Black asked when I arrived back.

"The camera, a Glock 19..." Not my favourite gun—that was a Walther P88—but we'd left the best stuff in a concealed lockbox on the jet. "An extra knife, comms gear, sunglasses, the coffee machine."

"You brought the *coffee machine*?"

"I have a feeling it's gonna be a long day. Doesn't appear that the cops have been inside, which means they haven't seen your wall. You really should consider doing everything electronically."

"Let them look at it. Al-Busari needs the education."

My first destination was Happy Fish, but the place was dark. Silent. The guy sweeping the path in front of the Sweet Dreams Hotel next door said Gunther never got there before ten, which meant I had at least an hour to kill before I could tackle our new number one suspect.

Should I find a way in and snoop around? As well

as the beachside seating area, Happy Fish occupied a two-storey building across the promenade that held the kitchen on the ground floor, together with a few indoor tables and a counter for picking up takeout. Fuck knows what was on the next floor up. A slaughterhouse? The windows were filthy, covered with years of dust and grime. No cobwebs—spiders were one thing you rarely saw in Dahab.

Sweeping-dude kept watching me, which I suspected had more to do with my ass in the shorts I was wearing and less to do with me sizing the place up. In the dark with nobody around, I'd get into the building in a heartbeat, but with an audience? Tricky.

Black could hear me through a microphone built into my necklace, and I could hear him via an earpiece.

"I want to go in," I said.

"Of course you do."

On the left, the building joined to the one next door, but there was an alley on the right with room to park a car. A shabby door led inside. A good setup if you wanted to abduct somebody—knock them out in the restaurant, then bundle them straight out and into a waiting vehicle. I paused. The *swish* of a broom on stone told me sweeping-dude was still busy out the back. The door itself was secured by a simple mortice lock, and I was about to get out my lock picks when a man turned into the alley. Not Gunther. This guy was a local in chef's whites.

"You are looking for something?" he asked.

"Yes, actually. Is Gunther here?"

"Not now. He comes later."

"You work here?"

"Yes, I cook."

"Do you know where Gunther lives?"

"Assalah." The chef pointed left along the promenade. "He walks that way."

"Do you have an address?"

A shrug followed by a shake of the head. "He comes soon."

Dammit. Foiled again.

"New plan," I told Black. "I'm going to get breakfast. Do you want anything?"

Happy Fish might have been closed, but the café on the other side of the Sweet Dreams Hotel was open for business, so I plopped onto a seat and ordered an Egyptian breakfast of falafel, eggs, cheese, and ful medames—mushed fava beans, for the Hannibal Lecter fans amongst you—served up with pitta bread. When in Rome and all that.

Who worked there? What did they know?

"You want coffee?" the waiter asked. A young guy, more of a kid. He couldn't have been older than sixteen.

"I *need* coffee. And I also have a couple of questions."

He came back with an insulated jug and poured me a generous cup, then perched on the chair opposite.

"What questions?"

"Did you hear a man got killed the other day?"

"*Naam*, by the water plant? I heard."

"Yes. I'm part of an exchange program with the Dahab Police Department—you know, some of their people visit the UK, and we come over here—and I'm helping to investigate the case." I fished out the flyer with Duncan's picture. "Have you ever seen this man?"

"That is Mr. Duncan." The kid's eyes widened. "This

is who died?"

I nodded. "How do you know Duncan?"

"He came here for dinner with his family. Lunch, sometimes. He always gave me a big tip."

"As far as we can tell, he was last seen somewhere along the seafront here, walking back to Assalah. Were you working on Friday evening?"

"The day the American girl disappeared?"

"Yes."

"I was here, but I didn't see Mr. Duncan."

"Was anyone else working that night?"

"My father and my brother."

"Could we ask if they noticed him walking past?"

We could, and they didn't. The father seemed too frail to manhandle a guy Duncan's size, and the brother had one leg in a cast. A fall downstairs, apparently. I couldn't honestly imagine any of the trio committing our murders.

It was a similar story at the next two restaurants along the seafront—no likely suspects, and nobody who'd seen Duncan—and I began to get jitters from all the caffeine. Ten fifteen. Was Gunther back yet?

The door was locked, but when I knocked on the window, the chef ambled through from the kitchen and fumbled with the catch.

"He's not here yet."

"The guy next door said he came at ten."

"Sometimes eleven, sometimes twelve. There was a big group here to eat last night, and he stayed late. Maybe he sleeping?"

Should we try calling him? We had his number from earlier in the investigation, but if he *was* our culprit, I didn't want to scare him off. I was just about to consult with the oracle when his voice sounded in my ear.

"You're not gonna believe this. Zena's gone missing again."

"YOU'RE KIDDING?" I muttered, careful to keep my voice low. "Gone? *Again*?"

"Bob just called. She's not in her room, and they can't find her at the hotel."

"They've tried calling her?"

"Phone's turned off. And with everything that's been going on, they're understandably worried."

If she'd run away again, I'd kill her myself. "Any arguments this time?"

"Apparently not. But Lynn says she hasn't stopped begging for a dog, and Chris reckons there's a hundred bucks missing from his wallet."

"I bet she's come into town to look for the damn mutt." She probably took the cash to buy it a rotisserie chicken or something. "Have you tried Aurelie?"

"She's not answering. I've left a voicemail."

For a moment, my chest tightened, but then I relaxed again. Aurelie had never visited the hospital. Without a blood test, she wouldn't be on the killer's radar.

"Do you want to head over there, or shall I?"

"Let's both go. If Zena's loose in town, I want to find her quickly."

So did I. Joking aside, there was a nasty niggle at the back of my mind that Zena had been to the hospital recently. If she'd been targeted, we didn't have any time to lose. I jogged down an alley, found Black in the pickup on el-Melal Street, and jumped into the passenger seat.

"Did Bob say how long she's been missing?"

"No one's seen her since last night."

Last night? Fucking hell.

"According to the chef, Gunther worked late yesterday evening. And Bergeron had his lady friend staying." So both had been otherwise occupied.

"I'll call Khaled and get him to spread the word."

Shit, shit, shit. I hated when people close to me got wrapped up in the middle of nasty stuff. It had happened in the past with Tia, my ex-boyfriend's sister, who had an uncanny ability to get herself kidnapped with no bloody warning. Twice I'd rescued her, and the second time, I got shot in the chest. I'd been wearing a bulletproof vest, thankfully, but it still stung like a bitch.

"Khaled?" Black had the phone on speaker. "We've got another problem."

"You heard already?"

"That Zena's missing again? Yes."

"No, about the body."

My spine went rigid, and Black's knuckles turned white where they gripped the steering wheel.

"What body?" he asked.

"At the Blue Hole. A woman's body. Someone just reported it. My colleagues are on their way."

"Where are you?"

"The captain is making me update the Twitter. He says I should not have helped you."

"We're on our way to the Blue Hole. Just get

outside and look for Zena." Black hung up. "Fucking Twitter."

The road to the Blue Hole clung to the edge of the shore with the mountains on one side and the sea on the other. Occasionally, the beach widened enough for a hotel or a café, but in places, there was just a drop from the tarmac into the water.

Black floored it around convoys of scuba divers, busloads of tourists from Sharm el-Sheikh, and locals dawdling along in ageing taxis and pickups. The driver of a water tanker blasted his horn as we swerved in front of him, narrowly missing a car coming the other way. After the Canyon dive site, the tarmac ran out, and we bounced over the rocky desert. It was a good thing I didn't have any fillings because they'd have come loose.

"If this turns out to be Zena, it won't just be us her killer has to deal with," Black said. "Bob's gonna gut him."

"Well, I'll help to hold the fucker down."

Often, looking at Bob in his sandals and Bermuda shorts, it was easy to forget he'd been Black's commanding officer in the Navy SEALs. He may have lost some of his edge in semi-retirement, but he still kept in shape and went out to the desert regularly to practise shooting. I wouldn't want to face him in a fight.

The suspension rattled as Black took off over a rocky lip, and the engine didn't smell too happy either. A girl in a bikini riding a mangy camel hurled a mouthful of abuse as we roared past, missing her by inches, but Black didn't slow down until we reached the small strip of restaurants and shops that had sprung up around the Blue Hole. I was out and running before he'd stopped the vehicle.

"Hey," I called to the nearest man. "I hear they've found a body here?"

He shrugged, confused, and replied with a Russian accent. "Not speaking English."

Fine. I tried Russian. "Has somebody found a body here?"

"A body?"

"Like a dead body?" What did he want, a fucking biology lesson?

"I haven't heard that."

At the other end of the beach, I spotted a cluster of white uniforms against the sandy cliffs. Their black epaulettes told me they were Khaled's colleagues, but I didn't recognise any of them. Friend or foe? I didn't particularly want to find out. The second person I asked was no help either, or the third, but a Bedouin who'd overheard my question stepped out of a tiny supermarket.

"There is no body."

"Really? We heard from the police that there was."

"It was a jacket in the water. A woman thought it was a person and began screaming, and somebody called the police. But it was just clothing."

Oh, thank goodness. I didn't know whether to be happy it wasn't Zena or pissed because we'd wasted time driving over there. Probably we owed Bob a new transmission too. In the end, I settled for feeling relieved, and I ran back to Black, who was striding in my direction.

"It's not her. It's not anyone. Somebody made a mistake."

He closed his eyes for a brief moment. "Good.

That's good. Everyone's jumpy right now."

"We need to get back to town. Perhaps a bit slower than we came here."

It was almost as if Black hadn't heard me, but as we approached civilisation, he didn't have any choice but to hit the brakes because the traffic in front of us had ground to a halt. He cursed as we ended up parked behind a pickup filled with air tanks and scuba gear. Two Bedouin kids riding on the back hopped off and knocked on my window, trying to sell us bracelets.

"Not now, kids, okay?"

"What the hell is going on?" Black asked.

"I can't see a thing. Maybe someone hit a goat or a camel. I'll go and take a look."

Except before I could climb out, my phone rang. My heart jumped. Every call at the moment seemed to bring drama, and we desperately needed good news. An unknown number from the Netherlands flashed up on the screen, and I eased my door shut again.

"Hello?"

"Emerson Black?"

"Yes, that's me."

"My name is Beatrice Marten. You asked me about Gosia?" Beatrice spoke carefully, precisely, her English fluent and her Dutch accent thick.

I relayed the story for what felt like the millionth time that week, expanding on what I'd written in my email to Beatrice. "So we were wondering if you recall seeing her any time that week?"

"Oh, yes, of course. She took my produce order, but my box never arrived."

"Didn't you think that was odd?"

"Not really, because I saw the posters saying she'd

gone missing."

"You didn't contact anyone to say you'd seen her?"

"Should I have done that? We only had lunch. I didn't think it was important."

"You had lunch? On the twenty-seventh of June?"

"Yes, I checked my calendar. I had a business idea, and she agreed to talk with me about it."

"What kind of business idea?"

"I make jewellery, and we discussed her delivering flyers for my pieces with her produce boxes in return for a commission. But then she disappeared, and I got a contract to write for a travel blog, so I left Dahab for a while. I'll go back in the spring."

How did this fit? "Lunch would have been what, about twelve o'clock? One o'clock?"

"Around twelve o'clock. My painting class finished at eleven thirty, and I'd just got back home. If Gosia had come any earlier, she'd have missed me."

"Did you talk about anything else? Did she mention any unwanted attention? Maybe something that made her uncomfortable?"

"No, we just ate, and then she said she had to rush off to see Gunther at the fish restaurant by the Sweet Dreams Hotel because he'd promised her a big order that week."

Wait. What? "Are you certain? Gunther at the fish restaurant? Because he said she came earlier and spoke to one of his staff."

"Definitely Gunther. I know him."

"How do you know him?"

"Sometimes I ate there. He asked me to go for dinner with him once, but I said no."

"He gave you bad vibes?"

"Not really, but he was loud and I prefer women."

Fair enough. "He misjudged that one, didn't he?"

Beatrice chortled. "Sometimes men look but they don't see. Gosia didn't care for Gunther either. She hated that he served fish in his restaurant, but she viewed his custom as a necessary evil."

"I think you might have been the last person to see Gosia alive."

"Apart from Gunther, you mean?" She paused as my words sank in. "You can't honestly think Gunther killed her?"

"His name's already come up for other reasons. Why don't you think it was him?"

"I'm not sure. I think... I guess... He was always happy. Always smiley."

You know who else was always smiley? Keith Hunter Jesperson, and he killed at least eight people in Canada.

"I promise we'll look into this carefully."

"But—"

"There's another girl missing, so I really have to go. But thanks so much for calling, and I'll give you an update when I know more."

I hung up, stabbing the phone screen so hard my finger hurt. Fuck. *Gunther*? I got what Beatrice meant —he was kind of irritating, but despite the little clues pointing in his direction, he didn't give off creepy serial killer vibes.

"Gunther lied," I said. "And if he lied about the time, it means our route for Gosia on the twenty-seventh was wrong, and she never talked to Carmela—"

"And Carmela was never in Dahab City that day, therefore we wasted our time on Bergeron," Black finished. "Plus his sister's involved. She was his alibi that day."

"Murder. A family enterprise."

"I'll get Mack to shift all the Richmond team's focus to those two."

He dialled, and the ringtone filled the cabin. Five a.m. in Virginia—had Mack gone to bed yet? Left to her own devices, she was practically nocturnal.

"Hey, y'all." Mack's Texan drawl filled the cabin. "I was just gonna call."

"Why?" I asked. "Did you find something?"

"Maybe. D'ya have time to talk?"

"We're stuck in a traffic jam," I said.

"In that case... I divided the list of hospital employees into four and split the quarters between me, Luke, Agatha, and Mouse. Agatha's grandfather came from Berlin, so she speaks German, and she's got her hooks into a bunch of German databases I've never looked at, so she took anyone from the list who sounded German."

"And? What did she find?"

"One of the nurses at the hospital is married to a doctor who got suspended from the German Medical Association—the Bundesärztekammer—for ethics violations."

"What kind of violations?"

"Taking bribes from patients on the transplant waiting list."

Holy fuck! We had him. "What's the nurse's name? And the surgeon's?"

"Magdalena Fleischmann. And her husband's Stefan Fleischmann."

"Magdalena?" I remembered that name. "She was

the nurse who stitched Zena up when we took her to the hospital."

Black rested his head against the back of the seat and closed his eyes. "Magdalena. Maggie. Maggie and Stefan. She's Gunther's sister." Fuck. "We need an address for him—he lives somewhere in the Assalah section of town."

"I'll get right on it."

I opened the door again. "And I'll try to find out what the hold-up is."

Up ahead, the scuba divers had got out of their truck, shorty wetsuits dangling around their waists. Two of them were smoking as they chatted in French.

"Any idea what's going on, guys?"

"*Oui*, there's a roadblock ahead."

"A roadblock? What for?"

Please, say the police were actually doing their job for once and looking for Zena.

"Apparently, two tourists are running around impersonating police officers, and there's a rumour they were seen at the Blue Hole." He shook his head, and ash dropped onto the ground. "What kind of person pretends to be a cop?"

Ah, shit. "I have no idea."

"It's crazy, no?" He chuckled and held out a packet of cigarettes. "Gauloise?"

"No, thanks. I don't smoke." But at that moment, I was really, really tempted to start again. "Guess we'll just wait then."

Black was watching me as I hurried back to Bob's truck.

"It's bad news?" he asked.

"Yup. Al-Busari heard we were at the Blue Hole,

and this roadblock is for us."

CHAPTER 37 - EMMY

BLACK TWISTED TO look into the back of the crew cab pickup.

"What?" I asked.

"Seems we've brought Mr. Murphy along for the ride."

Ah, yes, Mr. Murphy of Murphy's Law fame, otherwise known as "what can go wrong, will go wrong."

"I've got a gun with me. Right now, I'm not sure whether that's a good or a bad thing."

If one of al-Busari's pet cops found it, they'd try to cart me off in handcuffs. "Try" being the operative word, because having the gun also meant I could shoot my way out of there. The biggest problem was the number of civilians around. The Egyptian police carried rifles, and I was willing to bet they weren't very good at aiming them.

Yes, I could easily drop the gun into the sea along with the rest of our gear, but then I wouldn't have it to shoot Gunther with. And going through the checkpoint would cause a delay. Perhaps not for me because I'd changed my appearance and had a fake passport to match, but for Black. That was the problem with looking like a living fucking god—he stuck out like a sore thumb, and new documents wouldn't help much.

"I can take a detour," he said, reading my mind. "Climb through the mountains. You need to get to Gunther's place and find Zena."

"Swimming would be faster if you went underwater past the checkpoint."

"True."

"Or maybe we should both swim? This line's taking forever, and how far is Assalah? A mile? A mile and a half?"

A twenty-minute swim for Black, and probably twenty-five for me in calm water. Today, it was choppy, but the south-easterly wind was with us and we'd be staying near the shore, away from the worst of the currents. Dammit, we were so close I could practically taste blood. The land curved, meaning we could see the Assalah shoreline across the bay from where we stood—houses, tiny dots of people moving about, and a few white boats bobbing up and down in the high tide.

What other options did we have? We could call Khaled, but he didn't have a car, and by the time he commandeered one, Gunther would've had time to reach Cairo.

"Let's do it," Black said.

I took a deep breath. This was all or nothing because when we came ashore in Assalah, dripping wet and barefoot with weapons strapped to our belts, there was no going back. The police would hunt us down. The only question was whether we could find Zena before we got slung in jail.

Black stripped down to his shorts while I thanked my lucky stars I'd worn a bikini as underwear today. I strapped on my thigh holster and checked my gun. Racked a round into the chamber. Dropped the magazine, filled the empty slot, then slammed it home again while Black swapped out our covert comms gear for something sturdier, a pair of custom-designed long-range waterproof headsets that would allow us to talk not only to each other, but to the team back in Richmond too.

"Nate?" Black said.

"What's up?"

Nate's voice came through loud and clear. The three of us would have each other's backs through anything, but Nate made no secret of the fact he thought I was a bad influence on his closest friend.

"We're about to swim a mile through the Gulf of Aqaba, then take on a serial killer while evading seventy-five percent of the Dahab Police Department. Mind being our backup?"

"Was this Emmy's idea?"

"Possibly, but only because she thought of it first."

Nate muttered something that sounded suspiciously like, "Fuck me," then cleared his throat. "What do you need?"

"Real-time information—Mack's already looking for the address we want. And possibly bail money at some point in the future."

"Man, I'm not giving you bail money. I'll come over and break you out myself." See? He had our backs. "Okay, I've got you on GPS. Are you ready to go?"

"Yes," we both said in unison.

And then everything changed.

Black and I both stared at my phone as it rang on the dash. *Zena calling.* I dove for it and answered.

"Zena?"

"Emmy?"

She was whispering. That wasn't a good sign.

"I'm here. Where are you?"

"I'm not sure." Even at a murmur, her voice trembled in fear. "Aurelie didn't message to say she'd fed Patch like she promised, and when I rang her, she didn't answer, so I came to feed Patch myself and now I'm stuck."

"Stuck where?"

"In, like, a shed."

"Where?"

"Along that path by the sea. Patch ran into this shack thing, and then I saw some men who worked for Grandpa coming towards us, so I followed her and hid inside. But then she started digging, and there's a freaking body in here!"

There weren't enough expletives in the world for this day. Motherfucking shitnuggets. Trust Zena to adopt a stray who was also a wannabe cadaver dog. Had the mutt been watching *CSI* with Khaled?

"Leave. Just open the door and run."

"I can't! The people who live in the house came back, and they keep walking across the yard carrying stuff. I think they're loading a car. There's a woman, and she's the nurse who stitched my forehead." Zena's words came out garbled, panicky, and I couldn't blame her.

"Keep away from the windows."

"And one of them's smoking right outside. I can smell it."

Black grabbed his camera and got out, using the zoom lens to scan the shoreline.

"Okay, stay where you are. We're on our way, but we're gonna have to swim."

"*Swim*?"

"It's a long story."

"I've got smoke," Black murmured through the open window. "There they are. Surprise, surprise—it's Gunther. Plus the sister and another white male."

"We know where you are," I told Zena. "We're coming to get you."

"It's not only a car they're loading," Black said. "It's a boat. A small walkaround, twenty-five feet or so, and I don't like the look of those two outboards. Suspect three's just carried a suitcase on board. He's Gunther's brother-in-law, I presume."

They were making a run for it, which was both a curse and a blessing. At least if they left, Zena would be safe. We'd just have to catch them afterwards, and if they were heading for Israel or Saudi Arabia, that could be a tricky task. Saudi was closed off and challenging to move around in, whereas Israel had some of the best-trained forces in the world. I'd dated an Israeli guy once, and in between screwing him and eating in fancy restaurants and posing in the buff while he painted me, I'd learned more ways to torture a man than I'd ever thought possible. No, I didn't want to go to either of those countries if there was a way to avoid it.

A dog barked in the background, and Zena's terrified voice whispered, "Oh no."

More barking followed by a yelp, the *thud* of a door, and Black's all too audible, "Fuck," told me everything I needed to know. Zena had been caught.

Chapter 38 - Black

IN THE GRAND scheme of things, a mile wasn't far, but stuck on the other side of the bay, watching helplessly as Stefan Fleischmann marched Zena over the reef and onto the boat with what looked like a knife digging into her back, that mile might as well have been an ocean. In front of Emmy and Black, the traffic inched forward at last, but it was too little, too late. Even if they reached the front of the line and drove through the roadblock in a hail of bullets, they wouldn't make it.

Black had to hand it to Gunther and co. They'd picked the perfect location for their killing spree, and even their getaway seemed well-planned. That type of boat had a top speed of forty-five knots or so, fast but with a shallow enough draft to float right over the reef at high tide so they could load their unwilling cargo right outside the back gate. They'd still have to die, obviously, but there was a certain admiration there.

While Black watched the scene in the distance, Emmy was scheming. He recognised that furrow in her brow, and her devious mind was the reason she'd managed to head up Blackwood's Special Projects team for over a decade without dying in the process.

"Nate, are there any satellites over the Gulf of Aqaba that can track a small boat and find out where it goes?" Black asked. "Best guess is that it's heading for Israel or KSA."

Security wasn't so tight along the Saudi coastline since there was a far greater distance for the authorities to patrol, but Black recalled the Star of David he'd seen Gunther wearing when they first met. The family might have more contacts in Israel.

"I'll check."

Emmy climbed onto the hood, scanning the vehicles around them. What the hell was she doing? Looking for a motorbike? Because he'd already done that and come up empty.

"Nate, go through my contacts. There's a cop called Khaled. Tell him you know me, and explain the situation. Get him to go to Gunther Krause's home in Assalah and secure it as a crime scene. And we need the jet ready at Sharm el-Sheikh airport."

Emmy leapt down. "Bring your wallet, and grab an air cylinder off that truck in front."

What? Black hesitated for a second, but only a second. He knew better than to question his wife. There were times in life you just had to do what you were told, and this was one of them. He'd get his own back in the bedroom later, assuming they survived that long.

But he was curious about what the hell she was doing. He grabbed a cylinder, ignoring the shouts of the Frenchmen who owned it, and jogged after her.

She stopped beside a truck three vehicles behind theirs.

"Hi." Her smile was more cunning than friendly. "We need to borrow some of your stuff."

She didn't wait for an answer, just strode to the back of the pickup and began unloading. Black realised what she was up to, and he would have kissed her if they weren't so short of time.

"Hey, what are you doing?" the guy in the passenger seat yelled. "You can't take that." He leapt out, a big man, only two or three inches shorter than Black, but when he saw the gun strapped to Emmy's leg, he threw his hands up and backed away. Smart move. "On second thoughts, take whatever you want."

Black zeroed the camera in on the boat once more. It was moving slowly away from the shore, but he only saw three figures on board—Stefan, Magdalena, and Zena. Where was Gunther? He caught sight of him walking back into the villa. Why wasn't he going with them?

"Nate, when you speak to Khaled, get him to put out an APB—or whatever the fuck they call it in Egypt—on Gunther Krause. He's stayed behind. Consider him dangerous."

"Got it."

Black used the air cylinder to inflate the kite sails Emmy had dragged from the truck. With a foot pump, it took a couple of minutes, but thanks to the magic of compressed air, they were rigid in seconds. The driver of the truck had climbed out too by then, and Emmy reached for Black's wallet.

"Here's three thousand bucks and our car keys. Buy yourself some new equipment, and I'd be grateful if you could drop our truck back at the Black Diamond Hotel."

The smaller man stared at the money in his hands. "Are we being Punk'd?"

"No, honey. Tell the hotel staff Emmy sent you, and they'll give you lunch."

Black strapped on the harness, tightening it because the owner clearly didn't go to the gym. A small crowd gathered as they connected the kite bars and lines, but nobody followed them as they grabbed their borrowed boards and ran for the sea. A quick glance towards Assalah showed Stefan's boat going east rather than north, which meant they were heading for Saudi Arabia and not Israel.

Emmy's idea was genius, but they also had the weather on their side. The wind blew towards Saudi's Hijaz Mountains, hazy on the other side of the gulf, and farther out to sea, the swell grew higher. The boat might have a top speed of forty-five knots on paper, but it would have to ride the waves while Emmy and Black could skip between them.

With seventeen miles between them and Saudi Arabia, they'd catch their target.

"Nate, we're riding kiteboards after the boat," Black said. "Call Bob and get him to follow us in the *Blue Tang*. Tell him Zena's on board."

"For a moment, I thought you said you were chasing a boat on a kiteboard."

"It's fun. You should try it sometime."

"Was that Emmy's idea as well?"

"Most definitely."

Shouts came from behind them, and Black glanced over his shoulder long enough to see half a dozen white-clad idiots waving at them from the roadblock. He turned and waved back. Sayonara, assholes.

Emmy cleared the chop with Black right behind her, and they settled in for the ride. The boat started off as a speck, but it grew bigger, not smaller, as the minutes passed. He didn't want to catch up too fast.

Somewhere right in the middle of the gulf would be ideal, out of sight of prying eyes from both sides.

Nate's voice came through his earpiece again, breaking up slightly as Black dodged a wave.

"Khaled's somewhat hesitant."

"He still has issues with authority."

"Doesn't respect it?"

"No, scared of disobeying. Tell him to make a damn decision—does he prefer bureaucracy or justice?"

"Got that. Bob's on his way to the jetty, and Mack's on hand to direct him." Coffee cups clinked. "Thanks, Sloane. Anywhere there's fine."

Did Black wish he was in Virginia sipping Colombian roast from a china cup? No, he didn't. Chasing criminals across the sea was far more entertaining, and judging by Emmy's grin, she was enjoying herself too.

"Are you having fun yet?" she shouted.

"Now, *this* is a vacation."

Black saw the moment Stefan and Magdalena realised they had company. Magdalena's mouth dropped open, and she whacked her husband on the arm so he turned too. Zena tried to get up from her seat, but Magdalena shoved her back down and yelled at her.

"What the hell is she doing?" Emmy shouted.

"Beats me."

Magdalena was struggling with the suitcase Black had seen them carrying earlier, trying to hoist it into her arms. Was she planning to lighten the load? Because one suitcase wouldn't make much difference, even if it did look heavy. What the fuck was in it?

He cut his eyes sideways to Emmy, but she shook

her head. She didn't know either.

Magdalena finally heaved the suitcase onto the side of the boat, where it teetered for a moment before toppling overboard.

"There's someone in it!" Zena yelled, only to be silenced by a backhand from Stefan.

What the fuck?

Emmy and Black didn't have to discuss it. Each knew the role they'd play. Black was stronger in the water, so he ditched his kite, kicked his board away, took a breath, and dove after the sinking suitcase.

Emmy? She jumped a wave and carried on to the target.

CHAPTER 39 - EMMY

WELL, AT LEAST we knew how the sick fuckers had transported their victims. Suitcases? In Dahab, those wouldn't warrant a second glance.

Stefan jammed the throttle open, and the boat slammed bow-first into a wave. Nice driving. The jolt unbalanced Magdalena, who pitched forward onto a seat before righting herself and staggering to the stern.

"Come any closer and we'll kill the girl," she yelled, kneeling on the seat and spreading her arms as if that would ward me off. "I'm serious."

So was I. I pulled up alongside the stern, jinked sideways, used the kite to jump out of the water, raised my legs, and hit Magdalena square in the chest with the kiteboard. She made a satisfying splash as she landed in the sea.

One down, one to go.

I left Magdalena choking on salty water and quickly released myself from the kite and board. Then I grabbed my gun. Even so, in the few seconds that took me, Stefan had hauled Zena in front of him as a shield, the point of his knife pressed against her carotid artery.

"Drop the gun or she dies!"

Oh, so unoriginal. And also unrealistic.

But I couldn't shoot him, not with the boat bouncing over waves and swinging from side to side as it carried on sans pilot. And to give Stefan his credit, he'd got Zena positioned quite well. I only had the smallest slivers of bad guy to aim for.

Zena was pale, her eyes wide, and a yelp escaped her lips as Stefan pressed the blade in harder. A thin trail of crimson ran down her neck.

"You can't win!" Stefan yelled. "You've got nowhere to go."

Wanna bet?

I fired three rounds into each outboard, and as they sputtered and died, I emptied the rest of the magazine into the bottom of the boat. Nine neat little holes, now with water bubbling through. This time, it was Stefan's eyes that went wide.

"What the hell did you do that for?"

Instead of answering straight away, I dropped the mag out of my Glock, kicked it out of the way, and took a seat.

"Maybe now we can talk about this like adults."

Or not. Stefan acted more akin to a petulant toddler as he shoved Zena to the side and came at me with the knife, roaring like a wounded bear.

He died mid-cry, crumpling into an untidy heap with a small black hole in his forehead.

"You forgot the round in the chamber, asshole."

Zena began screaming, but at that moment, with the danger neutralised, I was more concerned with checking on Black. Stopping the boat and killing Stefan hadn't taken more than a minute, but he was already a couple of hundred yards back. And he wasn't alone. Thank fuck for that.

Who was the woman with him? She turned for a second, flailing her arms, and I caught a glimpse of her face. Aurelie. *Aurelie*?

"He's dead," Zena rasped behind me, her face ashen.

"It's okay, honey. It was the best thing for him. Did he hurt you?"

Her hand went to her neck, but the trickle of blood had slowed. The knife hadn't nicked anything vital.

"It's okay. You'll be okay. But the boat's sinking, so we have to get out of here."

"Bob's on his way," Nate said in my ear. He tended to keep quiet and let me get on with my job, but he'd been doing his own in the background. "The *Blue Tang*'s just left the jetty. Nice work, by the way."

"Ta. How's the girl with Black?"

"Shaken but unharmed."

A noise from the port side of the boat attracted my attention, and I glanced across to see Magdalena splashing past, heading for Saudi Arabia. Since she still had ten kilometres to go, I figured dealing with her could wait. Zena was more important.

What did this boat have that we could use? Water lapped around my ankles as I rummaged in the locker under the rear seat and came up with life jackets and a flare gun. There was a picnic cooler too, and I almost didn't want to open it, but I had to look.

"What's in there?" Zena asked, curiosity getting the better of her despite the trauma.

"Cash." About a million bucks, if I had to guess. Black was right. Murder boiled down to three motives— sex, money, or revenge—and we'd just found ours.

Four life jackets... I wrapped two of them around the cooler and tied them in place with a spool of red cord I found, trying not to think of what else it had been used for. The water was up to my calves now, and Zena sat on one of the front seats, crying, knees drawn up to her chin, as far away from Stefan's corpse as she could get.

"Here, you need to put this on." I helped her into a life jacket. "We'll have to go into the water in a minute, but your grandpa's coming, okay?"

With Zena ready, I heaved Stefan's limp form into an empty locker and tried to shut the lid. Damn the guy for being so porky. I jumped on it a couple of times—don't judge me, he fucking deserved it—and finally the latch caught. I didn't want his bloated body washing up on a beach in the next few days because some awkward sod would ask questions about the hole in his skull.

Black was nearly at the boat now, swimming on his back while he towed Aurelie along. She'd gone silent, and that worried me more than Zena's quiet sobs.

"We need to put this on her." I grabbed the remaining life jacket. Black and I would be fine without. The water temperature was in the mid-twenties—or the mid-seventies in Black-speak—and Bob was on his way.

The water on board had passed my knees and was lapping around Zena's ass on the seat as I reached under Aurelie's armpits and hauled her onto the edge of the boat. It'd sink soon, but she'd be able to rest for a minute or two.

"Are you okay here?" Black asked, glancing towards the Saudi Arabian shoreline.

"Yup. Go for it."

Black took off after Magdalena, his arms slicing cleanly with each stroke, as at home in water as he was on land. I almost felt sorry for the bitch. Drowning was a horrible way to go.

But enough about her. I wrestled Aurelie into the life jacket and cinched it tight just as the boat started to go under.

"Won't it suck us down?" Zena asked, suddenly panicked. "I saw *Titanic*."

"It's not big enough. Just relax and float, okay?"

"Bob's ten minutes away," Nate told me.

Zena kicked her legs a bit as her seat disappeared, but when I gave her what I hoped was an encouraging smile, she stilled and did as she was told for once. The cooler floated free, but I'd tied a length of cord to the handle like a dog leash, so I was able to keep hold of it while it bobbed about like an oversized cork. Aurelie still worried me. She'd gone limp and kinda grey.

"How are you feeling?"

"I thought I was dead," she whispered, almost too quietly for me to hear. "I thought I was dead and no one would ever find me."

"You're not dead. An hour, and you'll be back on dry land."

"He said he'd cut me up. I heard them talking. He said he'd cut me up because they'd already sold my heart."

A wave washed over her, and she spluttered, squeaking in fear. I grabbed her hand, and the last tiny piece of the puzzle slotted into place when I caught sight of her bracelet. Her medical alert bracelet. I flipped over the tag. *Aurelie Butler - Blood group AB+ - Allergic to gummy bears*. No next of kin. She wore her blood group on her freaking wrist for all to see.

A white dot appeared over the next crest, and I raised my head to get a better look. Was that the *Blue*

Tang? Say it was the *Blue Tang*.

"Nate, we've got a boat approaching from the west. Is that Bob?"

"Hold on. I'm not hooked into his GPS, but I'll get his coordinates." Twenty seconds passed. "That's him."

Thank fuck. I fired the flare gun into the air, then settled back to wait.

CHAPTER 40 - EMMY

"WHY DID YOU leave the hotel, Zena?" Chris asked, hands on his hips. "Do you realise how much trouble you've caused?"

Five minutes, we'd been back at the Black Diamond. *Five minutes.* Did the man have no tact? Lynn rushed forward to hug her daughter while Chris kept tutting.

"The whole of the staff's been out looking for you. Lunch is late. Rooms haven't been cleaned."

"I left a note," Zena said.

A note? Good grief.

"Where?" Chris wasn't giving up. "I didn't see any note."

"I pushed it under Emmy's door."

The door of the villa we weren't in. Brilliant.

"That's just not good enough. You need to apologise to each and every person whose time you've wasted today, and you can start with your grandfather."

Outwardly, Black was calm as he held Aurelie up, but his gaze had hardened. He was itching to kick Chris into the swimming pool, as was I.

"Zena saved a woman's life today," I said. "She deserves some thanks for that."

"Whose? Whose life?"

Aurelie spoke up, the first word she'd uttered since

she got off the *Blue Tang*. "Mine."

Chris looked her up and down. "Who are you?"

Bob appeared, having parked Sondra's SUV and found a pile of blankets. I gently took Zena's damp towel and wrapped her up in something warmer. Although the sun was up, there was a danger of both girls going into shock, and the last thing either of them wanted to do was visit the hospital.

We'd spent the trip back going over our story, that terrible moment when Stefan and Magdalena, having held us at gunpoint, sabotaged the boat with us still on board and took off in a RIB with an accomplice from Saudi Arabia who'd come out to meet them. Where were they now? We had no idea. None whatsoever.

"It doesn't matter who she is," Black told Chris. "What matters is that you're behaving like an asshole to two women who've been through enough today."

"Who are you calling an asshole?"

"Do I have to spell it out for you?"

"How dare you tell me how to speak to my daughter?"

"She's not your daughter."

"In two days, she'll be as good as," he snapped. Zena broke free of my arm and ran towards the villa, gulping back a sob. "Now look what you've done."

What *Black* had done? With that remark, Chris made it all the way into my top ten of self-absorbed douche-canoes. But I didn't stop to congratulate him—Zena was more important, and I jogged after her. By the time I reached the terrace, she'd retreated into Crash's run, and the bunny was sitting in her lap as she sniffled.

The cop on guard outside the villa reached out an

arm to stop me from going any farther, but I just shrugged a lot and jabbered at him in Italian. Since he was looking for an English woman, he shrugged and let me past. I crawled into Crash's palace and wrapped an arm around Zena's shoulders.

"I hate Chris," she said. "He's a giant dick."

"Can't disagree with that. Is he like that all the time?"

"At home, it's not so bad. He mostly ignores me. I'm only his 'daughter' when it suits him." She used finger quotes around the word. "Like the time his work held a family quiz night and I knew all the answers. We won a five-night vacation in Miami, but he left me behind and just took Mom. Then when they got back, he complained I'd used his credit card to order a pizza. It's not my fault I memorised the number."

Getting pizza in seemed like a perfectly reasonable move to me.

"Do you want me to try speaking to your mom?"

"She won't listen. I already tried that, and she just says I'm being melodramatic. But Chris is always nice to me in front of her. Today's the first day he's behaved like a total jerk while she's watching."

And I'd seen her face. She hadn't been impressed. There was a glimmer of hope, but I hated to leave anything to chance, and we only had one day until the wedding. I made a mental note to call Mack—if she'd dug up anything I could use as leverage, maybe I'd be able to convince Chris to go easier on his soon-to-be stepdaughter.

"I'll see if there's anything I can do, but you need to play your part too."

"I always—"

"Shh. Let me finish. Chris is a grade A twat, but he was right about the note. Why didn't you ask somebody to go with you?"

"You weren't there, and I couldn't find Grandma or Grandpa, and I figured if I asked Mom and Chris, they'd stop me." She wasn't wrong about that. "And I don't know what happened to Patch." Another sob. "Stefan kicked her, and she ran away."

"We'll find her. But Black and I are in a teensy bit of trouble with the police at the moment, so we have to fix that first."

"What kind of trouble?"

"The police captain isn't too happy that we decided to investigate the case on our own."

"But you saved my life, and Aurelie's."

"It'll get sorted out, don't worry. But you have to promise not to run off again for the next few days. Gunther's still on the loose."

Unless Khaled had staged a coup. We hadn't heard from him since Nate told him to pull his finger out, and when Black tried to call him from the *Blue Tang*, there'd been no answer. Our next task, as soon as Zena and Aurelie were settled, was to find Gunther and make his life a misery.

Zena stiffened beside me. "You think he'll come back to hurt me?"

"Honestly? No. Now that everyone's looking for him, I think he'll run like his sister. But we're not taking any chances. Promise me you'll stick like glue to either me and Black or your grandpa until this gets sorted."

"I promise."

"And Aurelie could use a friend too."

"What should I do?"

Zena seemed to be holding up remarkably well, all things considered. And while being kidnapped at knifepoint had undoubtedly been a scary experience, she'd known Black and I were on our way, that help was coming. Aurelie had been completely alone, bundled into a suitcase like dirty laundry and tossed into the sea. Terrifying didn't even begin to cover it. And at the start of this, she'd lost her best friend too. She'd need a lot of help to pick up the pieces.

"Just be there for her. Introduce her to Crash, see if she wants to watch a movie, make sure she has something to eat. We'll be back later."

"You're leaving?"

"You want me to find Patch, don't you?"

"I'll come with..." She caught a glimpse of my expression and trailed off. "I'll stay here and watch TV with Aurelie."

"Good girl."

"Can we use your villa?"

"Just let me move some stuff first." Because no way did I want them seeing Black's murder wall in all its technicolour glory. "Sit tight for a minute."

"Can we get room service?"

"Sure."

"And premium movies?"

"Yup. But stay off social media, okay?"

"Okay. Emmy?"

"Yes?"

"Do I have to wear that horrible dress tomorrow?"

Oh, I was such a sucker, wasn't I? Give Zena an inch and she'd take a mile. But it was such a hideous dress, I felt I'd be doing Lynn a favour by keeping it out of her wedding photos.

"No, you don't have to wear the dress."

"What about the first one?"

"We'll sort something out."

Great. How was I going to find a replacement dress in less than a day? I needed help. Our friendly kitesurfers had dropped Bob's truck back and were now in the dining room, hoovering up the lunch buffet like a pair of starving locusts, so at least we had our phones again. I tapped out a text.

Me: Bradley, I need some assistance.

WHERE THE HELL was Khaled? The man wasn't answering his phone, and neither was Gamal. Nobody at the hotel had heard from him either, including his cousin, who was busy pruning bushes by the tennis court.

"We need you to stay in here for a few hours while we tie up loose ends," Black told Aurelie, leading her into the villa. She didn't have any family for them to call—her father had never been in the picture, and her mother died when she was nineteen. When Black voiced the question, that had brought a fresh round of tears. Did they have enough tissues left? "Bob's going to wait outside, and nobody's coming through that door."

Bob was currently arguing with the cop who'd parked himself on the sunlounger, who wasn't sure whether to call al-Busari or arrest Black himself.

"Does 'loose ends' mean Gunther?"

"Yes."

"I trusted him. He acted like my friend, and then he...he..."

Tried to kill her. When Gunther saw Aurelie passing with food for the dog, he'd called out to say it was in his garden. Apparently, they'd had a nice chat about the pooch the previous afternoon over coffee, less than a day before Gunther revealed he was acting as broker for the Middle Eastern version of Burke and Hare. Aurelie had stuttered out the basics on board the *Blue Tang*, but the details would have to wait until later. First, Team Blackwood had to track down two missing cops and a homicidal German.

Zena managed a shaky smile when they walked into the living room. The murder wall was empty, the sheets of paper presumably torn down and moved into the bedroom by Emmy, a tattered reminder of an investigation that had cost so much for so many.

"Hey, come and take a seat," Zena said to Aurelie. "Do you want a drink? There's fruit juice or coffee, or tea, but if you want something else, I can go—" Zena glanced in Emmy's direction. "I can call somebody to bring it."

Aurelie shook her head and sank onto the sofa, arms wrapped around herself. Work was needed there. They'd find her professional help at the earliest opportunity.

"Emmy, you ready?"

"Yup. Assalah?"

"Yes. We'll have to go out through the bedroom window. There's a small situation on the terrace."

"Life's never boring with you, Chuck."

Black had expected the streets around Gunther's house to be teeming with law enforcement officials, trampling over the crime scene or at least scratching their heads, but the area was deserted. The white pickup Emmy had seen him driving was still in the driveway, but fresh tyre tracks in the sand indicated a second vehicle had recently been parked in front of it. The dark-coloured SUV Khaled had seen, Black was willing to bet.

Why had Gunther struck out on his own instead of leaving with Magdalena and Stefan?

The pickup was empty—no personal effects, no trash, no satnav that might give a clue as to where Gunther had been or where he was going. The door of the shed where Zena had hidden hung ajar, and Black checked inside. Sure enough, there was a hole with bones visible at the bottom, a neat arrangement of phalanges and metacarpals belonging to an as-yet unidentified victim. How many more would they find?

Behind Black, Emmy peered through the first-floor windows of the darkened home.

"It's quiet. Unless Gunther doubled back and hid in a closet, he's not here."

Black joined her, walking around the other side of the building to look at a tidy European-style kitchen that spanned from one end of the house to the other. Or did it? There was a discrepancy between the walls visible inside and the length of the building. Not a huge disconnect, but Black estimated there was an eight- to ten-foot difference. Suddenly, the idea of Gunther doubling back to hide didn't seem quite so far-fetched anymore.

"There's a secret room in there."

"Then what are we waiting for?"

If it hadn't been for Khaled's radio silence, Black would have held off. Perhaps asked the Cairo office to send over their RANGE-R device, a handy little unit that used radar to "see" through walls. There was a reason Black and Emmy's Virginia homes had a layer of metallised wallpaper underneath the patterned stuff

Bradley chose. Forget infrared. Those colourful pictures you saw in the movies? All bullshit. IR couldn't even see through glass, let alone brick.

But with Khaled's whereabouts unknown, time was of the essence. Emmy had a knife, and so did Black. They'd just have to improvise.

"Here." He passed his wife a pair of nitrile gloves. "Might as well go through the back door. Nobody's watching."

Emmy pulled out her set of lock picks. "Do you want to do the honours, or shall I?"

"Go right ahead."

Inside, Emmy gave the second floor a quick once-over while Black took the first.

"They left in a hurry," she whispered into his earpiece. "Clothing's strewn everywhere, but there's nothing else significant up here."

The police would have to go through the house properly at some point, but for now, Black had seen enough. Time to get into that secret room.

Which turned out to be easier said than done. It took ten minutes of searching before they found a latch hidden behind a bag of flour in a storage cupboard. Emmy crouched, waiting to spring while Black swung the door open, careful to keep the thick wood between him and anyone waiting inside.

"Fuck," Emmy whispered.

Gunther wasn't there. In fact, the tiled room was empty other than a stainless-steel table, a metal cart full of saws and scalpels, and a stack of picnic coolers that reached from floor to ceiling. They hadn't bothered to clean up after their last victim, and the metallic tang of blood filled the air. Luminol wasn't required to see the place had been used as a slaughterhouse.

"This makes Youssef's back room look positively hygienic," Emmy said before voicing the question on the tip of Black's tongue. "But where the hell is Khaled?"

They moved out, scanning the grounds before they stepped into the sunlight. A scratching noise came from the shed, and Emmy glanced at Black.

"It was empty before."

She went over to look, because of course she did, and came back with Zena's fucking dog in tow, dirt covering its front paws and the front of its snout.

"We probably owe her a biscuit or something. I mean, if she hadn't pestered Zena, Aurelie would be dead by now."

"We already have a dog."

"Well, we can't leave her behind." Emmy crouched down, and the mutt tried to lick her face. She laughed as she ducked out of the way. "Isn't she cute?"

They could have the dog argument later. Now wasn't the time, not when they were standing in the middle of a fucking crime scene. But part of Black relished the prospect of pissing off Lynn's idiot of a fiancé.

"Fine. Bring her along, but if she shits in the house, you're cleaning up the mess."

"Speaking of cleaning up messes, how are we gonna deal with al-Busari? If we do a runner, that could cause problems for Bob and the hotel."

"I've got a plan for that."

"I'm all ears."

"What's the one thing Captain *Al'abalah* values above all else?" On second thought, Captain Idiot was too tame a name for the man. Captain Wilfully Negligent seemed more appropriate.

A slow smile spread across Emmy's face as she realised where Black was going with this.

"I'll call Mack."

Zena squealed with happiness when Emmy led Patch inside, which validated the decision to bring the dog along. Even Aurelie half-smiled.

"Before you let her lick you, she needs a bath," Emmy told her. "She's been digging again."

"I'll do it."

"And I'll help," Aurelie offered.

But the joy was short-lived. They had company, and from the hammering on the door, it wasn't friendly.

"Captain al-Busari. How can we help?"

He started by jabbing a finger in Black's chest, then shook his hand in pain when it turned out to be more solid than he thought.

"You are under arrest! You've corrupted my officers, interfered in police business, and evaded capture."

"Evaded capture? I don't follow. You'll have to explain."

"You ran from an official roadblock."

"Ran? I don't think so. Traffic was bad, so we decided to liven up the wait with some kitesurfing. The wind was great today."

"I don't believe it."

"That's up to you. I can only tell the truth."

"I heard you chased a boat."

"We did come across a boat, yes. Two of our friends were on board, and they didn't look happy to be there, so we followed. A few miles out, the boat was met by a smaller craft, and the helmsman and a female accompanying him holed the boat and escaped."

"You're lying. Where are these so-called friends?"

"Right here." Black waved at the couch. "Maybe you want to ask them?"

"It happened exactly like he said," Zena piped up. "I was walking my dog when some crazy guy grabbed me and shoved me onto a boat."

"Why would he do this?"

"Who knows? He just kept talking to himself like he was loony tunes."

"It looked as if he was making a planned escape," Black said. "Even had a suitcase on board. He probably wanted a hostage or two in case things didn't go according to plan."

"Where is this man now?"

Black gave a deliberately careless shrug. "Last seen heading for Saudi Arabia. This is just speculation, but it's possible he's got something to do with all the bodies that keep turning up."

"We already have the man responsible for that in custody."

That was news. "What man?"

"Gunther Krause. Two of my men caught him this afternoon."

Two men? Khaled and Gamal? If so, then why hadn't they been in touch? And why hadn't anyone secured the crime scene at Gunther's home? Khaled knew how important it was to preserve evidence. It was policing 101, and after the last two weeks, Black had been hoping that Khaled had stepped his skills up a gear.

"Terrific. Then those men are both heroes."

"No, they are not. They deliberately disobeyed a direct order not to leave the police station, and then they stole a vehicle to chase the suspect. The owner is very angry."

"So where are they now?"

"In detention. They will be dealt with accordingly, and so will you." Al-Busari fumbled around his belt for a pair of handcuffs. "You are under arrest."

"Really? For what?"

"Impersonating a police officer."

Aurelie and Zena gasped, but Black held out his hands to be cuffed. With Gunther in custody, the danger had passed, and sometimes it was fun to fuck with a man's mind. To lull him into a false sense of security before giving him a metaphorical kick in the balls.

"Sure, let's go."

Even al-Busari looked surprised, as if he'd been expecting a fight. But this battle wouldn't be won with fists, it would be won with cunning.

CHAPTER 42 - BLACK

BLACK, KHALED, AND Gamal sat in a row on the other side of al-Busari's oversized desk while the captain read the riot act. So far, he'd broken every protocol in the book, and Emmy's laughter echoed through Black's earpiece. No, al-Busari hadn't bothered to search him beyond a cursory pat-down that missed the knife in his boot, the garrotte threaded into the waistband of his shorts, and the microphone built into the leather-and-silver bracelet on his right wrist.

The two privates hung their heads as al-Busari announced their suspension, effective immediately. Apparently, one of Gunther's neighbours saw him heading out of town, so Khaled had borrowed the nearest vehicle with the keys left in the ignition, which happened to be a souped-up truck belonging to the son of the local auto shop owner.

Gunther had made it through the first checkpoint, and Khaled had to make a decision. North or south? Recalling that Gunther was Jewish, Khaled had guessed—correctly—that he'd seek sanctuary in Israel rather than trying to flee via Cairo or Sharm el-Sheikh and headed north towards Taba and the Israeli border. They'd caught up with Gunther's SUV, rammed him off the road, arrested him, and brought him back to Dahab to face the music. Only to be detained themselves.

And Black's fate? He was to be escorted to Sharm el-Sheikh and deported.

Finally, al-Busari stopped ranting. "So? What do you have to say for yourselves?"

"This isn't a fight you want to start."

"You're a foreigner. You can't tell me what to do."

"No, I can't, but I can talk about what you've done. Have you checked your Twitter feed lately?" Ah, that delightful look of confusion. "The departmental Twitter feed. Look at it. And Facebook too, while you're at it."

Al-Busari reached for his mouse.

Mack and her team had been busy, keeping Black updated on progress as they worked. When al-Busari opened Twitter, he'd find his mentions full of hastily written but thorough articles about the bungled police investigation in Dahab, all with his name featured front and centre. The words "incompetent," "global implications," and "oversight" were mentioned. Facebook was the same, with the added benefit of comments expressing disgust at the man's actions.

Black used the key taped to the back of his watch to undo his handcuffs, but when he dropped them onto the captain's desk with a *thunk*, al-Busari barely noticed. He was too busy click, click, clicking, no doubt trying to remove the scathing posts from Facebook.

"It's called a botnet," Black told him. "For every one you delete, ten more will appear in its place."

"This cannot be happening."

"The way I see it, there are two ways of spinning this. The first is that the man in charge of the Dahab Police Department, a lifelong officer who's grown complacent over the last few years, fucked up the investigation of an organ theft ring, resulting in the deaths of a number of foreign visitors. Then, because he's scared and stupid, he tried to blame his shortcomings on the two junior officers who used their own initiative to catch one of the men responsible. How does that sound? I can have someone type it up and post it on Twitter in 280-character chunks if it makes it easier for you to digest."

Al-Busari just stared at him. It made a pleasant change to see the man speechless.

"Or we can go with option two. Captain Mohammed al-Busari joined forces with investigative consultants from the US and the UK, fostering a spirit of international cooperation while tackling a tricky case. The culprits were identified thanks to innovative detective work, and two of his brave officers improvised when one of the suspects attempted to flee, resulting in an arrest. Those two officers received promotions and recognition for their excellent work, and the captain would like to reassure all visitors that Dahab is once again safe and open for business. Personally, I prefer that story. If we go with option one, the bots might start demanding overtime pay."

Khaled and Gamal were staring at Black, mouths open. Seemed nobody had stood up to their boss before, with the exception of his wife, obviously. Meanwhile, al-Busari's face went redder and redder. What was that shade? Plum? No, plum was more purple. Maroon? Russet?

"'Local hero' has a nicer ring to it than 'disgraced former police chief,' don't you think?"

Emmy snorted in Black's ear. "Nate's just come up with a new hashtag—DismembermentInDahab. What do you think?"

"Is DismembermentInDahab trending yet?" he asked al-Busari. "If not, then don't worry. We've got plenty more where that came from."

"This is *my* town. You can't march in here with your demands and—"

"It's not your town, it's everybody's town. And I didn't march in here. You brought me in handcuffs, remember? Now you've got a chance to do something great here, to leverage this case for additional resources and training. Give Khaled and Gamal more responsibility. Let them question Krause and tie up the loose ends in the investigation. Skilled individuals make the whole department stronger, and that'd reflect well on you. Far better than the alternative."

"But—"

Black tapped his watch. "Time's ticking. You've got five minutes to make a decision."

"Will you take down all these tweets and posts?"

"We can do that. Will you promote Khaled and Gamal?"

A minute passed. Two. Black recognised the internal struggle of a man used to throwing his weight around to get his own way, but he sat it out. Al-Busari had to make the decision himself. Bureaucracy or justice.

Eventually, the captain gave a single nod. "It will be done. Now get out of my office."

It was nine o'clock when Black slipped through the door of the villa. Emmy had her feet up on the couch, a glass of wine in her hand, but when she saw him, she rose to her feet, gave him a high-five, then wrapped her arms around his waist.

"Missed you, Mr. Black."

"Missed you more, Mrs. Black."

He picked her up, but before he could push her against the nearest wall, she pressed a finger to his lips.

"Shh. We've got company. Zena's on what's left of the bed in my old room, and Aurelie's in the other one."

"What happened to the mountain of junk?"

"Bob had his staff tidy it. Honestly, solving this case was worth it just for that."

In that case... Black walked them through to the master bedroom, pausing to sweep the remains of his case notes off the bed before he lowered Emmy onto the mattress. When he kissed her skin, it tasted of sweat and seawater, the lingering evidence of the day's adventure. This should have been a vacation, a much-needed break from the chaos of their daily lives, except now they had one day left in the sun and most of that would undoubtedly be spent answering questions and attending the wedding from hell and taking care of Aurelie and Zena and the rabbit and the damn dog.

"I'm sorry," he whispered against Emmy's temple.

"What for?"

"If there was a prize for the least vacation-y vacation, this trip would win hands down."

"It's not over yet. We've still got twenty-four hours left."

And he'd spend that time taking care of her—not because she needed it, but because he wanted to. He undressed her, kissing each sliver of skin as it was revealed, then picked her up and carried her into the shower.

"Is this a subtle hint that I stink, Chuck?"

"Just shut up and give me this, Diamond."

Months had passed since he washed her hair, and he'd almost forgotten the soft moans she made when he massaged her scalp. This was sweet Emmy. The girl she might have been if life hadn't fucked with her from the moment she was born. Black combed conditioner through her hair, then squirted shower gel into his hands and started on the rest of her body. She'd gained lumps and bumps over the years, most of them barely perceptible unless you were up close thanks to skilful repairs by the best cosmetic surgeon money could buy. The faint ridge of an old knife wound on one arm. A tiny pucker of skin where a bullet had gone through her shoulder. The rough patch on her ass where she'd skidded along the highway after leaping from a moving vehicle. Every mark told a story. Their story. His dick hardened, but he ignored it until she dropped to her knees.

"Emmy, no. This is about you."

"Exactly. It's about me, and I want your cock in my mouth. Shut up and come, old man."

Ah, fuck. He loved this woman. Love. An emotion he'd never thought himself capable of until she ran into him one dark night in London all those years ago.

He leaned against the tiled wall, water cascading over his chest as she took whatever she wanted from him. He'd give her anything. *Anything.*

Until death do us fucking part.

CHAPTER 43 - EMMY

"YOU'RE NOT GONNA believe this."

Why the hell was my ex calling at...at five thirty in the fucking morning? I pressed the phone to my ear to avoid disturbing Black.

"Luke, the part I can't believe is you're calling me at this time. I'm not even awake."

"You'll definitely forgive me."

"Please, just get the talking over with. I need to sleep."

Black stirred beneath me, one arm tightening around my waist. He'd earned a lie-in with his efforts last night.

"This had better be good," he mumbled.

Yes, it had.

"Mack asked me to take a look at Christopher Holt," Luke said. "Said he was getting married to a friend of yours today?"

"Sort of. A friend's daughter."

"Well, I doubt his other wife's going to be too happy to hear that."

"His...what? What are you talking about?"

"Esther Holtz. She lives in Kansas with their teenage daughter."

"Holtz? With a Z?"

"He seems to have dropped the Z, but the rest of the

details match. Social security number, bank accounts, employment history."

Holy fuck. "How sure are you about this?"

"I'd say ninety percent. Esther tried sending a private detective after him when he skipped his alimony payments, but the chap didn't get far before she ran out of cash and the search got put on hold. Dan just called him—he'd be *very* interested in knowing Holtz's whereabouts."

"What can you send me to back this up? I mean legal stuff?" As opposed to the fruits of his slightly dodgy hacking habit.

"Court filings. A marriage certificate. The PI's supposed to be sending more info to Dan."

"Legend. Consider yourself forgiven."

I flopped back on the bed, digesting that little titbit of information. Christopher Holt was a wannabe bigamist? Bloody hell. Tempting though it was to fly Esther Holtz to Egypt and have her pipe up when the officiant asked whether anyone had any objections to the marriage, I couldn't do it. Mostly because the jet wouldn't fly fast enough, but also because I refused to embarrass Bob and Zena like that. Uh, and Lynn.

"Does this mean the wedding's off?" Luke asked.

"I hope so."

"Because I hear the stylist Bradley arranged has just landed at Sharm el-Sheikh airport with a cargo of dresses."

Ah, shit. "It never rains but it fucking pours."

Luke choked back a laugh. "And Mack found out why Gunther didn't go to Saudi Arabia, in case you want to know."

"Go on, tell me."

"It seems..." Another laugh. "It seems he got caught a decade ago trying to smuggle alcoholic chocolates through King Khalid Airport. Due to an administrative mix-up, he made it onto a plane out of there, but he got sentenced to six months in jail and fifty lashes in his absence, and there's still a warrant out for his arrest."

"Chocolates? They arrested him for chocolates?"

"I guess it's another reason to cut out the junk food."

I hung up and tossed the phone back onto the nightstand. It was too early for this. But my busy mind was already wondering whether we could somehow drop Gunther off in Riyadh with a case of champagne and half a dozen gay porn magazines.

"What was that about?" Black asked.

"We need to have a chat with Bob."

"I'll kill him. If I do it at sea, I can make it look like an accident."

Bob paced back and forth across his office, fists clenched at his sides, and I felt a tiny bit sorry for Chris. We'd printed off the worst of what Luke and Dan had sent through, and the papers were spread out across Bob's desk in a slideshow of damnation. Dan had even found a wedding photo, which was a nice touch.

"Did he tell Lynn he'd been married before?" Black asked.

"No, he did not. He said he'd been consumed by his job, but now it was time to take a step back. You're sure he never got divorced?"

"We can't find any evidence of it. And refusing to pay alimony to his ex is a low move."

Right. In a weird twist, I'd managed to stay on good terms with all my exes. I guess I figured that if I liked them enough to date them in the first place, it'd be sensible to keep them as friends. Luke was a case in point—look at the way he'd helped us this morning.

"Motherfucker," Bob muttered. "I need to find some concrete blocks and fuel the *Blue Tang*."

"We should probably talk to him first," I suggested. "And Lynn. Chris just disappearing could be awkward. What if Lynn thinks he's dumped her?"

Bob slumped into his desk chair. "Before she met him, after she divorced asshole number two, she went through a massive depression. What if it hits her again? Helping her from here was difficult. Sondra wanted to move back to the US, but this place is our livelihood, and we need to be on hand to manage it. And then there's Zena..."

"Zena won't be as upset to see the back of Chris as you think, trust me. But we need to act sooner rather than later. Lynn's supposed to walk down the aisle in six hours."

"Will you talk to her? It might be better coming from another woman."

Why me? "What about Sondra?"

"She'll be too busy removing Chris's gonads with nail clippers."

Somebody knocked on Bob's office door, and we all swivelled in that direction. The reception manager poked his head in.

"Mrs. Black, there's an Italian man with a *lot* of luggage here to see you."

"Okay, uh..." My head hurt and I needed coffee. "Hide the bags and offer him breakfast, yeah? I'll talk to him in a minute."

But what was I supposed to say? I was no good at the touchy-feely stuff. That was Bradley's domain, and it was times like this that I really missed him. There, I admitted it. I missed him.

"Emmy, how about we talk to Chris and you talk to Lynn?" Black offered. "And then I'll take you out for lunch. Just the two of us. No teenagers, no dogs, no murderous Germans."

"Can that lunch be in, say, Greece?"

Because this trip to Dahab was jinxed. Every move we took, something went wrong, and I still had to work out what to say to Lynn.

An hour later, I stood at the edge of the beach, watching as Lynn had words with the florist who'd fastened all the roses to the gazebo. That saccharine voice—it still annoyed the crap out of me.

"They're supposed to be blush pink to match the sash on my dress. These are more bubblegum."

The guy took a pace back as she turned to face him, hands on her hips. "I am sorry."

"How are we gonna fix this? The wedding starts in five hours." She glanced at her watch. "Four and three-quarters."

I stepped forward. "Actually, I've got a bit of good news about that."

"What news?"

I explained as succinctly as I could, and Lynn's

focused expression turned to devastation. She dropped the clipboard she was holding, and her eyes glistened with the telltale sign of tears.

"Here, I brought tissues."

"Are you sure? What if there's been a misunderstanding?"

"There's no misunderstanding."

Black had called me five minutes ago. He'd taken the lead in questioning Chris, and the snivelling little rat had admitted everything before Black hit him where it hurt—in the wallet. They'd let him live on the understanding that he'd pay every cent he owed in alimony, with the same amount going to Lynn in compensation. He'd also pack up her and Zena's things from his house and store them until she was ready to have them sent to a destination of her choosing. Considering who he was dealing with, I'd say he got off lightly.

Lynn chewed her bottom lip, biting it hard enough to draw blood. "I think I found a picture of her once. The wife and the daughter. Chris told me she was a colleague." Lynn laughed, but there was no mirth in it. "I guess deep down, I always thought he was too good to be true, but I just wanted a nice life for me and Zena. Oh, heck—what's Zena gonna say?"

"I think that sometimes, teenagers are more understanding than we give them credit for."

Zena was gonna have a fucking party.

I half expected Lynn to crumple onto the sand, but instead, she straightened. Perhaps she took after Bob in some ways after all.

"I'm gonna kill him."

Yup, she definitely took after her father.

"We're already taking care of it."

"No, I'm gonna pull his brain out through his freaking nose."

Whether he had a brain or not was debatable, but we'd seen enough blood this week already. Lynn turned to run off, and when I grabbed her around the waist to hold her back, she started slapping at me with both hands. Ouch! I hooked her legs out from underneath her and we both ended up on the ground, which was definitely not how I'd planned this conversation going.

"Get off me!"

"Not until you calm down."

"I'm perfectly freaking calm!" she shrieked.

"What's going on?" Zena called from the path that ran alongside the beach. "Why are you wrestling with Mom?"

"Good news about the dress. I think the wedding's off, so you don't have to wear it."

"Off? *Off*?" Lynn growled. "His freaking testicles are gonna be off."

"Your mom's a bit upset."

Zena's laughter didn't help matters. In fact, Lynn didn't stop struggling until a shadow fell over us and an Italian voice asked, "Did I hear you say the wedding's off?"

We both looked up. The speaker was tall, in his early forties at a guess, and dressed in an Italian suit that looked made to measure. A silver fox.

"Are you the stylist?" I asked.

He nodded and held out a hand. "Leonardo."

Lynn reached up and let him help her to her feet. "Yes, the wedding's off. He cheated on me!"

Technically, I'm not sure whether that was correct,

but the sentiment was there.

"Don't worry," I told him. "You'll still get paid."

"Then I should do something to earn my money." He smiled at Lynn, her hand still held in his. "Let me take you to breakfast."

"Uh, okay."

Zena and I stared after them, open-mouthed, as they walked away. A little way up the path, Leonardo dropped Lynn's hand and wrapped an arm around her shoulders instead, and she leaned into him, giggling. Well, that escalated quickly. Sometimes the heart just fucking knew, right?

"Did Mom seriously ditch Chris for an Italian stallion?"

"Sure looks that way. Let's hope he likes animals, eh?"

Epilogue

I shivered as I rushed through the door of Little Riverley, my Virginia home. Mid-January, and a cold front was passing over the eastern United States, bringing snow, sleet, and fender benders. I'd just flown in from the Caribbean, and I couldn't say I was glad to be back.

Bradley greeted me in the hallway, wearing the fluffiest boots I'd ever seen.

"What happened to your hair?" he asked.

"It's called wind. How many polar bears died to make those boots?"

"None! It's faux fur. Ishmael created them for me."

His friend Ishmael was a fashion designer, most famous for making a dress out of orange peel and hiring gymnasts to walk down the runway on their hands.

"They could audition for *Sesame Street*. How have things been?"

"Did you see the TV? That crazy German guy you caught in Egypt escaped from prison in Cairo. They caught him heading for Port Said on a bicycle." Bradley shuddered. "A *bicycle*. So sweaty."

Good grief. Couldn't he at least have taken a taxi? I

was almost disappointed they'd dragged his sorry ass back to jail because if he'd still been loose, I could've tracked him down for a little chat. Ah well. Maybe next time.

Miracle of miracles, Captain al-Busari had kept his word, and, still more concerned with his image than police work, he'd promoted both Khaled and Gamal to lieutenant. Now they headed up Dahab's fledgling investigations unit, although other than the Krause/ Fleischmann case, they'd mostly been dealing with petty crime.

The easy schedule had given them plenty of time to devote to Gunther before his trial. At first, he hadn't been keen to talk, but after Black taught interrogations 101 over Skype, the details had begun to trickle out.

Like the names of the victims.

Our last afternoon in Dahab hadn't been spent having a leisurely lunch. Instead, we'd helped to secure and process the murder scene in Assalah. DNA from fourteen people had been found there. With Gunther's assistance plus a bit of help from Dan's forensic anthropologist friend, they'd all been identified, although the only victims Gunther had shown any remorse over were Gosia and Carmela. He swore he hadn't wanted to kill them, but they had the right blood types, and Stefan had insisted. Little bro-in-law had Gunther by the balls, apparently, because he'd bailed him out when the restaurant got into debt. Happy Fish belonged to Stefan, not Gunther, and Stefan liked to throw his weight around.

Ironically, it was Stefan's pushiness that led to his downfall. Why? Because of the scarab amulets. Gosia had told Gunther the history of her little trinket, about the Weighing of the Heart and the journey to the afterlife. So when Carmela died at his brother-in-law's hand, Gunther had tucked one of Magdalena's holiday souvenirs into Carmela's bra in the hope that it would protect her too.

It didn't, of course, but it *had* helped to hint at the link between the two girls, the link that nudged us to connect the dots and gather the evidence to bring their killers to justice. Our investigation had caused the trio to panic, to advance their schedule to fulfil orders—fucking *orders*—and that led to mistakes. Who knew how long they'd have carried on otherwise, quietly bumping off a tourist here and there while they pocketed thousands in blood money?

But now the families of the dead could get closure, although we were still missing six bodies. Duncan's remains had been found—Black had called in a favour and gotten the oxidation ponds drained under the guise of maintenance—but some of the earlier bodies were still to be located. The bones Patch had dug up were the trio's first victim, apparently, but they soon realised there wouldn't be enough room in the yard for everyone.

In his interview, Gunther had cursed his brother-in-law for leaving the shed door open on the day of their attempted escape. They'd used the small building to store fuel for the boat, and Stefan had gotten careless while he was packing to leave. Good for us, not so good for them. According to Gunther, Stefan and Magdalena had disposed of the other remains in the mountains, but he didn't know exactly where. The search was ongoing.

Speaking of Stefan and Magdalena, the Jordanian

police were investigating them too. Back when they lived near Amman, there'd been several unsolved disappearances, and I knew from personal experience that parts of the Jordanian desert were desolate enough to lose a body. Magdalena's bloated remains had washed up on the Egyptian coast a week after Black snuffed her out, and taking a leaf from al-Busari's book, the police in Taba had deemed her death an accident. When Stefan's remains didn't follow, nobody looked too hard.

As for the Saudi Arabian doctor who'd purchased the stolen organs, he'd gone unpunished so far. Governments of the "donors" were pursuing him through diplomatic channels, but at the moment, the Saudi King wasn't playing ball. I'd heard a rumour that the Israelis, upset at the death of a young Jewish artist who'd been one of the Fleischmanns' early victims, were considering taking matters into their own hands.

I'd keep my fingers crossed.

"Guess Gunther didn't want to get into another car chase," I told Bradley.

"I hope he got road rash from the asphalt when they took him down. That horrible man caused far too much pain. But did you see the email from Louise? She sent a picture of Katie's first day at preschool."

Before we left Dahab, I'd offered Duncan's widow the use of our jet and Bradley's services to facilitate her move home to Scotland. We couldn't bring her husband back, but we'd been able to make her life just a tiny bit easier.

"I've literally just walked in the door."

"I thought you might've checked your messages on the plane."

"I was flying the plane."

"What happened to multitasking?"

"Do me a favour and make coffee, would you? I've been awake for eighteen hours and I've got to join a conference call before I can go to bed."

"Colombian, Kenyan, Guatemalan, Ethiopian, Costa Rican, or Jamaican?"

"Whichever one's quickest."

"Cappuccino, espresso, flat white, long black, macchiato, mochaccino, or latte?"

"Do you really have to ask?"

"Quadruple espresso, coming right up."

In the living room, I collapsed onto the sofa and closed my eyes. It'd been a long week. Black was in San Francisco, but he was flying back this evening, and we'd have a few days together before the next crisis hit.

In the meantime, I was left with Bradley and Miles, who'd come to stay in Virginia for a week. Archaeologists got vacations, it seemed. I was clearly in the wrong line of work. Miles wasn't particularly happy with us at the moment since we'd given Gosia's heart scarab to Selmi rather than handing it over to a museum, but as Black had pointed out, the amulet's job was to facilitate safe passage to the netherworld, and it wasn't going to do that stuck in a glass case.

I shared Black's view—the beetle was hardly Tutankhamun's mask, and if it brought Selmi some comfort to keep it close, then he should have it.

Everybody deserved peace.

Where was that picture from Louise? I was glad she was putting her life back together, that Katie seemed to be coping after the tragedy. And I appreciated the updates. So many times, all I saw was the bad in the world, and I craved happiness like anybody else.

And there was the picture. A snapshot of a tiny girl wearing an oversized backpack and grinning as she waved to the camera, her hair done up in neat plaits fastened by sparkly bows. Louise gave her enough love for two people.

I didn't recall much about my own first day at nursery school, just my mum shoving me off the bus and through the gates with no lunch and no idea where to go. I'd been terrified. Yes, those memories were better off forgotten, and I shoved them to the back of my mind.

Footsteps sounded in the corridor outside, and Bradley hurried in with my coffee.

"Here you go. I brought you a cookie too."

"Lifesaver."

"Ooh, you found the picture. Did you get the message from Aurelie too?"

"Not yet. Is she still in France?"

"No, Australia. Akeem *loves* her."

Aurelie had stayed in our villa in Dahab while the dust settled, helping Zena and Bob to make improvements to the town's animal shelter. Black and I figured we might as well put Stefan's cash to good use. Half would help Patch's buddies, and we'd find a way to funnel the rest to the victims' families. An anonymous benefactor had already donated twenty thousand pounds to an online fundraiser set up by Louise's friends.

But Aurelie had begun getting itchy feet, her desire to see the world battling against the fear instilled by the kidnapping. Katie might have bounced back, but Aurelie still had a way to go.

It was Bradley who'd come up with the perfect solution—a way to improve Black Diamond's well-being offering and help Aurelie to fulfil her dreams at the same time—and now she travelled between our hotels teaching yoga and meditation. The clients loved her, the staff took care of her, and I liked to think that little by little, her life was getting brighter.

"Akeem knows she's still fragile, right?"

"I explained everything, and he's taking her sightseeing in Brisbane at the weekend."

"Good, that's—"

Wait, what was this? A wedding invitation?

Together with their families, Leonardo and Lynn invite you to celebrate their marriage.

12th May at two o'clock.
The Black Diamond Hotel, Dahab.
Reception to follow.

Bloody hell, it was happening all over again.

"Did you see this?" I asked Bradley.

"See what?"

"Lynn's getting married to that Italian bloke. Maybe it'll be fourth time lucky, eh?"

"A wedding? OMG! We'll need outfits and flowers and gifts..."

"Bradley, please stop. *Please.*"

Lynn's invite was swiftly followed by an email from Zena.

Sender: Zena T
Subject: Did you see?

Mom's getting married again!

She wanted me to wear another ugly dress, but Leonardo convinced her it's important for me to express my personality through my clothing, so I'm wearing shorts instead.

Crash and Nibbles and Patch have to stay behind in Piacenza with the pet-sitter, but Leon says I can adopt another dog from Dahab and bring it back with me. Isn't that awesome?

Are you coming?

Z

Were we going? Good question. Black had promised we'd take a proper vacation soon, but I wasn't sure he'd be thrilled by the prospect of another Dahabian adventure. On the other hand, there was sun and sand, and perhaps we'd get to make more than one dive if we didn't find any dead bodies? Maybe it would be fun...

WHAT'S NEXT?

My next book will be *Copper*, the seventh book in the Blackwood Elements series, releasing in the autumn of 2019.

When Tai Beaulieu impulsively hands in her notice by text message one dreary January morning and sets off in search of adventure, the last place she expects to end up is Africa.

But soon she's in Egypt, home to ancient tombs and spectacular temples. Plus friendly locals, a rather nice English businessman and, an American tourist who doesn't know when to butt out.

Along with roommate Tegan and archaeologist Miles, Tai sets out to explore everything the city of Luxor has to offer. But soon, she's keeping a terrible secret, and she's not the only one.

For more details: www.elise-noble.com/copper

If you'd like to read about the Fidda Hilal murder Emmy mentions, you can find that story in *Trouble in Paradise*, the first book in my Trouble series.

When Callie Shawcross's wedding plans fall apart, a friend convinces her that a relaxing break in the sleepy Egyptian town of Fidda Hilal is just what she needs.

As she arrives in the former Bedouin fishing village, Callie feels a sense of peace. The sun is shining, the locals seem friendly and the sparkling azure sea is calling out to her. The day she meets a sexy stranger, she finds a welcome distraction from the life she left back home. But as her feelings for him get more serious, events in paradise take a dark turn.

After a series of mysterious disappearances, Callie is left hunting for answers, and during her frantic search, she finds out it's not only the town that has secrets.

For more details: www.elise-noble.com/trouble-in-paradise

If you enjoyed Stolen Hearts, please consider leaving a review.

For an author, every review is incredibly important. Not only do they make us feel warm and fuzzy inside, readers consider them when making their decision whether or not to buy a book. Even a line saying you enjoyed the book or what your favourite part was helps a lot.

WANT TO STALK ME?

For updates on my new releases, giveaways, and
other random stuff, you can sign up for my newsletter
on my website:
www.elise-noble.com

Facebook:
www.facebook.com/EliseNobleAuthor

Twitter: @EliseANoble

Instagram: @elise_noble

If you're on Facebook, you may also like to join
Team Blackwood for exclusive giveaways, sneak
previews, and book-related chat. Be the first to find out
about new stories, and you might even see your name
or one of your ideas make it into print!

And if you'd like to read my books for FREE, you
can also find details of how to join my review team.

Would you like to join Team Blackwood?

www.elise-noble.com/team-blackwood

END OF BOOK STUFF

The town of Dahab has cropped up in a few of my Blackwood books now, and was also the inspiration behind the fictional town of Fidda Hilal in Trouble in Paradise. I first travelled there in 2012 for a last-minute beach holiday because I was craving some sun. Problem is, I'm not really cut out for sitting around doing nothing, and I lasted one day on a sunlounger before I got bored. A sign nearby offered free introductory scuba dives, and as I squeezed myself into a borrowed wetsuit, I didn't realise quite how addictive diving could be. Honestly, parts of that first week weren't particularly pleasant—days spent doing mask-off/kit-off drills underwater and evenings spent studying for tests—but by the time I left, I'd got my open water qualification. And I was hooked.

I've been back every year since, and I figured it was about time I wrote a story set there. Emmy and Black's adventures aside, crime rates in Dahab are actually pretty low, and the town itself is special. It's not modern and shiny, and that's part of its charm. The weather's nearly always good, the sea's awesome, and the people are super friendly.

After loads of requests for another Emmy and Black book, I figured last year that I'd better pull my finger out and get it done, so I decided to use my holiday as a research trip. And of course, people helped because that's what Dahabians do. This story definitely turned into more of a team effort than usual!

First problem, I needed to work out where to dump Carmela's body, and who better to ask than a bunch of divers. Big thanks to Eid, Hamed, and Thorsten from Sinai Divers Backpackers for all the brainstorming! After a bunch of discussions, we decided on the spot by the Caves, and one day when we were out on the boat, Eid came sprinting outside and herded me over to the railing. "Look! Do you think he's dumping a body?" Sure enough, there was a white pickup parked in exactly the right spot, but I wasn't about to dive down and find out.

The kitesurf chase came to life one tipsy night in Jackie's restaurant (the Mexican restaurant by the bridge). The lighting wasn't so good, so we were basically sitting in the dark eating tacos. At that point, the local police's theme was "thou shalt not drink alcohol," so Jackie's got these neat little hollow stools with lift-off lids for people to hide their booze if the cops came. Needless to say, the stools were pretty full that night.

At first, I was going to have Emmy and Black borrow a boat to hunt down the bad guys, but that seemed so tame. Then Toby and Fiona, both kitesurf instructors, pointed out that kites can go faster than boats and the new idea was born. Thanks also to veterinarian Liz for reminding me how much blood there would be, *everywhere.* Even Jackie, who's a technical diver when he's not running his restaurant, got involved, supplying churros and information on the kit Emmy and Black would need on their little expedition.

To share the Dahab love, my lovely friend Kristina took photos of the places that inspired the book, and I've put them on my website. If you'd like to take a tour of the town and see the places Emmy and Black visited, you can do that here:

www.elise-noble.com/stolen-hearts-dahab

Sadly, I couldn't find a transplant scientist in Dahab, but I did bump into one a few weeks later in the UK. Thank you, Alasdair, for answering my questions, even if it was a strange conversation to be having at a funeral! And yes, a few years ago, people really did carry organs in picnic coolers across London on the Tube!

I hope you enjoyed Emmy and Black's first thriller book. I had a blast writing about them again, and if there's enough interest, you may see them back in another adventure. Watch this space!

Elise

OTHER BOOKS BY ELISE NOBLE

The Blackwood Security Series

For the Love of Animals (Nate & Carmen - prequel)
Black is my Heart (prequel)
Pitch Black
Into the Black
Forever Black
Gold Rush
Gray is my Heart
Neon (novella)
Out of the Blue
Ultraviolet
Glitter (novella) (2019)
Red Alert
White Hot
The Scarlet Affair
Quicksilver
The Girl with the Emerald Ring (2020)

The Blackwood Elements Series

Oxygen
Lithium
Carbon
Rhodium
Platinum
Lead

Copper (2019)
Bronze (2019)
Nickel (2020)

The Blackwood UK Series
Joker in the Pack
Cherry on Top (novella)
Roses are Dead
Shallow Graves
Indigo Rain
Pass the Parcel (TBA)

Blackwood Casefiles
Stolen Hearts

Blackstone House
Hard Lines (TBA)
Hard Tide (TBA)

The Electi Series
Cursed
Spooked
Possessed
Demented (2020)

The Trouble Series
Trouble in Paradise
Nothing but Trouble
24 Hours of Trouble

Standalone
Life
Twisted (short stories)

A Very Happy Christmas (novella)

Printed in Great Britain
by Amazon